The Master of Seduction . . .

"Are you saying that you are London's Least Likely to fall for me?" Blake asked, towering over her.

Emma stepped back, until the bookshelves dug into her back. Blake placed one hand on either side of her, effectively boxing her in.

"That is exactly what I am saying," she said.

The duke was so arrogant. He set her nerves on edge. He played with her affections and her very grasp on reality. He made her heart race, and he made her crave kisses that drove her to dizzying heights of pleasure.

"And yet some say I am a master of seduction," Blake replied in a low voice that sent a shiver shimmying up and down her spine.

"And yet here I am, hardly seduced," Emma replied. *Breathlessly*. Damnit.

"[illegible] fix that," Blake murmured, tracing [illegible] edge of her bodice an[illegible] breasts. She fo[illegible] valiantly to re[illegible] that she *not* be[illegible]

Romances by Maya Rodale

THE WICKED WALLFLOWER
SEDUCING MR. KNIGHTLY
THE TATTOOED DUKE
A TALE OF TWO LOVERS
A GROOM OF ONE'S OWN

From Avon Impulse
THREE SCHEMES AND A SCANDAL

MAYA RODALE

The Wicked Wallflower

AVON
An Imprint of HarperCollins*Publishers*

This is a work of fiction. Names, characters, places, and incidents are products of the author's imagination or are used fictitiously and are not to be construed as real. Any resemblance to actual events, locales, organizations, or persons, living or dead, is entirely coincidental.

AVON BOOKS
An Imprint of HarperCollins*Publishers*
10 East 53rd Street
New York, New York 10022-5299

ISBN 978-0-06-223114-7
www.avonromance.com

First Avon Books mass market printing: November 2013

Printed in the U.S.A.

10 9 8 7 6 5 4 3 2 1

For all the bluestockings.
And for Tony,
who wooed me with books and
who reads almost as fast as I do.

Acknowledgments

WHILE I AM tempted to take sole credit for this book, I cannot. I am completely indebted to Sara Jane Stone, Amanda Kimble-Evans, and Tony Haile, who read early drafts and offered valuable feedback.

Many thanks to the team at Avon for getting my books into people's hands, especially Jessie, Pam, Shawn, and Dana. Thank you to Tom for another gorgeous cover. Most of all, thank you to my lovely and talented editor, Tessa.

I am grateful to my fellow authors Caroline Linden, Miranda Neville, and Katharine Ashe for friendship and conversations one can only have with other romance authors. When I need a break from the nineteenth century, I turn to my friends and fans on Facebook, who were tremendously helpful when it came to suggesting character names and providing the titles for Emma's books.

I'd also like to thank my family, my agent, my husband, and my darling dog, Penelope.

The Wicked Wallflower

Prologue

London, 1821

ANY MINUTE NOW Lady Emma Avery's life would truly begin. Glittering parties, rakish rogues, breathtaking romance . . . all those things that only ever happened in books would finally, *finally* happen to her.

Any minute now Emma would be announced at her first London ball. The great husband hunt would finally, *finally* begin. She'd spent four years preparing as a student at Lady Penelope's Finishing School for Young Ladies. She spent the entire afternoon forcing her brown hair to curl and enduring fittings for a lovely ivory silk and lace gown, even though she would've rather been reading.

All the preparation would be worth it when some rogue swept her off her feet in a whirlwind of romance, which would happen, oh, any minute now.

"Lord and Lady Avery. Lady Emma." The butler at Lady Wrotham's ball announced their arrival. No one in the crowded ballroom took note.

Emma kept her head held high. She was new to London.

At the first opportunity, Emma found her two dearest friends from Lady Penelope's: Lady Olivia Archer and Miss Prudence Payton. They had staked out a position in the corner of the ballroom, where they watched the other couples dancing, flirting, and conversing.

"I hardly have any names on my dance card," Emma said, slightly despairing. This was not how she imagined her debut.

"There are just four names on mine," Olivia said. "But I think the gentlemen only agreed to escape my mother. I really can't blame them."

"I haven't any," Prudence replied glumly.

"The night is still young," Emma declared. "And this is only our first ball of our first season."

"I wager *her* dance card is full," Prudence said. They all turned to look at Lady Katherine Abernathy—blond, beautiful, and *mean*—surrounded by a gaggle of young, handsome suitors. She smiled like a cat in cream.

"Oh, hello!" she called out to them. The three tensed, for Lady Katherine had never, in the history of their acquaintance, had a kind word for any of them.

"My friends from Finishing School," she explained to her swarming pack of beaux. First she introduced Lady Olivia and Miss Prudence. Then Lady Katherine paused to smile wickedly. "And Lady Emma. But we all called *her* the Buxom Bluestocking."

The gentlemen, desperate to please or perhaps mistaking this cruelty for wit or humor, burst into uproarious laughter. Emma felt her cheeks flame red. She had actually prayed for Lady Katherine to drop that horrid nickname. And this was how God answered.

"Have I died and gone to hell? Tell me I have," she pleaded to her friends.

"I'm afraid this is actually happening," Prudence said sorrowfully. Olivia clasped Emma's hand.

"This is not how the evening was supposed to go," Emma said through clenched teeth. It was bad enough that she blushed while everyone laughed at her—tonight, of all nights.

She. Would. Not. Cry.

Through their laughter, Emma didn't hear the orchestra begin playing the third waltz. But she did see a handsome gentleman awkwardly attempting to push his way through.

Mr. Benedict Chase. They had been introduced earlier. He was one of the few to pencil his name on her dance card. She wouldn't blame him if he cried off. Who could possibly want to waltz with a girl known as Buxom Bluestocking?

But no, as Lady Katherine and her suitors watched, he bowed before Emma and then led her to the dance floor.

"The Buxom Bluestocking?" Mr. Chase inquired.

Emma bit her lip and looked away.

"I love a woman who reads," he said kindly. Emma's gaze locked with his; she saw he wasn't teasing. He liked her—when everyone else laughed at her expense. She also noted that he was handsome. He looked at her mouth as if he wanted to kiss her.

Emma promptly fell in love with Mr. Benedict Chase.

He whirled her around the ballroom; she felt dizzy from it. Or was that the heady, intoxicating sensation of true love? She smiled happily. Her cheeks were still pink—but from pleasure, not embarrassment.

This is what she had prepared for. If only this moment could last forever.

This moment came to an abrupt stop when a large, hulking masculine body stepped backward and bumped into her. The force of their collision sent her sprawling to her knees on the parquet floor.

Emma peered up at the horrible, inconsiderate brute and found herself peering at the most breathtakingly handsome man she had ever seen. He could only be the Duke of Ashbrooke, an infamous scoundrel who made frequent appearances in the gossip columns.

"My apologies. Didn't see you there," the duke said with a smile that was renowned for melting hearts and weakening women's resolve.

Emma just scowled.

He had ruined her perfect moment with the man she loved.

Then, like a gentleman and not the rogue he was reputed to be, the duke offered her his hand. Not to be outdone, Benedict did as well.

Emma glanced from the duke to Benedict, each reaching out for her hand. She didn't hesitate. Her choice was clear. She chose the man who *saw* her. She chose love.

Chapter 1

The graduates of Lady Penelope's Finishing School for Young Ladies make excellent matches . . . eventually.

—Promotional Pamphlet

London
April, 1824
Lady Emma Avery's Bedroom

As graduates of Lady Penelope's Finishing School for Young Ladies, it was expected that Lady Emma Avery and her friends, Lady Olivia Archer and Miss Prudence Payton, would make good matches on the marriage mart within a season or two of their debut. They had done no such thing.

Having endured Lady Wrotham's ball celebrating the start of the 1824 season earlier that night, the girls returned to Emma's house, procured a bottle of sherry, and proceeded to face a dire truth.

"To our *fourth* season," Emma said with a sigh, raising her glass. Reluctantly, Olivia and Prudence did so as well, clinking the cut crystal goblets together and taking small ladylike sips.

"As of tonight, there are just three months until

Lady Penelope's Anniversary Ball," Prudence said, giving voice to the dreadful fact that had been weighing on all of their minds.

At the end of every season, all the graduates—*and their husbands*—gathered to celebrate the anniversary of the school's founding, as well as announce the matches made that season and pray for those yet unwed.

To miss the event was simply not done.

To attend the event without a husband was excruciating.

"Thus if we are not married by within three months time, we shall be the first batch of spinsters in the history of the school," Olivia said in a small voice. "No one has ever ended their fourth season unwed. Except for us."

Olivia, seated primly on the pale blue carpet, nervously fussed with her skirts. Emma leaned back against the bed, bumping her head on the post. Prudence sighed.

There was also the unspoken truth that they all *wanted* romance, love, families of their own and happily-ever-after. With each year that went by, it became harder and harder to smile at another of their classmates' weddings or the birth of another baby. Inside, the same aching, desperate feeling: When will it be my turn? When? *When?*

"In the one-hundred-year history of the school, it was bound to happen," Prudence said. "Mathematically speaking."

"Lady Katherine Abernathy is also still unwed," Olivia pointed out.

"By choice," Emma replied. "She has refused numerous proposals. She need only say yes to one of them." Beautiful, blond, and despicable Lady Katherine Abernathy had delighted in tormenting Emma and her friends at Lady P's with cutting remarks, cruel pranks . . . always followed by demands for help with her lessons from the Buxom Bluestocking.

"I suppose it doesn't need to be said that we haven't received any proposals. At all. Whatsoever," Olivia said glumly.

"No, it doesn't," Prudence said. "I am well aware that I have received none and shall not receive any, so long as the ton calls me Prude Prudence."

"At least you are not known as Prissy Missy," Olivia replied. "The name does not seem to entice gentlemen. Surprisingly."

"Neither of those are as bad as the Buxom Bluestocking," Emma said, shuddering at the horrid nickname she had earned thanks to her figure and her penchant for reading.

With life on the marriage mart cruel to a girl known as the Buxom Bluestocking, she had retreated even more into her books, which only made things worse.

Prudence refilled their empty glasses and raised hers in toast. "To London's Least Likely," she declared wryly.

Olivia pursed her lips and Emma groaned. The prior season, the "gentlemen" at White's had concocted a cruel new game in which they named London's Least Likely to Cause a Scandal (Olivia), Misbehave (Emma), Be Caught In Compromising Position (Prudence).

The revelation of this did not enhance their marital prospects.

They weren't *tragic.* They just weren't *it.*

"Something must be done," Olivia said. "I cannot bear the thought of standing there while our class takes a bow and we are the only unmarried ones in the lot. My mother will probably weep openly at what a failure I am."

"That ball is the least of my worries," Emma declared. "I have overheard my parents arguing, for we cannot afford another season in town. If I do not marry soon, I shall have to rusticate in Lincolnshire. For the rest of my life. Unless . . ."

"Unless you can make Benedict come up to scratch," Prudence finished.

Emma nodded. Benedict had been her one and only beau for three seasons now. When everyone teased her bluestocking tendencies, he asked her about the books she'd read and her opinions of them. He *liked* that she was bookish—when her mother despaired of her and the rest of the ton teased her. Benedict and she dreamt of a town house they might share, possessing a well-stocked library with a roaring fire, large windows overlooking a garden, and children tucked in a nursery upstairs.

Other than Prudence and Olivia, he was the

one person she could just be herself with. Emma loved him desperately.

It was only a matter of time until he proposed—*everyone* thought so.

But then disaster struck.

"If only it were that simple," Emma said with a sigh. "His father has recently made a disastrous investment and is now insisting that Benedict and his brother marry heiresses."

"If he would have proposed last season this wouldn't be an issue," Prudence said.

"Or the season before *that*," Emma added. Indeed, she and Benedict had a sort of understanding for three seasons now. He'd asked her father for permission to court her—all that was missing was the proposal. "I love him. But he is not the most enterprising of men."

"Which means *you* must do something, if anything is to be done at all," Prudence concluded. Emma nodded in agreement.

"If only you would come into a fortune," Olivia mused. "That would solve everything."

Emma smiled sheepishly and said, "I might have perused Debrett's to discern if I had any wealthy, elderly, sickly relatives I wasn't aware of. There were none."

"How does one force a man's hand anyway?" Olivia asked. "Besides being caught in a compromising position, which is always an option if we are truly desperate."

"Sometimes," Emma whispered, leaning in conspiratorially, "I wish that the announcement were just in the newspaper and done. Then he'd be honor-bound to marry me, fortune or not."

" 'Mr. Benedict Chase, second son of Viscount Rossmore, is pleased to announce his engagement to Lady Emma Avery,' " Prudence recited.

"We should do it," Olivia said. Then she giggled. And hiccupped.

"Are you mad?" Emma gasped. "You have had far too much sherry."

"Our situation is desperate," Olivia said. "Do you really want to be the only failure of Lady Penelope's in the entire *one-hundred-year* history of the school? Don't you wish to marry and have children and not be nagged about eligible bachelors?"

"I do want all those things," Emma said fiercely. "But you must agree that forging a betrothal announcement is a bit much. Perhaps I might just confide my feelings to him. Or convince him that my meager dowry will be enough if we live frugally. Or perhaps I should settle. I could find a wealthy older man searching for a second or even third wife. Perhaps he will die and leave me a fortune before I grow too old."

The prospect did not enthrall.

"No, we mustn't settle," Olivia said firmly. "We have waited too long to settle. Lady Penelope would never wish for us to settle. We must do something."

Prudence crossed the room to Emma's writing desk in search of paper and pen under all the stacks of books Emma had read, or planned to read, or was in the midst of reading.

"Olivia, you write it," Prudence said, handing her the materials. "You have the best penmanship."

"Indeed, it is one of my many talents that gentlemen care not one whit about, along with my skill with an embroidery needle, watercolor brush, or my deft handling of a teapot," Olivia muttered. Then she asked, "What should I write?"

"Nothing!" Emma protested. "You should not write anything."

"'To *The London Weekly*,'" Prudence said grandly. "'Mr. Benedict Chase, handsome but impoverished second son of cruel Viscount Rossmore, is delighted to announce his engagement to the lovely Lady Emma Avery—'"

"Toss that in the fire immediately!" Emma cried, lunging for the paper Olivia held high above her head.

"Ladies do not attempt to steal the private correspondence of others," Olivia admonished.

"Ladies do not compose outrageous falsehoods for nefarious purposes," Emma countered.

"Speaking of fire, do you smell smoke?" Prudence asked, sniffing the air. "No, maybe not. I must be imagining things. Like your future happiness going up in flames."

"Olivia, you cannot be serious! You have had far too much sherry!"

"If you are going to send a betrothal announcement to the newspaper—" Prudence said thoughtfully.

"Which I am not going to do," Emma cut in firmly.

"—why settle for Benedict?"

Olivia's eyes went wide. Emma didn't even entertain the notion.

"Because I love Benedict," she said. She did love him, truly and deeply. She wanted to belong to him, and to live the life she imagined for them. She had the townhouse picked out, along with the china pattern, their children's names, and the fabric for the drawing room drapes. "I love him. Which is beside the point because I am not going to—"

"Who else shall we announce her betrothal to, Prudence?" Olivia asked, and ever the gracious and attentive hostess, refilled their empty glasses.

Prudence pursed her lips. She paused thoughtfully. She even sipped her sherry. Emma could practically see her compiling a list of eligible bachelors, evaluating them and dismissing them.

Prudence grinned. It was a wicked grin. One that made Emma's stomach feel as if it were turning cartwheels. Olivia leaned forward expectantly. Emma braced herself with another fortifying sip of sherry.

"Ashbrooke," Prudence said with a curve of her lips.

Emma spat out her sip of sherry—all over the letter announcing her betrothal to Benedict, thus completely ruining it with a smattering of red splotches.

"The Duke of Ashbrooke!" Olivia shrieked.

"Shhh," Prudence shushed her.

"You are absolutely, stark raving mad," Emma said flatly. "I should ring for the footmen to escort you to Bedlam."

"He's so . . . dreamy," Olivia said in a wispy voice.

Emma rolled her eyes and said, "He's a notorious libertine."

"He's the most eligible bachelor of the season," Prudence pointed out. "Of *every* season." It was the truth, but it was also irrelevant.

"Men like him do not associate with girls like us," Emma said, highlighting a far more pertinent truth. "Ashbrooke is out of our league. He's out of everyone's league, except perhaps oh-so-perfect Lady Katherine Abernathy. That is, if he even deigned to associate with debutantes. Everyone knows he is not the marrying kind."

"He just hasn't met the right woman," Olivia said.

"Because he's always with the wrong ones," Emma replied. "He has seduced the female half of London, effortlessly."

"Except for us," Olivia said glumly. "He's just so . . ."

"So virile," Prudence said, a blush stealing over her cheeks. "And masculine."

"Or arrogant," Emma said. That was one thing she loved about Benedict. His kindness, his open-mindedness, his humility. Benedict listened to her, and you could just tell that Ashbrooke didn't pause to consider anyone else, if he paused to think at all.

"How can you know what he is like?" Prudence asked. "Have you ever spoken to him?"

"Of course not. Men like him do not speak to girls like me. It's probably a universal law," Emma said. "Besides, men that handsome need not develop charm or humility because women and the world just fall at their feet, breathlessly, eager to do their bidding. He wins easily at everything, which means he's never had to work for anything. I'm sure he's a pompous, arrogant bore."

"But you agree he is handsome," Olivia said gravely.

"I am not blind. Or dead," Emma conceded. "But I love Benedict!"

"You must be the only woman in the *whole entire world* who is immune to the Ashbrooke Effect," Olivia said. "Amazing. You are a medical marvel."

"First of all, the Ashbrooke Effect is not an actual medical condition," Emma lectured, after another sip of her drink. "Secondly, I refuse to believe it even exists at all."

"I suffer from it even thinking about him," Olivia said. "My heart is fluttering and my skin feels hot. I must be blushing all over."

"That's probably all the sherry you've been drinking," Emma remarked.

"My knees are weak," Olivia sighed, with a dreamy look in her eyes.

"You're sitting," Prudence pointed out.

"It's an imaginary condition and I am immune," Emma said confidently. "If I ever meet him, I'll prove it to you."

•

"Do you smell smoke? Or is that my imagination?" Prudence asked.

"Can you just imagine if you were engaged to Ashbrooke?" Olivia said, with far too much excitement for Emma's comfort.

"I cannot. No one would believe it, even were it true. No, I wish to marry Benedict and we shall have a neat little townhouse with a library and we shall devote ourselves to his scholarly pursuits."

"Pfft," Prudence puffed dismissively. "Olivia, if you please, I shall dictate."

"What? No!" Emma lunged for the paper, but Olivia—even drunken Olivia—was too quick for her. "Oh bother it. No one will believe it anyway."

Prudence began her dictation. " 'To the surprise of everyone, the Duke of Ashbrooke announces his betrothal to Lady Emma Avery.' "

"Oh, please," Emma scoffed as Olivia wrote slowly. Hopefully her penmanship was rendered illegible due to the sherry.

"Where do you keep the sealing wax?" Prudence asked.

"I shan't tell you that. Both of those missives ought to go in the fire immediately," Emma said.

"Are you sure?" Olivia asked, the dangerous sheet of paper in her hand.

"Of course I am sure! I shall speak to Benedict," Emma said. "Perhaps I can talk him into eloping."

"That would be romantic," Olivia said encouragingly.

"But Ashbrooke—" Prudence started, before Emma interrupted.

"Wouldn't marry me even if that announcement did appear in the newspaper. Which it will not. Because we will burn it immediately." Emma held out her hand, expecting the letter.

"Speaking of fire, do you smell smoke?" Prudence asked. "I thought I did before, but I really do now."

Olivia even coughed.

Emma's bedroom door burst open, slamming into the wall. Her mother appeared, gasping for breath and clutching her chest.

"Girls! Come quickly! There is a fire in the kitchens!" she cried.

Three girls jumped up in a hurry, knocking over their glasses, bottles of black ink, spilling half the sherry bottle, and abandoning everything—including That Letter—in their haste to reach for shawls and escape the house.

Chapter 2

"Noooo!"

—Many marriage-minded mamas wailing dramatically upon reading the latest issue of *The London Weekly*

The Drawing Room, Avery House

No one ever paid much attention to Emma Avery. She did not have breathtaking beauty, sparkling charm, sharp wit, or fortune to recommend her above all the other beautiful, charming, witty, wealthy girls of the haute ton. She was fine. *Fine.*

But *fine* didn't quite cut it on the marriage mart. Thus, calling hours were whiled away in an empty drawing room, with the good company of the latest novel from the circulating library. It was not altogether an unpleasant way to spend the afternoon, though Emma could have done without the quiet sense of desperation.

And so on Saturday afternoon Emma sat down with volume one of *The Mad Baron,* which would hopefully provide a distraction from the empty drawing room and her looming, impoverished spinsterhood in Lincolnshire. Her mother read the newest edition of *The London Weekly*, beginning with the front page and proceeding to read each and every page.

The grandfather clock in the hall ticked loudly, marking the passing seconds and hours, reminding Emma that Judgment Day, otherwise known as Lady Penelope's Anniversary Ball, was fast approaching.

Already a week had passed uneventfully (and unromantically) since the night of Lady Wrotham's ball. Had it truly been seven days already?

Her brain must *still* be foggy from all that sherry she, Olivia, and Prudence drank that night. The kitchen fire had saved them from complete and utter drunkenness. Fortunately, it had been contained, but to be safe, the girls spent the night at Olivia's house. When Emma returned the next afternoon, her bedroom had been tidied completely and—

She gasped and slammed her book shut.

"What is it, darling?" her mother asked. She peered up from behind the newspaper.

"Nothing," Emma said. But her heart was pounding. Could her mother hear it from across the room? No, definitely not. But lud, her heart beat so hard she could feel it sticking in her throat.

The Letter. *What had happened to the letter?*

Her room had been cleaned within an inch of its life. The carpet had even been removed because of the ink stain—and presumably the stink of sherry. The glasses had been whisked away, the bottle, too. But The Letter . . .

What the devil happened to that cursed letter?

Emma closed her book. Her palms were damp. Her heart was still thudding like a drum in her chest. She should go search for it right now and burn it immediately.

"Mother, if you'll excuse me, there is something I must tend to—"

Emma quickly crossed the room before her mother could protest, but she didn't make it past the double doors to the foyer before Jenkins, the butler, stepped into her path.

"Lady Emma, you have a caller," he intoned.

"Is that so?" her mother asked curiously, looking up from the newspaper.

Emma closed her eyes and exhaled slowly. It was one thing to know one was "not quite." It was another thing entirely if your own mother thought so.

And it was another matter entirely when the most incriminating and humiliating letter ever composed was lurking somewhere and she had to find it immediately, and *now* she had a caller?

"Who is calling, Jenkins?" she asked in a small voice, while silently praying, *Please don't say the Duke of Ashbrooke.*

Ashbrooke House, London
The Duke's Library

Blake William Peregrine Auden, the ninth Duke of Ashbrooke, shrugged out of his jacket and rolled up his shirtsleeves, exposing the taut muscles of his forearms as he set to work on the confounding problem that had been occupying his attentions for days.

Portraits of disapproving ancestors looked down upon him. Understandable, given his usual activities.

Blake focused on the drawings and calculations on the pages spread out on a table before him. After entering the room, his idiot friend Lord Salem had given one look and declared it "incomprehensible rubbish" before availing himself of the brandy. What the fool didn't see were calculations for a machine that could revolutionize everything.

A second visitor, his cousin, heir, and good friend, George Parker-Jones, sat before the fire, newspaper in hand.

"First the Tarleton twins and now this," George lamented, shaking a copy of *The London Weekly* above his head.

It was not the problem that absorbed the duke.

"Are we still talking about the twins?" Ashbrooke asked, bored. "For the thousandth time, to be caught with one girl is to compromise her. But two chaperone each other."

It was only logical. The ton did not see logic.

"By all accounts they did not appear to have *properly* chaperoned each other, given the state of their hair, attire, and virtue when discovered with you," George said, grinning.

"I don't know if I should be flattered or insulted

that the ton thinks me capable of ruining two young, twin sisters in just a quarter of an hour," Ashbrooke said. Then, with a grin, he added, "Hell, I'm just getting started after a quarter of an hour."

"This may be a shock to you, but I am not interested in the details of your lovemaking," George declared. "Unlike the rest of the ton."

"Please spare us," Salem said. "I beg of you."

"I should publish my memoirs," Ashbrooke said. "I'd make a fortune."

"There's the funds for your Difference Engine," George pointed out, referring to Ashbrooke's latest, frustratingly slow project.

The Difference Engine was a machine that performed mathematical calculations perfectly every time, no matter how complex or difficult. The results would be free of human error.

Or rather, the Difference Engine would do that once he completed his calculations and designs and then secured the funds to build it. He estimated it would require fifty thousand pounds—an enormous sum that he wasn't about to bankrupt his estate for. Yet.

Then architects, ship captains, bankers, investors, inventors, and tradesmen could conduct their business based upon accurate calculations rather than the grossly infallible "ready reckoners" everyone currently relied on. Those huge books full of multiplication tables, fractions, and other mathematical calculations were riddled with human errors.

In his darker moments, Blake believed lives—

such as those of his parents—were lost because of this. Ships gone astray. Buildings collapsing. Dangerous machines. Fortunes lost.

In his waking moments—when he wasn't seducing women or living the high life of a duke in London—Blake worked on plans for the machine.

His efforts at soliciting the support of his friends in the government and of his peers had met with great success—and disastrous failure.

During a wild bachelors' only excursion at Lord Norton's country seat, Blake had busted into his lordship's priceless collection of rare vintages and imported brandies, much to the drunken delight of all the guests and much to the unbridled fury of Lord Norton.

The shipping magnate, Archibald McCracken, was irreparably offended when Blake was an hour late to their interview. Matters were only made worse by Blake's attire, which consisted of his wrinkled, smoke-stinking evening clothes and a limp cravat that had obviously spent the better portion of the previous night on a bedroom floor.

But the fallout from the Tarleton twins debacle had been enormous. Their enraged father withdrew his support and persuaded his friends to do the same. It seems that stodgy old blokes—the ones with the money and connections—did not want to do business with the kind of man who was caught in a compromising position with twin sisters. Duke or not, some things were just beyond the pale.

And that was just last week's scandal.

"If you would have married one of them, you wouldn't be in this situation," George, not helpfully, pointed out. "You could be building the engine rather than just laboring over the drawings and calculations."

Ashbrooke sighed and once again tried to explain, logically: "I couldn't marry one twin and ruin the other. Of course I cannot marry *both.* So I shall marry neither."

"They shan't marry either, it seems," Salem pointed out.

"I shall never marry at all," Ashbrooke stated. For the thousandth time.

"That's not what *The London Weekly* says," George said, with a cryptic smile. He rustled the pages of the newspaper. Even Salem was intrigued.

"Let me see that," Ashbrooke said, snatching the paper away. He flipped through until—but of course—he found his name in the gossip column, "Fashionable Intelligence."

He held his breath as he read what was very likely more disastrous news.

The Drawing Room, Avery House

Emma held her breath, awaiting what could only be disastrous news.

Jenkins cleared his throat and announced the callers: "Ladies Abernathy, Crawford, Mulberry, Falmouth, and Montague."

She would have scowled were she not paralyzed by a slow dawning terror. Ashbrooke would have been preferable to that pack of young women. As would a trip to the dentist, an attack by highwaymen, or being kidnapped, ravished, and murdered by a band of bloodthirsty pirates.

"My goodness!" Mother announced. "Show them in and send up tea."

A sweat now broke out on Emma's brow. She rather felt like she might be sick, right there on Jenkins's silver tray bearing the calling cards of Ladies Abernathy and Crawford, Mulberry, Falmouth, and Montague—all of whom had delighted in torturing her and her friends at Lady Penelope's Finishing School.

There was no reason for them to be calling on her, unless . . .

The Letter!

Emma had barely taken a seat when the five ladies burst into the drawing room in an explosion of girlish chatter, silk, lace, jewels, bonnets, feigned laughter, and deceptive smiles.

"We saw the news in *The London Weekly* and had to be the first to congratulate you!" Lady Falmouth exclaimed.

Out of the corner of her eye Emma saw her mother frantically flipping through the pages of *The Weekly* to see what they might be referring to. Unlike most mothers of the ton, Emma's actually read the parliamentary reports and did not skip straight to the gossip columns.

She watched her mother's eyes grow large. And

then she started coughing. Emma suspected she knew exactly what she had read. She prayed fervently that it was anything else.

"Are you alright, Lady Avery?" Lady Crawford inquired. "The prospect of planning such a grand affair must be so overwhelming."

"I cannot believe we had to read it in the paper—when we are your dearest school friends!" Lady Abernathy said sweetly.

"Yes, we were so close," Emma replied, just as sweetly. "Like England and China."

Lady Abernathy paused to puzzle over that.

Once, Emma had been selected to give a solo pianoforte performance at the school musical—a rare achievement. The morning of the show, Lady Katherine Abernathy had deliberately slammed her fingers in the schoolroom door, making it impossible for Emma to play and thus obtaining the solo opportunity herself. That was Lady Katherine Abernathy in a nutshell.

"Indeed," her mother said, clearing her throat. "It must be such a shock to read such intimate, personal news in the gossip columns. I really couldn't imagine it."

Ashbrooke House

It was nothing unusual for the duke to read intimate, personal news about himself in the gossip columns. Often it was pure fiction, fantasy, or a complete fabrication for the sole purpose of selling more copies. More often, however, his real life antics provided ample fodder for the gossips.

The week prior to the Tarleton twins debacle, Lord Doyle's mistress had been persuaded to share her favors with Blake, much to the fury of her protector. And the week before that he could scarcely remember, but it was surely something.

Which made what he read in *The London Weekly* all the more intriguing.

Ashbrooke read aloud, perplexed, amused, and annoyed by the words he uttered: "'To the surprise of everyone, the Duke of Ashbrooke announces his betrothal to Lady Emma Avery.'"

"Who is Lady Emma Avery?" Salem asked, clearly wracking his brain to match a name with a face. His recognition of women usually began and ended with their breasts.

"She is one of London's Least Likely," George explained, since he kept track of these things.

"Ah, the bunch of wallflowers," Salem said. "Is she the one voted London's Least Likely to Be Caught In Compromising Position?"

"No, that was her friend, Miss Prudence Payton," George corrected.

Salem looked blank.

"Prude Prudence," George explained, and then Salem's eyes lit up in recognition. "I believe Lady Emma was voted London's Least Likely to Misbehave."

"I'm still not sure which one that is. Can't picture her," Ashbrooke said. Well-behaved Wallflowers didn't quite capture his attentions; he made it a habit to consort with women *most* likely to misbehave. In bed.

"Given that you do not even know the lady in question, I presume you did not actually propose to her," George said dryly.

"I might have," Ashbrooke said with a shrug. The devil only knew what he did when he was deep in his cups. "But I doubt it."

Salem burst out laughing as the full implications of the situation began to register in his brain. An engagement announcement in the most widely read newspaper in London—and the bride and groom had never even met. "What are you going to do?"

"This is clearly some prank or a joke or an egregious error," Ashbrooke said easily. "Why should I bother myself with it?"

"Because everyone will be expecting a wedding," George said impatiently. "She'll be ruined otherwise."

"They shall be disappointed," Ashbrooke replied. "It happens in life. I'm given to understand it is not a fatal condition."

There would be no wedding. Not to the Tarleton twins or this Miss Aviary or anyone. Everyone knew marriage was for the creation of heirs, and he was resolved not to have any. No, he would leave a different legacy—one more innovative and daring than a bunch of squalling brats.

If he could just get the damned engine built.

The butler interrupted his brooding to announce a caller.

"Your Grace, a caller. Mr. Edmund Parks."

"Hello, cousin," Ashbrooke said, smiling as he greeted his cousin, who eyed him warily. Edmund was always formally attired, starched within an inch of his life, and exceedingly well-behaved—a perfect gentleman, though without fortune or title. The more proper he was, the more Blake felt duty bound to make mischief enough for them both.

"I suppose you have come to inquire about news of my engagement," Blake said, looking up from his calculations.

"You have my sincere felicitations," Edmund said with a dignified nod of his head. "I look forward to meeting your betrothed."

I as well, Blake thought. His polite smile faded at the words Edmund uttered next.

Edmund smiled and said, "I am also calling to see if we will have the pleasure of your company at this year's Fortune Games."

The Drawing Room, Avery House

"How fortunate that you have landed a duke! And Ashbrooke, no less! However did you manage it, Emma?" Lady Mulberry inquired, a tinge of malice in her voice. Truly, she implied, it was remarkable that Emma had landed anyone.

But London's Least Likely and London's Most Eligible? It just did not add up.

Well, now she knew where That Cursed Letter

had gone: directly to the offices of *The London Weekly*.

Mystery solved.

One-way ticket to America soon to be acquired. No, that wasn't far enough. Perhaps the Orient instead.

Emma glanced at her mother, who appeared to be woolgathering as she sipped her tea. Probably planning the wedding already.

"I was shocked to read it," Lady Katherine said, and there *was* malice in her tone, because she had set her cap for Ashbrooke and everyone knew it.

Perhaps it was unkind or untruthful of her, but Emma was still mad about the pianoforte solo and a hundred other devious manipulations she had suffered at the hands of the beautiful, wealthy, and charming Lady Katherine Abernathy.

Emma could not relinquish this moment of triumph over her rival, nor could she admit that it was a hoax.

"I can assure you, I was equally surprised," she said. Then she smiled, like she knew the most delicious secret in the world—which she did, though she would die a thousand torturous deaths before admitting the truth of the matter to her nemesis, and in her own drawing room. "I didn't realize word would get out so soon," she added. *Or at all.*

"When will the wedding be?" Lady Katherine asked politely, while shooting daggers with her eyes.

"We haven't set a date yet," Emma replied in a thickly sweet voice. Technically, this was not a lie.

Technically, she and Ashbrooke had not even met, but did Lady Katherine know that? No. And God willing, she would not.

"What of your dress?" Lady Crawford asked.

"I'm sure I shall wear one," Emma said confidently.

Jenkins appeared again, this time to announce even more callers. "Lady Archer and Miss Payton," he said, and Emma breathed a sigh of relief that she would soon have allies in this farce. Then Jenkins mentioned at least a half a dozen other names that Emma did not bother to register.

It was official: she'd had more callers in this one hour than in four seasons combined. Behold: the power of Ashbrooke.

With whom she was still not acquainted.

The whole scene repeated itself at least six more times—even though she, Olivia, and Prudence did their best to change the topic of conversation, and even though Emma did her very best to neither confirm nor deny the engagement. But with each gossipy miss and matron who passed through the drawing room, the more impossible it became to *not* marry the Duke of Ashbrooke.

With whom she was *still* not acquainted.

Ashbrooke House

Everyone in London was acquainted with the Fortune Games. A house party so strange, so devious, so absurd, with stakes so high, it would certainly be gossiped about. Extensively. But only the select few who had attended and survived truly understood.

Rather than simply leave her vast fortune to an assortment of close relatives and charities, Lady Agatha Grey invited a select group of family members to compete for the chance to be named her heir at her annual house party. Then she'd rewrite her will, leaving everything to that year's winner.

"Ah yes, the Fortune Games," Blake repeated dryly. "The highlight of every year in which twelve of the Ashbrooke clan debase themselves at a demented house party in order to be named a batty old broad's heir for one year in which they pray for her timely demise."

"That does accurately sum it up," Edmund replied. "But I can't bring myself to miss it. I would hate to disappoint Aunt Agatha."

"I'm going as well," George said. "One can hardly turn down the opportunity to be named heir of a ninety-thousand-pound fortune. Especially if one is in need of funds."

"I still haven't decided if I shall attend," Blake said casually, though he tightened his grasp on his pencil until it snapped.

He declined to mention that his invitation had still not arrived. Must have been lost in the post. Or his secretary, Gideon, must have misplaced it. He would die a thousand torturous deaths before mentioning a lack of invitation to his own, dear aunt's annual house party.

Especially when the letter had probably fallen off the back of the mail coach, or something.

"How is the matter even under consideration?" Salem asked. "If all I had to do to get a fortune was attend a silly house party, I wouldn't think twice about going."

Never mind that Salem wasn't in the habit of thinking once, let alone twice. Blake and his cousins shared a smile that commiserated over Salem's foolishness. The infamous Fortune Games were not for the faint of heart, dim-witted, or socially inept.

"The games start in two days' time," George said casually. "I myself am departing at first light tomorrow."

"You had best decide soon, Duke, if it's not too late already," Edmund said. Blake's gaze shifted from one cousin to the other, both in possession of a coveted invitation from Aunt Agatha, who, terrifying old dowager that she might be, was his favorite person in the world.

He suddenly felt a sharp pain in the region of his heart as the truth dawned: Agatha had not invited him.

If she had, and he had not replied, she would have scolded him about it in one of her weekly letters. Now that he thought about it, had he received a letter from Agatha lately? No . . . he didn't recall any. Not even a scathing set-down about his behavior with the twins, or concerning the Norton scandal, the Doyle scandal, or his general recklessness.

It must have been weeks since he last had word from her. He'd been too busy with his plans for the engine by day and with debaucheries at night to notice her silence until now.

Blake swallowed and shifted his stance.

It should also be noted that Gideon was paid too handsomely to ever misplace anything.

He was the Duke of Ashbrooke, which meant he was invited everywhere. Always. As a rule. Especially by his own aunt. Though all the facts dictated otherwise. He had been snubbed by the one person whose good opinion and favor mattered to him.

"Although," George said thoughtfully, "you of all people can afford *not* to attend, being a wealthy duke, and all."

Unlike the rest of us. The words, unspoken, were still understood.

"Which shall one day be yours, coz," Blake said, sweeping his arm to indicate the large majestic house stuffed with priceless objects . . . and just one of many that the Dukes of Ashbrooke possessed.

"Unless you and your fiancée should be blessed with children," Edmund pointed out. Blake ignored that point, given that he didn't know his fiancée. But George's eyes darkened and his brow furrowed in consideration. He stood to lose considerably if Blake ever did take a wife and sire brats.

"I'm sure Aunt Agatha would like to meet your betrothed," Edmund added. "That is, before . . ."

"Is she unwell?" Blake was genuinely alarmed at the prospect. She had raised him. She had loved him. She was his rock. Although given this lack of invitation, perhaps she wasn't anymore. He would be damned if he showed even an inkling of the panic he was feeling.

How could she desert him?

"There are the usual rumors about the health of an older woman with a fortune," George said. "But she is not getting any younger, much as she may insist otherwise."

"We are still celebrating her twenty-fifth birthday, are we not?" Blake inquired.

"For at least fifty years now, according to my estimation," George replied. "Not that I would be foolish enough to allude to that in her company."

"One wouldn't dare," Blake quipped.

"Especially not if one wished to win the Fortune Games," Edmund replied. "And enjoy all the good fortune bestowed upon the winner."

Blake felt his competitive spirit flare. He was the Duke of Ashbrooke, who won everything, as a rule. At a hunting party, he bagged the most birds. In a ballroom . . . he bagged the most birds there, too. There was not a wager, card game, sword fight, or game of charades that he didn't charm or wit his way to winning.

The only thing he had ever lost was the support of his investors and Parliament for his Difference Engine. Someone more respectable and trustworthy was required, they had dutifully informed him.

Someone who didn't find themselves locked in a wine cellar with buxom twin sisters.

Someone who didn't steal other men's mistresses, flirt with their wives, or inspire wicked thoughts in their daughters.

Someone who was not cut by their own family. It seemed even Agatha didn't trust him with her money.

Someone who didn't find himself betrothed to a complete stranger by way of an announcement in the gossip columns.

They wanted someone more like Edmund or George. Someone who would become engaged to London's Least Likely to Misbehave. Someone who played by the rules and won fortune and favor from his own aunt.

A gentleman, not a rogue.

Blake smiled as a perfect plan started to form. An engagement with London's Least Likely to Misbehave would put to rest matters of which Tarleton twin he would marry, in addition to soothing his reputation and appeasing Agatha.

A fiancée and fortune would be just what he needed. She would restore his reputation, and thus he could woo back his investors. Or she might help him win the fortune, in which case he would have no need to pander for the funds needed to make his dream—the Difference Engine—come roaring to life.

No matter what happened, he won. It was the perfect plan—save for one crucial detail. He was not acquainted with his supposed fiancée.

The Drawing Room, Avery House

Finally, the duke—her fiancé—finally deigned to arrive.

A hush fell over the drawing room as the Duke of Ashbrooke entered. Emma's heart began to pound again because he was *here* and he was real and she had never been so close to him before.

The duke's gaze swept over all the ladies in the room.

To say he was incredibly handsome or virile or masculine just wasn't enough. He was taller than most men, bigger, and undoubtedly stronger, too.

Benedict. Remember Benedict.

Ashbrooke's features were pure Greek perfection—all strong, straight lines from his jaw to his nose to the noble slope of his brow. Yes, she had just had such an inane thought, but she consoled herself that any thoughts remained in her head at all.

Benedict. Your True Love. Do Not Forget Benedict!

Ashbrooke's skin could only be described as sun-kissed. His hair was dark, like coffee or chocolate, and slightly unruly, as if he had just come from bed.

His eyes, dear God, his eyes. When his gaze rested on her, it felt like sunshine on her bare skin.

Benedict who?

Women of varying ages and marital status peered up at him with dazed and dreamy expressions, like a God was literally in their midst. Emma got the distinct impression that he only had to say the word and any one of them would do whatever wanton wickedness he wished.

Ashbrooke smiled at them all.

One could practically hear the hearts fluttering, even above the sound of dreaming and the heartfelt sighs of longing. It was ridiculous. Ridiculous!

It dawned on Emma that he didn't know who she was. In a moment at least one or two women would come to their senses and realize that as well, then the jig would be up. The scandal would be mortifying, and she would never recover from it.

"Your Grace. Hello," Emma said, mustering a smile and managing to stand. She was horrified to discover that her knees were actually weak.

Stupid, stupid Ashbrooke Effect!

He's not that *beautiful,* she told herself. *He's just a man, not a god.*

He was totally that beautiful. And more. And he was *here.*

For a moment it seemed he was rescuing her from this farce. But then Logic, Reason, and Universal Laws reminded her not to be silly. There could only be one reason he was here, and it couldn't be good.

Emma felt herself tense, every last inch of her, as she awaited his declaration that she was an outrageous liar or a desperate pretender, in front of everyone, including Lady Katherine, who inexplicably was still here.

They would all laugh at her, the girl who made up an engagement announcement to the sort of man who would never look once—let alone twice—at her. No one would believe her if she tried to tell the truth of the matter.

Benedict! She loved Benedict!

She wanted to shout this aloud. But she was tongue-tied around this hulking beauty of a man who was reaching out for her hand then pressing his lips to the delicate skin of her inner wrist.

"Emily, my darling," he murmured.

Her heart stopped beating. She stopped breathing. What was he doing? And who was Emily? Oh Goodness, she was Emily! She had nearly forgotten her own name. It was the Ashbrooke Effect and it was happening to her.

"Emma," she corrected in a whisper a moment later.

"How are you on this exceptionally fine day, darling?"

"Truth be told, I am rather overwhelmed, Your Grace," she replied. An involuntary laugh bubbled up and escaped her lips because he was here, and he wasn't making a fool out of her.

"Darling, I thought I had told you to call me Blake," he scolded affectionately. Then he gave her the most devastating smile.

Emma peeked past the duke and saw Lady Katherine's eyes nearly bugging out of her pretty, perfect face. This is for the pianoforte solo, Emma thought. She saw Olivia, grinning because she knew the Ashbrooke Effect was happening to every single female in that room, including Emma, who was definitely not immune.

"Forgive me, Blake. I must have forgotten," Emma whispered.

"My memory isn't quite what it used to be either, Emily. Not since I met you," Blake said. Lord Above and the angels, too, *the Duke of Ashbrooke was holding her hand!*

"Emma," she corrected. But he still didn't know her name. What the devil was he going on about, anyway? Calling each other Emily and Blake and he holding her hand. The room began to spin. *Why* was this happening? *What* was happening?

"Emma, shall we take a turn about the garden?" Blake asked.

"Yes," she replied. Dear God, Yes.

Chapter 3

"It's the inconceivable sight of the Duke of Ashbrooke fawning over the Buxom Bluestocking."

—Lady Katherine Abernathy, spitefully

In the Garden

Though they were in full view of everyone in the drawing room, they could not be heard, thanks to the French doors that the duke deliberately closed behind them—with an apologetic grin to all the ladies, of course. Not one of whom moved, other than to obtain a better view of the unfathomable sight of Emma strolling arm in arm with London's Most Eligible Bachelor of All Time Ever.

She inhaled deeply, discovering the duke's manly scent of fresh linen and wool mingling with the fragrant flowers of the garden. She exhaled slowly. None of this could be real. At any second now everything would return to normal, or perhaps even worse.

What cursed person had sent the letter? And heaven's above, what was the duke actually doing here, in her garden, his muscled arm linked with hers?

"It seems we are engaged," Blake remarked casually. As if he were only commenting on the weather. As if they were acquainted, and not complete strangers to each other.

"We did nothing to dispel the rumors," Emma replied.

"Rumors? It was printed in the paper."

"Very well, libel," Emma corrected. "But you could still cry off."

She so kindly gave him the opportunity to live down to her expectations. She found herself holding her breath and glancing up at his impossibly handsome profile while she still had the opportunity to do so.

"Do you not want to marry me?" he asked, as if that had anything to do with it. She had not even considered it.

"Your Grace, I don't even know you."

"A minor detail, and one that is easily remedied." Then he glanced down at her with dark eyes and a suggestive smile. "It would be a pleasure to become better acquainted."

He said this, of course, in a manner that left no doubt as to what sort of pleasure or acquaintance he intended. Emma felt her temperature rising but would not allow herself to engage in his flirtations. She did not want to be swept away upon some flight of fancy, only to come crashing down when the world inevitably restored itself to the proper order in which the likes of him did not engage with the likes of her.

"I should think our lack of acquaintance is a significant detail, actually," she said. "And one not necessarily in need of a remedy."

The duke paused, and turned to face her. She was struck by the perfection of him. She, who had a crooked smile and plain brown hair and perfectly fine features, could not even imagine possessing such beauty as he.

He didn't even seem aware of how utterly handsome he was, and how it made a girl lose her wits around him.

Emma resolved then and there that she would be immune to the Ashbrooke Effect. She would not be yet another simpering, silly girl that flung herself at his feet. While the world as she'd always known it no longer made sense, she stubbornly clung to one truth: the likes of her and the likes of Ashbrooke could not belong together. Therefore, there was no point in acting prettily, as if she could (1) suddenly learn to flirt and that (2) something would come of it.

No, she wanted Benedict and their little townhouse full of books and babies. She wanted to be with a man who was safe, steady, and constant.

"I have a proposal for you," the duke said, clasping her hands. His were large, warm, and he scandalously did not wear gloves.

"Another one?"

He laughed, a rich, low, velvety sound, and she was overwhelmed by a flush of heat and pleasure just from the vibrations of it. Though she might have fleetingly suffered a sensation that could have been the infamous Ashbrooke Effect, she would perish before admitting it.

They did not belong together. She would do well to remember that.

She promptly forgot as he dropped to one knee.

"What in blazes are you doing?" Emma tried to yank him up to stand, but he held onto her hand firmly. She glanced, panicked, at the group of ladies pressed up against the drawing room window.

The duke remained on one knee, peering at her with an earnest look in his eyes and a hint of a smile on his lips.

"Emily, will you marry me?"

"Are you mad?"

"Smile, darling, they're watching," he murmured.

"Your Grace, we both know this betrothal announcement is a joke. It's not real," she told him. That much had to be said. She owed him that.

"I'm not an idiot, Emma," Blake said frankly, though he smiled as if in the midst of a proposal, because he remained on bended knee. "I know that someone with a warped sense of humor or twisted idea of vengeance thought it'd be an amusing prank to announce an engagement between two people who have never met. I don't know what kind of unhinged person would do such a thing."

Emma declined to offer further intelligence on the matter. In fact, she vowed to take the truth of the letter's authors to her grave, just as she vowed to seek revenge upon the horrible person who had actually sent it.

"But now I am proposing in truth. I beg you to say yes," he said so solemnly, she almost considered it. She narrowed her eyes, finding this proposal highly suspicious. She'd wager that when the duke awoke this morning, he didn't even know she was alive. And yet here he was, on bended knee, insanely proposing that they marry. He could not be serious.

Perhaps he was insane.

Or perhaps the duke had an ulterior motive. While she did not want to be unwed at Lady Penelope's ball, she also didn't want to throw her life away on a whim to suit an addled aristocrat.

She wanted Benedict. The man she loved. The man who actually and truly *knew* her.

Benedict! Where was he? Why was he not here? Probably because he thought her engaged to a man who towered above him in rank. He probably thought she'd lied and deceived him, too. Which is why she had to end this farce and explain the truth to Benedict. They could then elope and live simply in the country or in that townhouse on Brook Street.

That was the happily-ever-after of which she dreamed. She would not be the plain and forgotten wife of an infamous scoundrel, notorious rogue, and dashing duke.

"Thank you, Your Grace. But I cannot accept."

She, a lowly, impoverished wallflower on her

fourth season had just done the unthinkable: refused a wealthy duke. She must have gone mad.

In spite of her rejection, Ashbrooke just smiled. Then he stood, towering over her, gently lowered his mouth to hers and brushed his lips across her own. It was only an instant, but she felt sparks.

She felt the snap and sizzle of a fire flickering to life.

And she became aware that she'd never felt that with Benedict.

A lot could happen in an instant.

"What are you about?" she asked, dazed. He gently pushed a lock of hair away from her cheek. It was the affectionate caress of a lover.

"A kiss to celebrate our betrothal. For making me the happiest man in the world when you said yes."

"I did no such thing," she declared. Good God, the man was daft. All beauty and no brains.

"According to the dozen gossips in there," he said, inclining his head and never once taking his eyes off her face, "you just did."

"They couldn't hear me—" she said as the truth dawned. He wasn't daft at all. He was devious, and she had just fallen neatly into his trap.

"But they could see," he murmured, devastatingly.

They could see that he had proposed on one knee—again, presumably. They could see that he had kissed her. They would never, ever, ever, ever, ever consider that she would refuse him.

Emma touched her fingers to her lips. They

burned. Still burned. One fleeting kiss in the garden and she was betrayed. Ruined. Like Judas and Jesus. One fleeting kiss and the Duke of Ashbrooke had robbed her of her hopes, her dreams.

They were as good as married now. There would be no more Benedict, no little townhouse. She'd be the lonely duchess, married to a man far more attractive than she, and always the subject of cruel whispers. *What does he see in her?* She could just imagine the gossip columns: *To the surprise of no one, the duke of Ashbrooke continues his rakehell ways despite his marriage to the Buxom Bluestocking, who at least has books to comfort her.*

It was not the life she had planned, nor was it a life she wished for.

She would never forgive him that.

I am a wallflower, she wanted to protest. *I love another.* But she was a smart girl. Thus Emma knew none of that mattered anymore. Not after a duke kissed her in the garden, in full view of at least two dozen of London's greatest gossips. In a way, that was more official than actually signing the marriage contracts.

"Welcome to happily ever after," Ashbrooke said, linking his arm with hers. "Allow me to explain."

"Please do," she said in a strangled whisper. Rage had a way of tangling up words.

"You are one of London's Least Likely," the duke said smoothly, and she bit down on her lip.

"Really, you are going to start with that? I had heard you were considered an expert seducer.

Clearly, that rumor is an outrageous exaggeration."

"As you pointed out, I have, over the years, acquired a reputation as something of a rake."

"That's an understatement," she said. "One might say a ruthless scoundrel, a notorious libertine, a horrible jackanapes."

"Think, Emma, of how this betrothal could serve each of us," Ashbrooke said, keeping his voice even and his grasp on her secure. "My reputation would be mended by an engagement with a respectable girl."

"Words every girl wants to hear to describe herself. Really, I cannot fathom how you got your reputation for being such a seductive charmer."

"On my arm, you will become a sensation," Ashbrooke said plainly. "Let us face the facts: no one noticed you before, but everyone will want you now. When you cry off in a few weeks, I shall be inconsolable and take an extended visit away from London, and you shall have your pick of suitors."

Hope flickered. Then died.

"I'm not sure the world works like that," Emma said. The world was a different place for those who were not charming, powerful, wealthy dukes. "I would be seen as the Duke of Ashbrooke's jilted fiancée. Hardly the stuff of other men's dreams."

"That's where you are wrong," he stated flatly.

"I knew you would be arrogant," Emma muttered. "I am not pleased to be proven correct."

"It's not arrogance, it's the facts," he said with an impatient sigh.

"Why should I not cry off now? Because I really would like to." She glared stubbornly up at him. She detected a hint of a smile, a spark of appreciation in his eyes. She scowled all the more.

"You could jilt me now," he said slowly. "Even though two dozen women are already spinning stories of our whirlwind romance and romantic stroll in the garden. Everyone will think this was just a joke. You will be no better off than before. You'd be worse, even. And if you cried off now, we wouldn't have the fortune."

Her breath caught. Hope flickered again.

"What fortune?"

"My dear aunt Agatha is holding a house party at which she shall determine who will inherit her enormous fortune. She is also ancient."

Hope flickered again, and a flame burst forth. And then it died again.

"Allow me to confirm that I am understanding you correctly," Emma said slowly. "You would like us to pose as a betrothed couple to swindle your wealthy, elderly aunt out of her fortune."

"It does sound nefarious when phrased like that, I grant you," he said, grinning. "But it's all part of the Fortune Games, a mad scheme of Agatha's own creation. Every year, she invites a select group of family members to a house party to compete for her favor—and her fortune. And every year after the games, she rewrites her will, naming one of the competitors her heir until next year's games or . . . It must be said that she is not getting any younger."

"Ah yes, Lady Agatha Grey's Fortune Games. I have heard the most intriguing things about it. You have never won, have you?" Emma asked, eyes narrowed. *Why should I team up with a loser*? She didn't dare say it, but she hoped her expression conveyed it.

"With you as my blushing bride I would," he said, so confidently. "We would."

"And then I may jilt you and keep my portion of the reward?"

"If that's what you wish," he replied, eyeing her curiously. He obviously could not fathom that *she* might not wish to be with him. She was not at all sorry to provide this rude awakening to him.

"It is exactly what I wish," she said firmly. It was her one and only one chance to still attain the life she dreamt of. So long as she won the fortune and didn't do something ridiculous, like fall for the duke.

"Is there anything you wish to tell me, Emma? Is there another man? Are you in a particular condition?"

"We might pose as a happily betrothed couple, but you should know my heart belongs to someone else," she said, oddly delighted that he thought she, London's Least Likely to Misbehave, could possibly have gotten herself ruined or in a particular condition.

"So you'll say yes," he repeated.

"Apparently I already have," she remarked dryly. *For the fortune. For Benedict.*

Ashbrooke broke into a smile, a grin of pure

happiness. The force of such radiant, beautiful joy hit her like a runaway carriage pulled by a half-dozen charging stallions.

The duke wrapped his arms around her, swept her off her feet and whirled her around—right there, in the garden, with all the gossips of London watching. And then he kissed her—another swift brush of his warm, firm mouth against hers. She thought of fireworks, and a strange feeling of warmth and desire surged through her. She did not think of Benedict.

She thought of the Ashbrooke Effect.

It was real. It knocked her breath away, along with her wits.

"Pack your bags, Emma Wallflower," Ashbrooke said in a happy, laughing voice. "We have a house party to attend and a dowager to charm out of her fortune."

Chapter 4

According to the betting book at White's, the odds are decidedly not in favor of Ashbrooke and his betrothed winning the Fortune Games. Dear reader, do not inquire how I came about this information.

—"Fashionable Intelligence" by A Lady of Distinction, *The London Weekly*

A few days later
En route to the Fortune Games

After an hour into the journey it became clear to Blake that he had betrothed himself to London's Least Interested in Him.

She didn't flirt, act coy, or lean forward to show off her bosom to its best advantage, as women were wont to do near him. Though her lovely and curvaceous figure had not escaped his notice.

Ever since their departure, Emma's attention had been fixed upon a *book*, while he alternated between staring out the window and stealing glances at the curious woman seated opposite him.

It went without saying that this was not the usual state of affairs when he found himself in a carriage with a woman.

After an hour, he could tolerate it no more.

"What are you reading?"

She replied without once taking her eyes off the page.

"I am reading the sort of sentimental novel men dismiss as rubbish but could actually stand to learn a thing or two from."

"That's an awfully long title," he remarked dryly. She peered at him, as if to discern whether he was bamming her.

"Indeed," she remarked dryly.

Outside the carriage, miles and miles of pasture and wheat fields.

Inside the carriage: a challenge. Could he engage her in conversation? Could he tease a smile from her lips? He was Ashbrooke, after all. A legend. Women loved him. The Buxom Bluestocking should be no exception.

"Have you any questions about the Fortune Games? Given that it's your first time, I thought you might be curious."

She placed a red ribbon upon the page she was reading and looked up, fixing her dark blue eyes on him. He noted that she had very beautiful eyes—large, intelligent, and tilting up ever so slightly at the corners. But they were dangerous, those eyes. Like she saw right through him.

"Yes, Your Grace, perhaps you could tell me what I might expect from my first time. My nerves are tingling in anticipation."

He grinned, and replied, "Some people find the event to be unpleasant business, but I've found that if one anticipates the pleasures it affords—and has the right partner—it needn't be a tedious affair." To her credit, she did not blush.

"I thought I'd just lie back and think of the fortune," she remarked, and he felt his mouth crooking up into a slight smile.

"That is one way, though there are more stimulating and pleasurable possibilities," he said smoothly, noting a faint blush stealing across her cheeks.

"You speak a lot of pleasure."

"Would you rather I show you?" He gave her one of his devastating smiles that tended to make women swoon right into his arms.

"I thought you were going to tell me about the house party," she replied, completely unaffected.

"Is that not what we were discussing?"

"I heard that Lily Beekman died one year. Is that true?"

Blake shifted uncomfortably. "I'm sure Aunt Agatha has now learned that snake charming lessons are best done without using poisonous cobras expensively imported from India. Regular garden snakes will do."

"I suppose card games cease to be amusing after a while. One must keep entertained at a house party."

"'Entertained' is one word for it. One year we were expected to learn juggling. With her priceless collection of Roman pottery and Ming vases. Another year we played a game of her own invention, Dueling Debrett's, in which we competed to see who could flawlessly recite the lineages of peers back two hundred years."

"I'd win at that," Emma muttered. "Any unmarried woman would."

"Come to think of it, all the unmarried ladies performed exceptionally at that task," Blake noted. "They didn't fare as well at archery competition. For targets, we shot at apples placed precariously atop portraits of long-dead Ashbrooke family members. But only the ones Agatha didn't like."

"This certainly is not a typical house party activity," Emma said.

"The Fortune Games are not for the faint of heart or foolish. For all we know, we could be sent home on the first night. Or perhaps nerves have gotten the better of you and you'd like to return to London now?"

"Or perhaps we might win," Emma said with fierce determination and an adorable tip of her chin.

He lacked the courage to tell her that they had not been invited.

Queen's Head & Arms Tavern
Somewhere in Sussex

At suppertime they arrived at the coaching inn where they would dine, rest the horses, and spend the night before the final stretch of their journey on the morrow. After securing two adjoining bedchambers, Blake turned to Emma.

"I'm starving," he declared. "Would you care to join me for supper?"

"Thank you for the invitation, but I'd prefer a tray in my room," she replied.

"I'll speak to the innkeeper about a private parlor," he said before her words sank into his brain, causing him to pause, register *a refusal from a lady,* and feel—possibly for the first time—a noxious mixture of befuddlement and embarrassment.

He expected that a bluestocking spinster wallflower would be immensely flattered by his invitation and say yes.

But she had refused him! Blake pushed his fingers through his hair, frustrated and challenged all the same. Having persuaded her to go along with the charade, he could persuade her to share her company for the evening.

"Perhaps a drink, then? Would you care for a glass of sherry?"

She pulled a face, revealing that he had said exactly the wrong thing.

"What's wrong with sherry? Besides the fact that it is revoltingly sweet. I thought ladies loved sherry."

"If I never have another glass of sherry so long as I live, I will be a happy woman. But thank you for the offer anyway," she said. She started up the stairs, obviously finished with his company.

"Are you forgoing my company to read quietly by yourself?" he asked, warily eyeing the book she clasped firmly to her breasts. For the first time in his life he was jealous of a book. A book! "Are you forgoing the pleasures of a duke's company for . . . *Miss Darling and the Dreadful Duke*?"

"It is a rather captivating story," she said with a shrug. "I was not able to finish it on our journey today."

"It must be," he muttered. "You know, you are the first woman to refuse my company."

"How strange that must be for you. Never fear, the tavern maid seems like she'd be more than happy to be entertained by you."

Yes, but he didn't want the tavern maid. He wanted London's Least Likely. The realization of which made him badly want a drink.

Later that night

After concluding *Miss Darling and the Dreadful Duke,* the wickedly good novel she'd been reading, Emma found herself wide-awake and restless. She had not heard Blake return to his adjoining room, and she suspected that he was frolicking with the tavern maid as she had suggested.

She had not expected the ensuing vexation by what was surely the natural order of things. But she wondered where he might be and with whom, and then her traitorous brain imagined what romantic activities they might be engaged in.

Emma settled into bed with a copy of *The Sights and History of Sussex: Unabridged,* which, as expected, was a rather large and heavy volume. Alas, it was not as sleep inducing as she hoped it would be.

In fact, she had reached chapter four, *The Flora and Fauna of the Region,* when she heard Blake barge into his chamber and address his valet, Jepson.

"Your Grace has enjoyed himself this evening," his valet remarked dryly. Emma slipped out of bed and crept over to the adjoining door, where she pressed her ear against it and eavesdropped on every word. Naturally.

"Hardly. But a man deserves a pint or two after a day of traveling with a woman," Blake said. Emma scowled. She'd hardly been a bothersome companion.

"Lady Emma seems like a nice young lady. You couldn't have chosen a better fiancée," Jepson said, and Emma's heart surged with affection for him.

"You know very well that I did not chose her," Blake replied.

"Someone has a remarkable sense of humor to have placed that betrothal notice. I wonder who has done so. Do you not as well, Your Grace?"

Do not wonder such a thing!

"I'm not sure if I owe them a note of thanks or if I should call them out. It depends upon how we fare at the Fortune Games," Blake replied easily.

"Have you informed Lady Emma that you were not invited to attend this house party?"

Not invited?

Emma gasped at his breathtaking deception. She had half a mind to burst in and give him a piece of her mind. The duke had ruthlessly persuaded her to leave London and her true love, to compete for a fortune when they had *not even been invited*?

She could wring his neck right now. Or perhaps she could bash his beautiful face with her copy of *The Sights and History of Sussex: Unabridged.*

Or she could keep quiet and keep listening. What else was this duke hiding from her?

"There's no point in telling her. The lack of invitation hardly signifies," Blake replied, and she begged to differ.

"What if Lady Grey chucks you both out?" the valet asked. "It's likely that she would."

"Then we travel back to London and break off the engagement and pretend the whole thing never happened," Blake said. "I don't know why this has to be such a difficult drama."

She would wring his neck *and* bash him in the head with *The Sights and History of Sussex: Unabridged—and* spread a rumor that he was impotent. She would send that gossip to *The London Weekly,* which clearly printed anything.

"I doubt Lady Emma will be able to pretend the whole thing never happened," the valet said. Had she mentioned her love for Blake's valet? His concern for her was the only thing mollifying her temper.

Which was in great need of mollification, especially given what the duke said next: "Lady Emma is not my most pressing concern."

She exhaled slowly. It took all of her self-restraint to keep listening instead of flying into quite a rage.

"Is that because she is not throwing herself at you, like all the other women do?" the valet inquired oh-so-politely. Truly, she LOVED HIM. She added Jepson to the list of possible names for her firstborn.

"What the devil are you talking about, Jepson? Just because she needed some persuading to go along with this sham, and just because she spent the entire day reading a blasted book, doesn't mean I couldn't have her in an instant," Blake said sulkily. "If I wanted to."

"Ha!" A burst of shocked laughter escaped her. She was right: he was as arrogant and cocky as she had suspected. She was glad she had spent the day with her nose buried in a book and that she did not reveal how achingly aware of him she'd been. Her mind had wandered to wicked thoughts of what else they might do in the carriage . . . but now she would keep her sights firmly set on that fortune and on making sure the duke knew that she was the one woman who would not fall into his bed.

"Of course," Jepson replied consolingly. "No woman under the sun is immune to the Ashbrooke Effect."

"Basically," Blake said.

"I think she is completely immune to you," Jepson said.

"I am," Emma muttered. Though she occasionally had momentary lapses when she was not at all immune, her pride would not allow her to surrender to the duke's flirtations.

"I'll prove to you she isn't," Blake challenged. "I'll seduce her by the end of the Fortune Games."

Emma's jaw dropped, her eyebrows peeked high.

He did *not* just wager upon seducing her! What a rogue! What a scoundrel!

"Your Grace, I will not participate in such ungentlemanly and base wagers," her beloved Jepson said. That's right, she thought. But truth be told, one had to marvel at the fact that the Duke of Ashbrooke was wagering upon his attempted—and to-be-thwarted—seduction of one of London's Least Likely.

They would marvel even more when she jilted him. And she would resist his attempts at seduction and jilt him if it was the last thing she did.

"Suit yourself, Jepson. I shall need a challenge to amuse me at the Fortune Games. Seducing Emma will be just the thing," the duke said.

That was, of course, the moment that the lock gave way, the door burst open, and she tumbled into his bedchamber, only to land on her hands and knees. In her unfashionable and unflattering white muslin nightdress.

Blake was not wearing a shirt. It had to be noted.

It also had to be noted that his chest was broad, muscled, tanned, and strong. She wanted to touch him.

It also must be noted that she was intent upon refusing him and ensuring that he never knew how he affected her. He could never know that the sight of him shirtless made her heart race and her skin flush.

"Eavesdropping, were you?" Blake inquired as she picked herself off the floor.

"Naturally. I was having trouble sleeping, but your conversation was just the remedy. Not even *The Sights and History of Sussex: Unabridged* put me to sleep so quickly. I must have drifted off while leaning against the door."

"I thought you were reading *Miss Darling and the Dreadful Duke.*"

"That was two hours ago, Your Grace. Do endeavor to keep up. I began on *The Sights and History of Sussex: Unabridged* because it seemed like an excellent sleeping remedy."

The duke's lips quirked up in a smile. She adopted a lofty expression and wished she were taller so she might actually look down upon him.

"Of course you need a remedy," he said. "You must be exhausted from sitting in the carriage all day."

"I found maintaining a polite interest in my company sapped my strength," Emma replied. She added a sigh, to demonstrate her weariness at being plagued by his insufferable (and maddeningly attractive) company.

"Do you find me dull, Lady Emma?" Blake said, taking one, two, three, four easy steps across the room to stand in front of her with all his towering, masculine, naked muscularity. She did not find him dull at all.

He did it to intimidate her. To affect her. To try to seduce her, just for the sake of it. Just because he wanted to win at *everything,* so she had to ensure that he lost at *this.* She would not be a pawn in his quest for glory.

Her heart was racing, but she wasn't intimidated.

"It's safe to say I don't find you as enthralling as most women do," Emma said. He was handsome, yes, but far too arrogant for her tastes.

"You should see a doctor about that. It can't be normal," Blake told her, and she laughed.

"Just so we're clear, Your Grace, not only am I *not* the slightest bit interested in you, but my heart belongs to another man," she said firmly. Yet her heart, which belonged to her beloved Benedict, was currently pounding away at a furious pace, all because of a certain arrogant, maddening duke.

Chapter 5

If I do not win the Fortune Games, I'm afraid of what I will have to do to survive.

—LADY BELLANDE'S TROUBLED INNERMOST THOUGHTS ON HER WAY TO THE GAMES

CASTLE HILL CAME into view after a few miles on the long, winding road shadowed by massive trees. Its namesake was obvious: a large castle perched high on the ridge overlooking the sea. Home.

Emma closed her book and peered out the carriage window.

Blake remembered the first time he'd made this journey as a lad of just eight, already a duke and very much alone.

The gnarled old oak trees still loomed large over the drive. Black and white sheep still dotted the lush green pastures. The sky was still blue, the lands still vast and impressive. The horses slowed as if sensing the end of the journey. He still felt the same mixture of relief to have arrived and dread, for he was not ready for what awaited.

He felt like a violin string, pulled taut and out of tune.

It was all the same except for the dark-haired girl peering out the window with wide blue eyes. It was all splendor to her. It was all something she might win.

It was everything he stood to lose if he was not victorious in the Fortune Games.

The carriage rolled to a stop before the house, and Jewkes, the butler, stepped out to greet them.

"Your Grace," he intoned as always, whether Blake was an eight-year-old orphan or a man of three and thirty. Whether he was arriving here to stay—home. Or whether he was here, one of a dozen, to debase himself by competing for Agatha's favor and fortune.

Agatha, the one woman who had ever loved and understood him.

And he was here to compete for what should be given freely. Hell, he hadn't even been invited. And he'd dragged an innocent woman into this mad effort to *not lose* Castle Hill, the one place he'd ever called home, as much as to win the fortune that would enable him to put an end to the tragic Ashbrooke legacy and create something newer, more powerful, more eternal in its place.

Jewkes just stood there, tall and firm, saying, "Your Grace" as if that were the only constant thing in the world.

To Blake's relief, they were shown to bedchambers where they might freshen up after the journey and dress for dinner. After a bath, a shave, and donning formal evening attire, he went to collect Emma.

He passed the stairs up to the fourth floor and thought of visiting the nursery. But memories ought to be left in the past.

That taut violin string pulled tighter, the tension stronger.

Blake knocked on Emma's door. He remembered being just a boy, knocking on Agatha's door, believing it his ducal duty to escort her to supper. Or because he awoke in the night, scared and confused. That was before Agatha had taught him how to analyze and master his emotions.

Emma opened the door, book in hand.

She wore a simple blue dress that made her eyes seem brighter. Her dark hair was done in one of those complicated arrangements with ribbons and pearls and whatnot that ladies favored. He only noticed a few wayward curls brushing against her cheeks, the nape of her neck, all those sensitive spots where a man kissed a woman. Perhaps he might press his lips there . . .

"You look lovely." He meant it. He'd spent a fair amount of time in the carriage discovering that she wasn't the plain girl he'd sized her up to be upon first sight.

Her lips parted, a slightly crooked smile that was charming and fascinating. He thought of kissing her.

"How kind of you to say so," she replied. Obviously she did not believe him. His compliments were not usually rebuffed.

He felt the violin string pulled tighter still, so far out of tune, so close to snapping. He exhaled slowly, not wanting to lose his temper or give her any indication that he was overset by nerves.

"What are you reading?" he asked, gesturing toward the book she held.

"*The Exhaustive History of the Ashbrooke Clan and Their Holdings*. A copy was left on my bedside table."

"Mine, too. But you couldn't offer me anything to read such boring old trivia. Are you ready? Once I introduce you to Agatha as my fiancée, there will be no turning back. We will have to compete. We will probably win—if you are up for the challenge."

He had to ask. Because once they stepped amongst the competitors, he would not accept defeat. Blake William Peregrine Auden, the ninth Duke of Ashbrooke, did not lose.

"I've made it all the way to Castle Hill. There is no turning back now," Emma replied. "Are you ready? Because I have every intention of winning."

The tension on the violin string lessened, slightly.

Blake led her through the corridor, down the massive staircase, across the pink marble and alabaster foyer, and onto the terrace—dodging ghosts and memories every step of the way.

In the stupidly pink foyer, he had been left alone with his dusty traveling trunks, just a young boy with a title longer than he was tall.

He had been a violent tempest of emotional turmoil.

Then Agatha arrived. She had coolly and calmly taken him by the hand and led him to the nursery. He still recalled his small, sticky orphan boy hand in her paper-soft old lady hand.

On a round marble table in the foyer stood the same monstrosity: a large porcelain urn, hand painted with pastoral scenes of Castle Hill and containing the ashes of Lady Agatha's fourth husband, Harold, otherwise known as "the one she liked." Some poor housemaid was tasked with dusting it each day, her job on the line if it should be anything less than perfectly maintained.

The hallway on the second floor, where she had pointed out her bedroom and said he shouldn't hesitate to disturb her. She was old and no longer had a husband, so he wouldn't interrupt anything, she had told him. He'd been confused then, but he understood: he was always welcome, her fierce little duke.

He hoped this was still true.

He held Emma's hand tightly, grateful for the comfort it afforded. He was troubled by feelings he couldn't have articulated even if he found himself at knifepoint, on the edge of a cliff overlooking a pit of man-eating crocodiles. Memories of the past haunted him, the warm touch of her hand keeping him grounded in the present.

Notoriously heartless scoundrel he might be, he held on for dear life.

Hand in hand they passed through the French

doors leading to the stone terrace, which overlooked the gardens and beyond that the water. One could see the blue line of the horizon, and the air carried the salty scent of the sea.

"The Duke of Ashbrooke and his betrothed, Lady Emma Avery," Jewkes announced.

The small, select crowd peered at the latecomers. George, knowing the truth about the engagement, grinned wickedly. Blake wondered if he could count on him to keep the information to himself.

The Copleys—second cousins—were there, looking peevish, as always. Cousins Archibald Pleshette and Lord Dudley stood off to the side, radiating snobbery. Blake noted the predatory gaze of Lady Bellande, the widow of his long deceased second cousin. It was how women other than Emma usually looked at him.

Emma's hand tightened around his, sending a surge of possessiveness shooting through him.

Then the crowd parted, revealing Aunt Agatha. Her white hair was done in an elaborate, towering arrangement that probably added eight inches to her height. As per her unique style, she appeared to wear the entire collection of Ashbrooke family jewels at once. Dangling ruby ear bobs, diamond necklaces tangled with strands of black pearls, a sparkling rock on every finger, gold and silver bracelets clinking on her thin, bony wrists.

Blake couldn't help it. He squeezed Emma's hand, hard.

Aunt Agatha was older, grayer. It was her eyes

that undid him, because they were as blue, keen, intelligent, and sharp as the day he first arrived. She had taken one look at him and said, "Well all right then, come along." There was no coddling or nonsense with Agatha. After a plethora of clucking, pitying aunties and cousins after the Accident, it was what he had needed. Desperately.

He remembered how she'd stood so tall, her spine so straight.

Though she still carried herself proudly, she no longer stood on her own. A footman held her arm, lightly, as if merely decoration. But Blake suspected that if the man let go, his beloved Aunt Agatha would topple over and shatter on the paving stones.

His heart clenched. Stupid heart.

Emma sighed as the footman approached. He was young, golden, brawny, and would be called handsome by any chit with a pulse. Blake took immense comfort in Agatha's choice of companion. The old broad had life in her yet. If nothing else, she obviously wasn't blind.

"The Duke of Ashbrooke deigns to grace us with his presence. I am beside myself with glee," Agatha said dryly, by way of greeting.

Blake exhaled with relief. Agatha was still Agatha. He had not been too late. But it had been too long.

"I fancied some extra spending money so I thought I'd drop by," he said. Beside him, Emma sucked in her breath sharply. She didn't know what he had just said meant *Hello,* and *I have missed you*, and a million other things that could never be put into words.

"As impertinent as ever. How predictable. How dull," Agatha replied. Then she rolled her eyes, which he knew meant that all was well in the world.

"My sincerest apologies," Blake said. Then he swept into a deep bow, and upon rising declared, "I forget we are all here for the amusement of a crotchety old dowager."

"You'll do well to remember it, Duke, lest I recall that you were not actually invited this year," she stated loudly. "Make a note of that, Angus."

The handsome footman did just that in the small red leather volume he kept close to his chest. One kept score in the Fortune Games, with Agatha awarding points for small triumphs and removing them at the slightest misstep. But in the end, she picked the winner based upon some formula that even he had never discerned.

The other guests had started to hum and whisper as they began to count their numbers. Emma smiled tightly in a *You'll pay for this, mister* way, so Blake treated her to one of his legendary smiles and kissed her hand.

"An oversight in your old age, and I forgive you for it," Blake said smoothly. "However, I thought you'd be vexed if I didn't introduce you to my betrothed. Dearest Aunt Agatha, please do meet my fiancée, Lady Emma Avery."

George started coughing. Blake hoped someone would smack him on the back, hard.

"I'm pleased to meet you, Lady Grey," Emma said.

"Are you really?" Agatha asked skeptically.

"I am also terrified and intrigued," Emma confessed.

"I suppose he warned you about the games," Agatha said, sounding totally bored. "Tell me, are you terrified or intrigued by those?"

"It can't be any more torturous than a wallflower's fourth season on the marriage mart," Emma replied without skipping a beat. Blake's heartbeat quickened. This had never happened—a woman who wasn't completely rendered spineless and spiritless in the presence of Aunt Agatha.

"But you are no longer on the marriage mart. You, a wallflower on your fourth season, have managed to snare this prime specimen of manhood," Agatha said with a dismissive wave of her old hand toward the prime specimen that was his person.

"Physically speaking," Emma conceded, with a glance that felt like a caress. Then she dropped her voice. "His wits, on the other hand . . ."

Agatha leaned in close, conspiratorially, and said: "Makes one wonder if he was dropped as a child."

Blake felt Emma lean in farther to whisper to Agatha, but he pulled her back to immediately put an end to a relationship that could only rain down terror upon him.

"While I am just delighted you two are getting along like a village on fire, perhaps Lady

Emma would like to meet the other guests," he suggested, even though the other guests were certainly the twelve most boring people who had ever walked the earth.

"I can't imagine she would," Agatha said. "They're a giant lot of boorish fortune hunters."

Said batch of boorish fortune hunters had the decency to blush, turn pale, and otherwise act dismayed by such a pronouncement.

But then Blake counted them, each and every one. There were only ten. Which meant that while no invitation had been extended to him—and his guest—he had been welcomed. Wanted. Expected.

The Dining Room

The guests—competitors—found their places around the long mahogany table in the dining room. Each setting contained numerous china plates, highly polished silver forks, knives, spoons, and crystal glasses. Blake glanced across the table at Emma and saw her pale at the setting. Odds were, a mistake would be made.

Odds were they would not make it through dinner.

That he and Emma were seated on either side of Aunt Agatha was probably not a mark of favor, but a trap. Many dismissed her as a mad old woman, impervious to logic or reason. Blake knew better.

She had introduced him to the comfort afforded

in rules and equations, whether etiquette or mathematical. There was no reason to fuss or fret. One had only to find the formula and proceed. Whether the seduction of a woman, the construction of the Difference Engine, or even the Fortune Games, Blake found and executed the formula.

"Welcome to the twentieth annual Fortune Games," she declared, standing with a bejeweled goblet in hand. Frail as she was, her voice carried to the far end of the table. "Undoubtedly you all have been shamelessly gossiping about the size of my fortune or the state of my health—especially you, Dudley. Don't think I didn't hear about what you said to Edmund. I have deducted two points from each of your tallies."

All heads swiveled to focus upon that wanker Dudley, whose cheeks reddened considerably.

"I can assure you, Lady Grey—" he began.

"Should you not provide some proof?" Edmund gently suggested to Agatha. "Perhaps a letter from your banker, or your physician?"

Emma gasped at his audacity.

"That would be the honorable thing to do," Agatha conceded. "But I'm a rich old woman so I can do whatever I please. Thus, if you doubt that there is in fact a fortune—and there may not be, wouldn't that just be hilarious—then you may leave at once."

No one made the slightest move.

Wealthy old woman + devious imagination – restraint = Aunt Agatha

"Some of you have played the games before,"

Agatha said. "Some of you have even won. Believe me when I say those years were some of the longest of my life."

"Then why did you invite us back?" Dudley asked, leaning back in his chair.

"Gives me an incentive to live longer, Dudley," Agatha remarked. She took a sip from her goblet and then carried on with her decrees. "The games shall last for three days. That is the maximum amount of time I can abide the lot of you. If you bore me, you shall be asked to leave and shall no longer be eligible for the fortune."

*Attention span = (entertainment value * novelty)*

"I chose the winner based on criteria I will not disclose. It is non-negotiable," Agatha said firmly. "If you do not think this fair, you may proceed to the library and write a letter to someone who cares. Do not address it to me."

Emotion = x
Do not solve for x

Agatha paused to sip from her goblet. Her footman hovered just behind her.

"Do remember that you are free to leave at any time. Nor was your presence here required. In fact some of your presences were not even requested," Agatha said with a pointed look at Blake.

Adopting an expression of utter innocence, he said, "Fortunately, we have corrected that appalling oversight."

"You're lucky you have a pretty face, Ashbrooke," Agatha said dryly. "Your manners are appalling. I don't know how your fiancée abides you."

"A little sherry gets her through the day. And night," Blake said. Emma's mouth dropped open and she shot him one of those looks that spoke of murderous rage and evil intentions. But then her lips curved into an adorably crooked smile.

"It's the only way to tolerate him," Emma replied as dryly as Agatha, to Blake's surprise and to the amusement of the others.

He saw Agatha's lips quirk into an approving smile.

"Indeed," she said, raising her goblet before taking a hearty sip. "Fortunately he had enough sense to betroth himself to a woman of wit and judgment. There is hope for your children yet. Now what was I saying?"

"That you are the queen of the Fortune Games, your word is final, and we have the choice to participate, which makes any complaints null and void," Blake declared.

"Well done," Agatha said plainly. "Your brain box works after all."

"Why don't you just declare him and his fiancée the winners and let us all go home?" Lord Pleshette muttered. "He was always the favorite."

"After everyone has traveled all this way?" Lady Agatha asked, aghast. "Besides, Lady Emma could still commit some unforgivable faux pas."

"Like Lord Anderson in 1816," Edmund said, shaking his head. "That was such a tragedy."

"Was he the one who had been caught in your dressing closet, in your corsets and petticoats?" Lady Copley inquired.

"No, that was Lord Wiltshire," George said. "Anderson was winning until he used the wrong fork at a luncheon. To be fair, it was a thirteen-course meal with separate cutlery for each course. The table setting monstrous. Not unlike this one."

"It's completely unforgivable," Agatha said. "I couldn't possibly leave my estate to someone ignorant in the most basic of table manners."

Everyone glanced nervously at the array of silverware, china dishes, and multiple etched crystal glasses upon the table. Dinner had not even begun.

"To the twentieth Annual Fortune Games," Aunt Agatha declared, bejeweled goblet raised and voice booming. All the guests raised their glasses as well. Emma, nerves getting the best of her, was the only one to drop hers, shattering the crystal on the china plate and spilling wine upon her best dress and the epic table setting before her.

Chances at winning the games = null

"Ah, the games have only just begun and we must already deduct six points from Lady Emma's tally. Angus, do make that note." Her footman wrote it down in the red leather volume. Emma's cheeks burned. And the games began.

THEY HAD NOT even survived the first course when disaster struck for the second time, in the form of a polite remark and simple question that caught both Blake and Emma utterly and foolishly unprepared.

"Lady Emma, Duke, I think I speak for all the guests when I offer my congratulations on your betrothal," Miss Montgomery said kindly from the far end of the table. Though she was a *Miss,* she was clearly at least forty years or more. A spinster.

Miss Montgomery was her, Emma thought, if she didn't play this game right.

"The news was such a surprise," George said with a sharp smile, reminding Emma of daggers drawn. "We never thought cousin Blake would be the marrying kind. We are all eager to know how you met."

"Indeed, we are all perishing of curiosity," Edmund said, and everyone murmured their agreement. Emma felt like a fox at a hunt. Surrounded. The snarling dogs closing in.

Emma looked to Blake, hoping the alarm she felt was not apparent in her expression. She thought of all those hours in the carriage when she deliberately avoided his conversation—and any temptation—by sticking her nose in a book.

They ought to have concocted a story. Instead they ignored each other.

When Blake did not rush to her rescue fast enough, Emma knew she would have to save herself. The games had hardly begun and she already had negative points—fewer than anyone else. She had to act daringly or risk falling further behind.

"It was the most romantic encounter," she said, and everyone at the table fixed their attention upon her. She took a deep breath and drew courage from Blake's curious gaze. Then she took the opportunity to commit them to the romantic story *she* wanted, and it was straight from the pages of *Miss Darling and the Dreadful Duke.*

"We met at a ball," Blake declared at the same time Emma stated, "We stumbled upon each other in an abandoned gazebo in Hyde Park during a sudden, severe thunderstorm."

"That's just like in *Miss Darling and the Dreadful Duke!"* exclaimed Miss Dawkins, a young debutante and fellow wallflower.

"Quite a coincidence, I assure you," Emma replied, smiling weakly. She nervously sipped her crisp white wine, gripping the glass securely.

"Where is there an abandoned gazebo in Hyde Park?" inquired Lady Copley, half of a bickering middle-age couple.

"Oh, it's on the far side," Emma answered, having no idea if one even existed. "I do enjoy a good constitutional walk in the morning."

"One wouldn't think Ashbrooke would," said Lady Bellande, who was the sort of painted widow that was every woman's worst nightmare. "One would think he were engaged in other pursuits in the morning."

"It was on my way home from an exclusive gaming hell," Blake explained, which tested the imagination of no one.

"How excellent you both enjoy long walks at first light," Lady Agatha said. "For I had planned a tour of the grounds tomorrow."

"Not all four hundred acres, I hope," Lord Pleshette quipped. "I should hate to wear my boots. They're from Hobbs, which makes the King's boots as well."

No one cared about his boots. Surely Emma wasn't the only one who felt ashamed of her unfashionable attire after he had given her a dismissive glance.

"What else have you planned for us, Aunt Agatha?" Blake asked. "Dragon hunting? Another game of Dueling Debrett's? Perhaps some jousting? It's just not done enough these days."

"A musicale. Perhaps a ball. Perhaps a circus," she said, sipping her wine and grinning devilishly. "I've heard some people are having the most remarkable luck training bears to do tricks! Wouldn't that be a wonderful talent to have?"

"Bears?" Miss Dawkins echoed in a very hollow voice.

"A musicale shall be lovely. Perhaps I might sing," Lady Bellande offered. "Ashbrooke could accompany me . . . on the pianoforte."

She said this in the sort of voice that led one to understand that she meant his accompaniment *literally on top* of the pianoforte, and not for a musical endeavor.

Emma felt her lips purse in a decidedly spinsterish fashion. An unexpected surge of possessiveness stole over her. She did not want her fictional fiancé to be unfaithful to her, nor did she want anyone to think so. Her pride revolted at the prospect.

Certainly the feeling of possessiveness had nothing whatsoever to do with wanting him for herself.

She was the first person to say that she and Blake made an odd and unexpected couple. She was a plain wallflower. He was a man so handsome that he sucked all the attention in the room toward himself, as if he possessed his own personal force of gravity.

But at the moment she fiercely wanted it to be true. Though she was still in love with Benedict and playing this game for her future with him, in the moment she longed to be something other than *not quite*. She didn't want to battle with the likes of Lady Bellande for her betrothed's attentions.

If she had the fortune . . . No one would overlook her then.

"Do you enjoy musicales, Lady Emma?" Lady Agatha asked.

"I do," she answered truthfully. Anything where she did not have to stand against the wall, awaiting a dancing partner while trying not to seem desperate for one.

"Do you play?" Lady Agatha asked, but Emma was distracted by Lady Bellande leaning in close to Blake. To *her fiancé*.

"I do play the pianoforte." Emma declined to mention she did not do so very well. She looked to Blake, hoping he might change the conversation before she was invited to perform. But she saw that Lady Bellande's hands had disappeared under the table and he did not meet her gaze. Oh, he could not ignore her now! He could not abandon her now!

She might be London's Least Likely to Misbehave, but she would not be the first loser in the Fortune Games.

"Speaking of musicals, Ashbrooke has taken up the flute," Emma told everyone. "I have encouraged him to learn in time for our wedding."

Lady Bellande removed her hands and gaped at the duke. Ashbrooke caught Emma's eye across the table. He gave her a wicked smile and her stomach flip-flopped. As if she had called him out, he rose to her challenge.

"Emma thought it would be romantic, and I live to please her," he said smoothly. "That's why I hope I may make a small request, Aunt Agatha. She is ever so fond of sherry. Perhaps we should be sure to include some at each meal."

"Even for breakfast?" Lord Copley asked.

"Especially for breakfast," Blake answered.

That rogue! Aware that everyone was looking at her, Emma smiled sweetly at him, when really she wanted to toss her wineglass in his beautiful face. He smiled in return, his eyes meeting hers over the flickering candles.

"Ashbrooke, you are too attentive to my every desire," Emma said darkly.

"That's what all the women say," he said with

a grin. Lady Bellande bit her red lip and gazed longingly at Blake. Emma fought the urge to roll her eyes.

"After your chance encounter in the Abandoned Gazebo in Hyde Park, did you propose immediately, Ashbrooke?" George asked smoothly, a grin quirking at his lips. "Or was there some courtship of Lady Emma that managed to escape the notice of the entire ton during one of the duller seasons in recent memory?"

"When a man knows he's found the woman for him, why should he wait?" Blake mused. A romantic sentiment? Or evading the question?

Definitely the latter.

"Perhaps he might like to know her better," Lady Copley said. "One should take the time to know their spouse before committing to a lifetime of marriage. It would save ever so much agony."

"Indeed," Lord Copley said strongly. "Though it pains me to agree with my wife."

No one else at the table knew quite where to look or what to say to that.

Save for Blake, of course.

"We know each other very well, " he said after a sip of wine. "For example, we all know Emma is fond of reading. So fond, she has earned the nickname the Buxom Bluestocking." *How dare he* mention her hated nickname! Her temperature began to rise, and it had *nothing* to do with a possible fleeting pang of desire for Ashbrooke. More like a slow boiling rage. And then he went on: "She loves sherry morning, noon, and night. She loves nothing more than to wake at dawn and take long walks at first light."

It was lies, all lies.

She would pay him back in spades.

"Lady Emma, what have you discovered about the duke that no other woman knows?" Lady Bellande asked. Was she *truly* asking for tips on how to seduce her fiancé? Or was she, like the rest, in utter disbelief that a man like *Ashbrooke* would ever bother with a girl like her? Well, she *was* one of London's Least Likely, after all.

"Is there anything?" Emma replied sweetly.

"Surely, there is something," Lady Agatha said.

"He's incredibly sweet, tender, and romantic," Emma said, thinking not of Ashbrooke, but of Benedict. And then she let her imagination take over. "He wept as he proposed. It was the most touching moment."

"Wept?" Blake asked skeptically. A few of the men quickly masked their laughter with coughs.

Lady Agatha cackled with amusement.

"I had to lend you my handkerchief, remember?" Emma replied, feigning innocence. "The one you requested I embroider with our initials entwined in pink thread."

Stealing a glance at her "fiancé," Emma saw that his brow was raised. Perhaps it was the wine, or perhaps it was his attention, fixed upon her, but her heart started to beat rapidly as if she were giddy. As if she were enjoying this dueling romantic story.

"How did he propose?" Miss Dawkins asked. Emma heaved a dramatic sigh before spinning a story of her own wishful thinking.

"On bended knee. At the gazebo where we had first met, on a warm, moonlit night."

"After I fought off a band of thieves," Ashbrooke said casually, leaning back in his chair.

"That pack of poor, unfortunate children? They couldn't have been more than twelve years of age. They were merely begging for bread," Emma replied, and he scowled mightily across the table at her. Much to her delight.

"They were heavily armed. A veritable artillery," he retorted. "I risked my life to protect your virtue."

"His nerves were overset that evening," Emma explained kindly to the table of skeptical—but riveted—faces. "Our courtship had been a whirlwind, and he was not sure if I would accept or not," she said, adding another outrageously unbelievable lie to the mix.

"It is amazing that no one in London discovered your courtship. What a *secret* whirlwind that must have been," Lady Bellande said, insinuating the very worst. Just when Emma was starting to enjoy herself.

"Oh, we traded numerous love letters," Emma said, thinking quickly. How else to explain a love match no one saw developing?

"I should love to have a reading of those," Lady Agatha said.

"They're private, Aunt Agatha," Blake said.

"Not everything under the sun exists for your amusement."

"An inconvenient truth I like to ignore," she said with a dismissive wave of her hand. "Where is your betrothal ring, Lady Emma? Don't tell me you didn't get her one, Ashbrooke."

"Oh, I must have left it in my bedchamber! I'm not used to wearing it yet," Emma said quickly.

He hadn't gotten her a ring! She glared at him across the table.

He shrugged, slightly.

They were horribly unprepared for this. They ought to have spent their journey concocting a story of how they met and determining the details of their fictional courtship. Instead he had thought about seducing her merely to prove a point, and she endeavored to maintain her virtue and dignity by refusing him.

If they survived this house party she would eat her bonnet.

Chapter 6

"Do you believe they are truly betrothed? The entire affair is highly suspicious if you ask me," Lady Copley murmured to her husband over tea in the drawing room.

"I didn't ask you. And it doesn't matter what I think. Only what your batty old Aunt Agatha thinks is true," Lord Copley replied.

Later that evening

"THAT WAS A disaster," Blake said flatly. He and Emma had bid good-night to the group after the conclusion of supper and the customary drinking of port and tea until the hour grew late.

For the sake of appearances, Blake linked arms with Emma as they quit the drawing room and proceeded past the monstrous urn in the foyer and onward to their respective bedchambers through shadowed corridors, dimly lit by the flickering candlelight contained in crystal sconces fixed high on the damask-papered walls.

Keeping his hands occupied properly would limit his ability to strangle her, which he desperately wanted to do after her theatrics at the dinner table. He didn't even want to know what outrageous tales with which she regaled the women over tea.

It was either that or kiss her hard so she was left breathless and unable to speak her own name, let alone make up any more ridiculous fictions.

"It was a complete and utter failure," Emma agreed. "We have probably lost the games already. I knew no one would believe us."

"They might have if you hadn't told the most absurd and unfathomable stories. You told everyone I fought a band of children."

He turned to glower down at her. She peered up at him, small and defiant.

"You said they were heavily armed! Poor, starving orphan street children!"

"And what of the nonsense about the gazebo? I'm afraid to ask how you came up with this rubbish. I shudder to think of what novels you have been reading that put such nonsense in your head."

"It's romantic. If we still have a chance of winning, it's because of my ingenuity. Besides, you have not offered a better idea."

She was a stubborn little thing. The problem was, he was, too.

"I said we could have met at a ball. Everyone knows I'm always disappearing with different women. It would have been completely believable."

"Except that I spend every ball properly in view just in case . . . " Emma's voice trailed off and he knew what she meant to say. Just in case someone asked her to dance.

Blake thought of all the wallflowers at balls,

their indistinguishable, hopeful-but-trying-not-to-be-desperate faces attempting to catch the eye of any gentleman who drew near. Occasionally he thought of waltzing with one of them just to give her a moment's happiness. But knowing that such an invitation would be tremendously misconstrued by the girl, her mother, and the entire haute ton, kept him at a distance.

"Not that I would ever be missed," Emma added darkly.

Blake was not inclined to pity. Not when every time he was "missed" resulted in some scandal or another. The ton's insatiable interest in his pleasure made it impossible for his business of securing funds for the Difference Engine.

"What's done is done," he said briskly. "Now I must learn the blasted flute and let it be known that I wept while proposing to you."

"We're even. Sherry makes me sick and now I shall have to drink it morning, noon, and night," she retorted.

"Hit the bottle too hard one evening?"

"Precisely," Emma said in a clipped voice.

"Now I am intrigued," he said. He tried to imagine her in the throes of a sherry-induced drunken spree and failed. She was London's Least Likely to Misbehave, after all.

"I'm not telling," Emma said darkly. So the wallflower had secrets and got into trouble, did she? He glanced down at the woman on his arm. No longer quite so plain. It wasn't just the candlelight or the port he'd drunk either.

"Pity, that you shan't regale me with stories of your debaucheries," he said. "In return, I could tell you about the time I drank an excessive amount of ratafia. The story involves a nun, a swan, and a portrait of the third Duke of Ashbrooke. I was only thirteen years old."

"Now *I* am intrigued," she said. Another glance at her told him she was intrigued in spite of herself.

Feminine resistance to his charms. What a novelty.

They had arrived before her door. Strangely, they lingered.

"Well I can't tell you here in the hallway," he said.

"We shall have plenty of time to converse on the morrow, when we walk all twelve thousand acres of your aunt's estate. Perhaps we could also use that time to concoct more stories. There are bound to be more questions."

"Everyone is far too curious," Blake said frankly, leaning against the wall. Emma's hand rested on the doorknob.

"Of course they are! Look at you. And look at me. We do not belong together."

The thing was, he had looked at her and they saw vastly different things. He saw a pretty girl; she saw a plain one. She saw a wallflower; he saw a girl who deliberately stuck her nose in a book when spending two days in a carriage with an eligible bachelor. No wonder she was unwed during her fourth season. But knowing women as he did, Blake knew better than to say any of that.

"It's nobody's damn business," he said.

"I can assure you," Emma said coldly, "no one heard about that law and no one is obeying it or enforcing it. I want to win this, Ashbrooke."

He sighed. "You had to mention love letters, didn't you." He had a reputation, and it did not include composing romantic drivel. Until now. He, too, wanted to win. He had a future to build and a past to redeem, all of which depended upon either a massive infusion of wealth or his reputation reformed.

He leaned in close. Her lips parted. He reached behind her. Twisted the knob and pushed the door open.

"What are you doing?" Emma asked in an appalled whisper.

"We're going to write some damned love letters and get our story straight, darling Emma," Blake murmured. "Even if it takes all night."

He tugged her into the bedchamber and closed the door behind them. He ignored all her protestations about propriety and what people would think. Instead he pointed out that it would serve their story if people thought them madly, wildly, dangerously attracted to each other.

An awkward silence fell over the room, disturbed only by the crackling fire in the grate. The drapes were open, allowing moonlight into the room. Candles flickered beside the bed.

His intentions had been pure, noble, not at all lusty or nefarious. Past tense.

Funny how, in spite of his talents with advanced mathematics, the presence of a bed and a woman added up to one and only one thought in his simple male brain.

Even though that woman was scowling at him. His instinct to charm, to soothe, to seduce did not fail him.

"It pains me to admit it, Emma, but you are right. We ought to get our story straight. God only knows what other embarrassing habits you will attribute to me. Though I can't imagine anything worse than weeping, fighting a band of street children, and playing the unmanliest instrument ever, save for, perhaps, the harp."

"The sooner we obtain this fortune, the sooner we can part ways," she said. Then she could run off to her mystery man. Who the devil did she prefer to him? It was a matter of pride, really. Certainly nothing other than the simple desire a man felt for a woman.

"So you agree we should write some lover letters," he suggested. "And confirm the details of our secret love affair."

"Now?"

"I suppose we could do it tomorrow," Blake mused. "In the drawing room. In front of everyone who stands to gain upward of ninety thousand pounds if they are able to prove our fraudulent engagement."

"Ninety thousand pounds?" Emma gasped. Her knees buckled slightly. It was an enormous sum. It was an unfathomable sum.

"Give or take a few," he said with a shrug. "Not

including the annual income. That's another forty or so, I believe. But I haven't perused the account books lately. Too busy with the Tarleton twins, Norton's mistress, and whatnot."

The point was, the fortune was A FORTUNE and possibly theirs, so long as no one—especially Agatha—ever uncovered their deception. Blake experienced a stab of pain somewhere in the region of his heart, which someone else might have attributed to guilt, remorse, or a sense of moral failing.

He ignored it and instead focused on Emma's surprisingly delectable backside as she bent over and rummaged through her things, only to then stand with her arms full of writing supplies.

Love letters it would be.

The only place to sit happened to be on the bed, and Emma glanced at him warily as he settled in beside her. Had she been Lady Bellande, she'd have crawled onto his lap and divested a few articles of clothing by now. But this was Emma, and she was proper and an Innocent, and he probably ought to offer her some reassurance.

"Yes, I am thinking of ravishing you because you are a female and we are on a bed," he said. "But I promise to keep my hands to myself and focus on composing odes to our secret love affair."

"I'm so glad we're clear on our priorities," she said, a faint smile upon her lips, handing him a sheet of paper and pen. With the writing box open on his lap serving as a desk, he began to write.

" 'Dear Emily . . .' " Blake began to narrate as he wrote.

"Emma! My name is Emma!" she said, not at all aware that she was adorable when she was exasperated—her cheeks pinked delectably—which only made him want to work her up into such a state.

"Shhh," he cautioned. "You don't want anyone to hear us, remember."

"If you cannot even get my name correct, how do you expect to fool everyone into believing that we are in love?" she asked in a furious whisper.

"First, I was teasing, *Emma,*" he said, looking her in the eyes. "Secondly, we are to be in love now?"

"Our whirlwind courtship, remember," she said, folding her arms across her chest. His gaze lingered over the swells of her breasts. He liked what he saw. Buxom indeed. "Only love can explain why you have chosen *me.*"

She didn't need to repeat that trite saying, "Love is blind," for him to know she was thinking it. He shook his head and kept writing. Silly girl.

" 'Dear Emma,' " he wrote. " 'When I happened upon you this morning at the abandoned gazebo, I was riveted by such beauty.' "

"No one will believe that," she said, utterly frustrated.

"Why not?" he replied, equally annoyed. Writing love letters was a blasted difficult thing to do, especially with the lady in question commenting on every line.

"I am not beautiful," she said frankly.

"You're one of those women. I should have known," Blake said.

"What do you mean?" Emma asked. He set down his pen and turned to face her.

"Some women have a warped sense of perception regarding their appearance, especially what they view as beautiful in contrast to what a man actually lusts after," he explained. Her lips parted, though she remained speechless.

He gazed upon her ready to offer assurance that she was pretty with all his tried and true phrases and his practiced expression of adoration.

He was prepared for that. He was not prepared for what actually happened when he fixed his gaze upon her face.

If one glanced at Emma, they would see a plain English girl. But when one looked at her, really looked at her . . .

Blake saw smooth, pale skin and high cheekbones with a pale pink blush. She had a heart-shaped face framed by hair she would probably describe as plain brown but a more poetic person might call chestnut, sable, or chocolate. It was fashionable to be blond and fair, but he'd always preferred the dark-haired girls. They were more clever, and thus more trouble.

Her mouth was a little rose pink bow, and she sighed, anxious under his gaze.

In her lovely eyes he saw the wish for his approval—he saw that often, it came with being a duke, and not an ugly one at that. But he also saw that she desperately did not want to care what he thought of her. There was a perfect storm of emotion in her deep blue eyes.

She was beautiful.

She just didn't know it.

He had only just discovered it.

"You are beautiful, Emma," he said softly. He kept looking at her, for there was more to see. The slender column of her neck, the delicate curve of her shoulders, the generous swells of her breasts (his gaze lingered there) . . .

"But—"

Given his vast experience with women, Blake knew better than to waste his breath trying to explain to her that she was pretty and he wanted to do naughty things to her.

Instead, he returned to the letter.

"'Dear Emma, when I happened upon you this morning at the abandoned gazebo, I was riveted by your beauty. The way your soaked gown clung tantalizingly to your breasts . . .'"

"You cannot write that," she said, aghast. "A gentleman shouldn't mention a woman's . . ."

His gaze slid leisurely to hers. She inhaled sharply. He grinned.

"Darling, men don't wax poetic over a woman's eyes," Blake explained. "They ogle their breasts, and that's just to start."

"Some do," she said defensively. Blake set down the pen, suddenly intrigued over which gentleman of her admittedly small acquaintance was in the habit of blathering about a woman's eyes.

Probably the one to whom "her heart was already engaged."

"Is this your secret beau for whom you require the fortune? Tell me, has he written poetry praising the beauty of your eyes, like deep pools of woodland springs, or the ocean or some other body of water?"

She scowled mightily at him, revealing that he had guessed exactly.

"I think my eyes are my finest feature," she said. They were fine: cool, blue, dangerously aware. And they saw right through him.

"They're nice, but your lips are far more alluring," Blake told her. "Your smile is slightly crooked, and my attention is drawn to it. Which means I have spent an inordinate amount of time focused completely on your mouth. Then my thoughts wander to what I could do with, and to, your mouth. I promise you'll like it. As will I."

"I don't think a gentleman has ever said anything about me was alluring," Emma remarked.

Men were such idiots. But then again, had he ever noticed Emma's mouth before she uttered the most devastating things to him? No.

He hadn't noticed her at all. And now he couldn't stop looking.

"There's a first time for everything," he said. He returned his focus to this ridiculous love letter. "Now where was I . . . 'I have been haunted by fantasies, wishing to claim you, to ravish you, to possess you, to show you such pleasures you have never even imagined.' "

He glanced up from the page to see her shocked expression: eyes wide, brows arched, her lips parted in shock. Very well, it was more erotic than romantic. But that was his kind of romance: the kind of pleasure that left both people calling to God and gasping for breath.

The clock ticked away the seconds, reminding them the hour was late. They were alone. On her bed. She was an innocent. And he was composing a love letter about pleasure and possession.

His brain knew it was fake. Other parts of him did not.

"What have you written, Emma?"

"'Dear duke . . . you shock me,'" she said slowly as she wrote.

"'I tempt you.' Write that down," he urged, peering over her shoulder. His gaze strayed from the page to her breasts. They'd fit perfectly in his hands, he reckoned.

"'You shock me. You tempt me. You drive me mad—'" Her voice had become breathless.

"'You desire me,'" he murmured. There was an infinitesimal pause in which she did not deny him, and he experienced an undeniable surge of triumph.

"'I count the minutes . . .'" she said, still writing.

"'Until we kiss again.'"

"'Until this farce is complete,'" she said firmly. She finished the sentence with a flourish. "'Never yours, Emma.'"

"Charming," he said dryly. She gave a little

shrug and started composing a new letter on a fresh sheet of paper.

"For this letter, why don't you imagine writing to your lover boy," Blake suggested. "Since I obviously do not inspire your romantic thoughts. Oddly annoying, that. But the important thing is that we convince everyone this is for real."

"Lover boy, really?" she drawled.

"Beau. Suitor. Gentleman caller," he said dismissively. "You have declared your affection for him. Furthermore, one doesn't participate in the Fortune Games for a spot of fun. No, they must have a reason. Also—"

"You're simply vexed that there is one woman in the world who is immune to your charms and would prefer to save herself for another man. A better man." Emma's delight and marvel at perceiving these rarities was undisguised. She treated him to that crooked smile of hers.

Vexed wasn't exactly the word for what he felt. Perhaps intrigued. Or perplexed. Or maddened.

He refused to believe it. And it would be easy enough to disprove it.

He leaned in close enough to whisper in her ear. "Immune to my charms? Are you certain, Emma?"

Blake let his lips lightly caress the soft skin just near her earlobe and breathed her in. He never could resist the touch or the scent or the taste of a woman. He was always deeply pleased when they shivered from a feather light caress. She proved to be no exception.

"Quite sure, thank you," she said briskly. "Now let's return to our correspondence."

With her head bowed and her attentions firmly fixed upon the letter, she did not see the firm line of his mouth—she had refused him, again. His expression devolved into a scowl, for he was Ashbrooke and he was never refused.

Especially by a wallflower who shivered under his touch, proving that she did feel a spark of attraction for him even if her heart was otherwise engaged.

Maddening, that.

Blake did not know heads or tails in a world where a woman refused him, or, for that matter, a world where Agatha did not invite him home. A world where he had to compete for a fortune and favor with that lot of "boorish fortune hunters."

A world where his roguish antics had finally caught up with him.

"You aren't writing, Ashbrooke. You ought to be writing about your everlasting love for me."

"'Dear Emma, I live for our every stolen moment,'" he said, writing. "'I thank God there is a sturdy trellis leading directly to your bedroom window, as if our midnight rendezvous were meant to be blessed by God himself.'"

"You cannot write that! I will be completely compromised if anyone were to see that! Also, I do not have a trellis outside of my window."

"We're betrothed, so it will be fine. And no one will check."

"It's bad enough that you are in my bedchamber at a house party when it is past midnight. We could be caught at any moment."

"Good. That will make our story more believable," Blake replied. "Perhaps I'll ring for a servant or give a shout."

Emma closed her eyes and exhaled slowly. Her lips were moving as if she were counting backward from ten.

"What are you doing?"

"I am thinking of my lover boy," she replied, eyes still closed. "And the fortune. And how you are insufferable."

"But not without a certain charm," he said, and then he leaned in close and pressed a kiss at that exquisitely sensitive spot just near her earlobe. He took his time about it, too, reveling in the warmth of her skin on his lips and that particular scent of a woman that never failed to entrance him.

He wanted her to want him. And not just in an "everyone wants me" sort of way. He wanted the pleasure of surrender—and he wanted her to experience it, too.

So he pressed another delicate kiss upon her sensitive skin. It was a kiss that was just a hint and a promise of more.

"What are you doing?" she asked breathlessly.

"Testing your resolve," Blake murmured, enjoying the wickedness of it all. The only problem was that it tested his restraint, too.

"Oh dear God," she huffed.

"Ashbrooke will be fine. Or Blake."

"You damned rogue," she murmured.

"You're not the first woman to call me that," he replied, voice low. He thought about kissing her full on the mouth. Or perhaps just a gentle caress from her wrist, higher . . .

"And surely not the last," she added. "Here, write a response to this letter."

Blake took the sheet and pretended to read. Instead, he did some simple arithmetic and concluded that this was the longest amount of time he'd ever spent in bed with a woman in which nothing had happened.

Nothing like his usual bed activities, at any rate.

But something tremendous had occurred. He had taken one long, thorough look at her and really seen Emma. Now he couldn't unsee her. Thus he was achingly aware of his proximity to a beautiful woman.

One who was utterly unmoved by his every overture, be it a look, a wicked suggestion, or an occasional brush of his hand against hers, his thigh adjacent to hers where they sat side by side on the bed.

Never yours. My heart is otherwise engaged. She did not want him. It was a challenge. He always rose to the challenge.

But now I want you. This revelation was not a shock. Of course he wanted her, and that wanting was intensified because she was playing hard to get, which was a novelty for him. Also, they were in bed, the hours were late, and they were both cloaked in shadows from moonlight and candles.

It was elementary mathematics and it all added up to one thing: desire.

The after-midnight hours passed in silence as they traded letters and composed replies. An entire courtship took place in one night.

She described fondly their first meeting at the ruins of an ancient gazebo in Hyde Park during a sudden summer thunderstorm. She wrote of waltzes where she felt swept off her feet and light-headed with delight. She alluded to kisses in the moonlight and soft laughter during calling hours and long chats before the fire in the library, with windows overlooking the garden.

Blake easily—far too easily—penned replies that were much less sweet and far more erotic. He imagined the way her gown, damp from that sudden summer thunderstorm, had clung to the luscious curve of her hips and the perfect swells of her breasts, and then he wrote it as if it were a treasured memory. In these letters, he waltzed her right out onto the terrace and into the secluded corners of the garden, where they indulged in stolen moments and passionate kisses. He composed odes to her blue eyes—whatever the lady wished—but also to her smile, the soft skin he had tasted, and he wrote not untruthfully about his burning desire to know more of her. All of her.

He handed her the letter and watched with satisfaction as her cheeks flushed pink.

EMMA HAD BARELY recovered from the shock of having the *Duke of Ashbrooke in her bedchamber* when to her great surprise the *Duke of Ashbrooke was on her bed.*

And then, unfathomably, the *Duke of Ashbrooke was writing her love letters.*

And then, defying all expectations, the *Duke of Ashbrooke kissed her.*

Gently. Barely. Not a proper kiss. But his lips—upon which legions of women had sighed over—had caressed her intimately as no one ever had. Not even Benedict.

These letters . . . she had to concentrate on these letters. But the duke was near, impossibly handsome and doing ridiculous things like describing her as beautiful and alluring.

If that was true, why hadn't anyone ever noticed?

He must not be right in the head. Yet when he looked at her, she felt as if she was truly being seen—for the first time in her life. As if she was alluring and beautiful and interesting. Not the buxom and batty girl who read too many books.

Thank God she had, for it informed the contents of the love letters she wrote. She wrote of waltzes and balls and romantic moments—all stolen from novels and tangled up with her daydreams of Benedict.

The duke wrote of passionate kisses that left her breathless just reading about them. His letters hinted of an erotic love she'd never imagined and suddenly had an outrageously strong craving to know. What would it be like to have him gaze upon her lustily? What would it be like to frantically kiss him in a moonlit garden?

She was London's Least Likely to have a duke in her bed. And yet . . .

Emma glanced up at Blake.

He was focused upon whatever delightfully wicked things he was writing.

He really was handsome.

"What is it, Emma?"

"Nothing. It's nothing." She just thought . . . what if? Perhaps they would never meet in an abandoned gazebo in Hyde Park where he would be riveted by her beauty. Perhaps he would never climb a trellis into her bedroom window at midnight because he could not bear to be apart from her. But what if they did kiss, just once?

"Nothing?" He turned to face her. Lifted one brow, as all the best rakes did.

She was aware that mere inches of air separated them.

She was aware of his lips pressing lightly against hers. She closed her eyes. She was aware of her heart pounding. And Blake deepening the kiss, slowly but deliberately. He tasted her; she tasted him. She was aware of a surge of heat within and an urgent need to be touched, everywhere.

Oh, how she wanted to reach out and thread her fingers through the dark locks of his hair. Oh, how she ached to feel the warmth of his chest and his heartbeat under her bare palm. Oh, how she wanted to know the feeling of being desperately desired and thoroughly loved.

But she was aware—too aware—of the stupid

wager he had made. She was aware that this wasn't true desire, it was just the Ashbrooke Effect, and legions of women had been similarly afflicted. It wasn't special.

She was painfully aware that this man was the Duke of Ashbrooke. He could have anyone. And she was London's Least Likely.

She put her palm on his chest, feeling his heartbeat.

"You should go," she whispered.

"Emma . . ." He whispered her name. If she didn't know better, she might have heard longing in his tone. But her imagination had run wild enough tonight. All this talk of love and beauty, gazebos and rainstorms, waltzes and passionate kisses, had gone to her head. But truly, none of it was real. It was all just pretend.

Chapter 7

The Fortune Games Scores:
Lord Dudley: –2
Lady Emma: –6
Everyone else: 0

Lady Agatha did nothing by halves. While everyone else strolled along the pea gravel paths of the house's manicured gardens, Her Ladyship was carried on a litter by four footmen best described as strapping young lads.

Their breeches were exceedingly fitted. Their gray jackets clung perfectly to their wide, strong shoulders. Crimson waistcoats highlighted their broad chests, which tapered to narrow waists. Each one stood at least six feet tall and possessed golden blond hair and chiseled features.

Families of the haute ton vied to have the tallest, most handsome footmen. Lady Grey won.

Emma, Miss Dawkins, and Lady Bellande, who had been amiably chatting together, fell silent when they appeared. They took a good long look. They heaved the most heartfelt sighs. It was too much perfect male beauty to pretend not to notice.

Lady Agatha just smiled like a cat in cream. She waved to her guests, bejeweled bracelets jangling and all the diamonds and gems glittering in the sun.

"Oh for God's sake," Blake muttered, bringing a smile to Emma's lips. While he was the only man in the group who compared to the lot of brawny young men, she caught him stand straighter and thrust his chest forward.

It was almost as if the duke felt competitive with these footmen. In Emma's mind, there was no competition.

Another brawny servant joined the group, and it soon became clear that his sole task was to hold a pink parasol trimmed with lace above Lady Agatha, shielding her from the mid-morning sun.

The group's progress through the grounds was not fast. They stopped, first, at the famous heirloom rose gardens, which had been effusively praised in Emma's book, *Sussex: The Quiet County*. There were over two dozen varieties planted, in varying shades of deep crimson, plump buds in bright pink, sunbursts of gold deepening into rusty orange, and feather white blossoms.

Butterflies flitted from flower to flower. Bees hummed. Birds chirped. All blissfully unaware that the group of people strolling in their midst were deep in the throes of competition for one of England's largest fortunes.

"Your gardens are lovely, Lady Grey. I particularly love these roses," Miss Dawkins said sweetly.

"That is a particular variety bred for the first

Duchess of Ashbrooke," Lady Agatha replied. "While the flower is beautiful, the stems possess an uncommon number of thorns. Much like the lady herself."

"Duchess Mary. Daughter of Marquis of Blandford," Emma said.

"You have read your Debrett's," Lady Agatha remarked.

"From cover to cover, under pain of death by my mother," Emma replied, drawing an approving smile from Agatha. She'd also read more of *The Exhaustive History of the Ashbrooke Clan and Their Holdings* this morning whilst her maid did her hair. The family was wealthy, and full of fascinating characters who were forever crossing the line of propriety. In that, Blake was no exception.

"Me, too," Miss Dawkins said. "Unfortunately, suitors do not seem impressed with a young lady's knowledge of the genealogies of all the great families in England."

"I believe this particular rose was for the second duchess?" Lady Bellande called out.

"That is a daisy, Lady Bellande," Lady Agatha said dryly.

"I must have spent too much time studying our family history instead of my botany," Lady Bellande replied with a tittering laugh. No one else joined in.

"She's probably spent too much time shopping instead of reading anything," Miss Dawkins said under her breath.

"Indeed," Emma replied, "but I would trade my encyclopedic knowledge of Debrett's for one of her dresses any time."

Miss Dawkins wholeheartedly agreed.

"Your variety is beautiful, Lady Grey," Emma said as she paused before a particularly stunning rose. It was large with snow-white petals tipped in red. The scent was strong and wonderful.

A patch of shade fell over her. It was Blake, and he expertly plucked a rose and separated the thorns from the stem with a knife that disappeared into his pocket as quickly as it had emerged.

"For you, darling *Emma*," he murmured, presenting it to her. There was just a hint of a smile on his lips. All it took was an instant for Emma to be swept up in the feeling of being wanted and wooed by this charming rogue.

Then she remembered this wasn't real. It was just a game.

She closed her eyes, deeply inhaled the flower's fragrance and pretended she wasn't disappointed.

"You could make a fortune selling these," Blake remarked.

"I already have a fortune," Agatha replied. "Besides, I would never stoop to engage in trade."

"Times are changing," Blake remarked. "One day the aristocracy will cease to matter."

The other guests ceased their chattering and peered curiously at Blake after he uttered such heresy.

"That may well be, but I am not changing. And I needn't encourage it," his aunt said dismissively.

Emma watched, intrigued, as Blake's features hardened.

She was struck with curiosity and the urge to console him. As if the tall, devastatingly handsome, charming Duke of Ashbrooke needed consoling about anything, ever. She couldn't quite imagine it, and yet there was an air of distance around him suddenly, and she wanted it to go away.

"Let's carry on with our walk," Agatha declared. "I would like to get to the ruins for lunch."

Blake and Emma fell in step together and he linked his arm with hers.

She was aware of everyone's watchful eyes, hoping they would make a mistake. The whispers didn't escape her notice either. She knew they puzzled over the shocking sight of London's Least Likely with the duke—except for Pleshette, who lamented the wear to his boots.

"What is it that you would like to change?" Emma asked when they had walked far enough ahead to be out of earshot from the group.

"I beg your pardon?"

"You looked peevish when Lady Agatha said she did not want to encourage change," Emma explained.

"I did not look peevish. Men do not look peevish. It's a natural law."

"You're right," Emma said obligingly. "Your expression darkened considerably, causing many a young maiden to tremble."

"Have you been reading more rubbish novels, Lady Emma?"

"Yes, in addition to the history of the Ashbrooke family. Riveting stuff."

Blake scoffed. "Hardly riveting. I haven't bothered to read it. The lot of it was drilled into me during my lessons as a child by Lady Agatha herself," he said.

"What of your parents?" Emma dared to ask. Was that too personal? He was her fiancé. In a way. He had spent most of the previous night in her bed, writing love letters to her. She could ask him about his parents.

"Ah, I see you haven't read up to chapter ten yet," he remarked.

"I'm only up to the third duke. But I will skip ahead to it upon our return," Emma said. "And you are avoiding the question of why your expression altered, indicating strong thought and feeling."

"Agatha won't like what I want to use the money for," Blake said with an affectionate smile. "Granted, she won't like what you intend to do with the money either."

THE RUINS AT Castle Hill had once been a fortress overlooking the water. These days naught remained but a pile of moss-covered stones alluding to walls and towers that once were. A terraced area and been reinforced to provide a lovely picnic spot with stunning views of rolling hills and the ocean below.

A long table had been set for a formal luncheon. Footmen poured wine, though at Emma's place there was a small glass of sherry in addition to a glass of chilled rosé wine.

The menu consisted entirely of pink foods: poached salmon, slices of ham, heirloom tomato salad, and roasted beets. For dessert, strawberries and cream. The men seemed resigned to the girlishly colored food, though someone grumbled about such light fare after such a long and taxing walk. That prompted Agatha to make a comment to Angus, who made a note in his book, and everyone effusively praised the meal after that.

"As we partake of this delicious luncheon, I should like you all to tell me what you would do with my fortune if you were to possess it," Lady Agatha began.

Emma shrank down in her seat. *Do not pick me. Do not pick me.*

"Let's hope she doesn't ask you," Blake leaned in and whispered in her ear.

"Indeed," Emma remarked dryly. She could never explain to Lady Agatha—terrifying, bejeweled, perspicacious—that she wished to jilt her favorite family member for another man.

If she could just make it through this meal without being asked, then she might still have a chance at happily-ever-after.

"Lady Bellande, you begin," Lady Agatha declared, and Emma breathed a sigh of relief. Beside her, Blake did, too.

"I would like to do good in this world," Lady Bellande said earnestly while leaning forward to better display her bosom to Blake. This rankled

Emma tremendously. "Which is why I would give all the money to various charities."

"You mean throw charity balls," Lady Agatha interpreted. Lady Bellande had the decency—or the acting skills—to look affronted by the accusation that she wished for all of London to drink and dance away Lady Agatha's fortune. For charity.

"That is one way of supporting a variety of institutions," she answered diplomatically.

"Tell us which charities you would host parties for," Lady Copley challenged. "I mean, support."

Lady Bellande's mouth curved into an approximation of a smile, but her eyes shot daggers. Discrediting each other in front of Agatha could help a competitor be sent home, or at the very least get another black mark in Angus's book.

A long silence ensued in which the table waited to learn which charity would first spring to Lady Bellande's mind.

"War Widows and Orphans," she finally said. "And other unfortunate women. It is a plight near and dear to my heart, as a widow myself."

"I wonder how much of it would be spent on champagne and ball gowns?" Lady Copley mused, sipping her wine and whittling away at her competitor's chance of winning.

"Probably the same amount as if you won the fortune, my dear," Lord Copley said, patting his wife's hand as if the affectionate gesture would disguise his cutting remark.

"Your snuff box collection is an investment, I suppose," his wife retorted. "Never mind all the money you spend on something you stick up your nose."

"Lord and Lady Copley: a cautionary tale for the marriage minded," Blake muttered under his breath so that only Emma might hear.

"Shhh. *We* will live happily ever after."

"You, with your lover boy. Me, with my lovers," he murmured.

"Something like that," she whispered, glancing nervously at Lady Agatha to see if she'd heard.

"Jewkes, do keep the wine flowing," Lady Agatha said. "People always say the most truthful things after a few glasses of wine, especially in the afternoon. Lady Emma, how is your sherry? Miss Dawkins, what would you do with the money?"

"Honestly?" she echoed in a small voice.

"Honestly," Lady Agatha said.

"I would use it to attract a suitor," Miss Dawkins said. "Failing that, it would keep me in funds until my old age. Perhaps I would buy a cottage by the sea."

"That's a lovely and sensible plan, my dear," Miss Montgomery said kindly.

Emma paused in lifting the sherry glass to her lips, struck by the realization that if she won the fortune it would be at the expense of Miss Dawkins or the sweet Miss Montgomery, who had thoughtfully reminded her to fetch her bonnet before setting out on the walk this morning.

Did she really deserve it more than Miss Dawkins or Miss Montgomery, whose prospects had dried up long ago?

Miss Dawkins was a sweet girl, a fellow wallflower. It was like stealing from Olivia, or Prudence, and it felt wrong. How would Miss Montgomery survive, forever dependent upon her relations? A feeling of unease crept over Emma. Could she enjoy her happily-ever-after knowing at what cost she had obtained it?

She sipped her wine, hoping that it would soothe her nerves and conscience.

"A cottage by the sea sounds just lovely," Lady Copley said. "Brighton is lovely and fashionable. I should love to have a cottage there as well."

"Yes, one just like the King's," Lord Copley remarked.

"Perhaps in a more traditional style," Lady Copley conceded. "The King's Brighton Pavilion is certainly . . . original."

"Blake, I'm sure we'd all love to hear what you'd spend my fortune upon," Agatha drawled.

"Gifts for his mistresses, for wagers and the latest carriages," Dudley jested. Seeing Emma's cheeks redden, he added, "I beg your pardon, Lady Emma."

Which only made things worse, as it drew everyone's attention to her and the sad truth that it was unbelievable she should have made a match with the duke. She knew that. Yet it still stung, like a slap across the face, to hear conformation of it. In public.

After the events of last night, she'd had fleeting moments of believing that maybe, just maybe, the duke might find her beautiful and alluring and want to do all the wickedly pleasurable things he had described in their letters. For a moment she dared to believe that perhaps she was lovely and had only been overlooked.

Back to earth she fell. Thanks to Dudley.

Then Blake's hand closed over hers protectively. That little kindness melted her heart toward him.

"I think you meant to say gifts for my beloved wife," Blake said smoothly, with a hint of a lethal threat in his tone. *The Duke of Ashbrooke championing her!* Emma never imagined it. Never imagined she would feel it in the triple time beat of her heart. Never imagined how warm and lovely and protected it would make her feel.

"I beg your pardon," Dudley said, chastised. "I think I did mean that."

"In addition to showering her with jewels and whatever feminine frippery Emma wants, I would also use the funds to construct my Difference Engine," Blake said.

A hush fell over the table—what a queer thing for him to say!

"Are you still going on about your ridiculous engine?" Dudley sneered. Blake felt every muscle in his body tense. He willed his voice to be calm, his demeanor cool.

"Yes, Dudley, I'm still going on about a machine that would revolutionize nearly every industry in England."

"I just don't see a need for it. We have the ready reckoners," Dudley replied.

"Calculating all the sums does keep many men employed," Edmund added.

"Men who make errors that have devastating consequences," Blake countered. His own parents had been victim to a stupid miscalculation in architectural plans that had been drawn up from erroneous figures in the ready reckoner. They'd been buried alive, practically. "Those men could construct the engines instead."

"Oh, now you want to build more than one? You haven't even built the first one," Dudley scoffed, accompanied by an incredulous laugh.

"I have a working prototype," Blake said firmly. "I have plans, designs, and calculations for a full working machine. I need only the funds to hire someone to draw up construction plans and build the engine."

Blake said all of that, aware that no one heard him. People looked at him and saw *duke* or *reckless scoundrel* or *notorious seducer.* He supposed it was his fault; that was the version of himself he presented to the world. It was the version Emma—and potential investors, and his peers—had judged him on, before they even met.

In moments like these he began to regret all the brandy, women, and scandals.

When it really mattered, no one believed him.

Blake glanced at Aunt Agatha. Surely she would understand. *Find the formula.* She liked control and to triumph over emotion and human fallibility. Above all she knew *why* this mattered to him.

"I don't like these newfangled machines," she said, bracelets jangling as she sipped her wine. With that, he feared the Fortune Games lost. Oddly, it paled in comparison to the loss of her support for his endeavor.

EMMA THOUGHT THEY might have just lost the games. Lady Agatha—and everyone else—clearly hated Blake's Difference Engine. She didn't see a need for the machine in her own life—the numbers she dealt with never added up to much—but she didn't think it was a terrible use of the money.

It was certainly no worse than Miss Dawkins's plans to attract a suitor. Even Lady Bellande's charity balls would require many expensive gowns, keeping the dressmakers employed.

Emma might have managed to get through the luncheon without sharing her own selfish reason for wanting the fortune. But she was no longer confident that she deserved it. And if she truly didn't deserve it, what was she doing here? She ought to return to London and convince Benedict to elope with her before anyone discovered her scheme with Blake and she became a pariah.

It was imperative no one know the truth.

Such were her thoughts when Blake clasped her wrist and led her away from the others and down a tangled path through a thicket of trees leading to a small clearing. Sunlight filtered through the canopy of leaves overhead. The ground was covered in leafy green ferns and soft pads of moss.

She immediately feared for her life.

Then Blake smiled, a wicked grin playing on his mouth, his eyes alight with mischief, and she immediately feared for her virtue.

She couldn't cry for help, not without ruining the ruse. If she were madly in love with her fiancé, she would delight in a moment alone with him—not scream for protection. So she bit down on her lip and tugged her hand away. As if retreating from a wild animal, she took one small step back, and then another, as Blake slowly walked toward her until her back was against a thick tree. He blocked her in by placing his palms against the trunk on either side of her head.

"What are you doing?" Why, why, *why* did her voice have to be so breathless around him?

"I want to show you something," he murmured.

"We will be separated from everyone else. We *are* separated from everyone else. We should return to the group."

She could hear Olivia in her head: *Young ladies did not find themselves at the mercy of a rogue.*

His body was inches from hers. She was acutely aware of the slight distance and her traitorous desire for him to be even *closer.*

"Perhaps I wanted to be alone with you," Blake murmured. "Or perhaps this is part of the ruse, Emma."

But no one can see us. And then Blake untied her bonnet strings and let the hat fall to the ground. He pushed a wayward strand of hair away from her face, tucking it behind her ear, his fingertips gently grazing her cheeks. The gesture was so tender, so promising, she felt herself softening.

"What are you doing?"

Blake began where he had started last night: a kiss, ever so lightly, upon the delicate place just by her earlobe. Who knew the warmth of his lips touching there would send shivers tingling up and down her spine?

She knew. It was so strange that she knew.

Blake did not stop there. Emma stood still, save for the thunderous pounding of her heart. The words *no* or *stop* or *we shouldn't* or *young ladies do not* evaporated on their path from her brain to her lips.

He pressed more kisses along the delicate skin of her neck. She felt his warm breath and the touch of his lips. His hands inched closer, his body pressed nearer.

Emma closed her eyes.

She tried to conjure thoughts of Benedict but found she didn't have a memory that could compare to this real, sensual moment. This moment, the likes of which she and her fellow wallflowers had only dreamt of. She ought to experience it, nobly, if only to tell them about it.

Blake's trail of kisses continued scandalously along the edge of her bodice, where the muslin ceased to cover her skin. She abandoned all thoughts of her friends or Benedict or even the disapproving look Lord Pleshette had given her day dress, which suddenly felt far too confining.

"Wait," she gasped. "What is . . . what are you . . . ?"

A few little kisses and her wits were completely dissolved. Damned Ashbrooke Effect!

"I am tempting you," Blake murmured. She gazed into his eyes, trying to find a reason why he was making her feel these things, and found no answer.

Benedict. She must think of him. She must save herself for him.

"I am not tempted," Emma said. Her voice was appallingly breathless and the words were a complete lie. She was impatient and curious to know what this accomplished rogue would do next. These little kisses and touches already had her dizzy and weak in the knees. She couldn't even imagine how she might survive anything more.

She was tempted, yes.

She was curious, oh yes.

But resolved.

Benedict, think of Benedict! Think of her pride and Blake's stupid wager!

Above all she mustn't think about how her skin felt warmer when Blake gazed at her.

"Are you sure?" he murmured. "You are not tempted even slightly, Emma?" As he carried on with the kisses, his palm found her waist and skimmed up, up, up, leaving a sense of delicious warmth and then a lonely cold.

Would his hand go higher, to her breasts? Emma caught herself arching her back and wanting to feel the wicked hands of this rogue upon her everywhere.

"My heart belongs to another. I told you."

"But you're not thinking of him now, are you?"

Blake pulled back, taking away those wicked little kisses. But still, he boxed her in against the tree so that escape felt impossible.

"I can think of nothing else. I am thinking of him."

She was thinking of Benedict, but it was taking every shred of her concentration to do so. Where Blake's dark eyes gazed down wickedly at hers, she forced herself to conjure Benedict's blue eyes bright with happiness when first seeing her at a ball.

Both made her heart beat faster. Who knew she was so wanton?

Blake looked at her mouth possessively and she involuntarily licked her lips. Was he going to kiss her? It seemed like he would. Why else would he stare so brazenly at her mouth with such a wicked smile on his lips? He was toying with her, she just knew it, and he was enjoying himself, too.

Well, all the other women in the world might fall all over themselves to have the infamous Blake Auden, Duke of Ashbrooke and All He Surveyed, looking for all the world like he was about to ravish them against a tree. But not she.

Benedict, think of Benedict. They had kissed. She knew about kisses.

She just didn't know about kisses like the one

Blake seemed to promise—wild, dangerous, devastating.

She tilted her head up to Blake. Was he going to kiss her or not?

Chapter 8

Aunt A will inevitably sniff out Blake and Lady Emma's deceit. Wouldn't it be something if I were the winner for once?

—INNERMOST THOUGHTS OF
MR. GEORGE PARKER-JONES

The Dining Room

THE GROUP ARRIVED at dinner to find that only ten places had been set. Yet there were thirteen among them—twelve competitors and Lady Agatha herself.

"Hmmph," Agatha said upon entering the dining room. "Mr. Parker-Jones, why don't you spend the evening at the local tavern on your way back to London."

George nodded politely and took his leave—but not before exchanging a loaded look with Blake. Truth be told, while Blake was sorry to see him lose, he was glad the only other person who knew his engagement was fake was now out of the games.

Emma had gasped, and Blake shared her shock. George was much less loathsome than the other players who remained. Aunt Agatha couldn't possibly mean to leave her fortune to, say, despicable Dudley. And yet he was still a contender.

Perhaps Aunt Agatha was just a batty old woman and Blake sought a rational formula where none existed.

Agatha's eyes narrowed at those remaining in her personally selected boorish lot of fortune hunters. At least two more would be cut before supper. Blake met his aunt's gaze, defiant but troubled.

He ought to go, for he hadn't even been invited yet had brazenly showed up with a fiancée on his arm. The question of *why* his beloved aunt hadn't invited him nagged. Especially when she seemed exceptionally frail and completely reliant upon the arm of her brawny footman; in short, especially when it seemed her time of terrorizing the family was coming to an end.

He wasn't ready for a world without her.

Agatha met his gaze and held it.

He couldn't quite bring himself to wink or give a charming grin or play the part of dashing rogue. Did she not want to spend those last days with him?

Could he not be like everyone else, fixated only on the fortune, and not seeking reassurance and acceptance from a batty old broad?

"Blake . . ." Agatha said his name slowly before issuing her challenge. "If I recall correctly, you were not invited this year."

He never resisted a challenge. Never met a

woman he couldn't charm either. And he knew her better than anyone else—which made this whole lack of invitation so troubling—and thus he knew that fawning and flattery didn't fly with her.

"You say it as if it were a problem, dear aunt. Really, you ought to thank me for gracing you with my handsome face and winning personality."

"Hmmph." He grinned as Agatha tried not to smile. "Miss Montgomery, Sir Pendleton, thank you for playing the Fortune Games. Good day."

Just like that they were gone.

The remaining competitors were in a somber mood over dinner, which consisted of seven courses of entirely white foods. And by the time they all adjourned to the music room for that evening's entertainment, tension was high.

Anyone, at any moment, could go.

No warning, no reason.

No goodbyes.

The Music Room

Ah, a musicale. Finally, an activity that should not destroy my new jacket. Or gloves. If I could only say the same for my boots after today's walk.

—Private thoughts of Lord Pleshette

After supper the guests quietly found seats in the music room for that evening's performance. A statuesque opera singer by the name of Angelica Scarlatti would perform, accompanied on the pianoforte and violin. Agatha sat upon a chair as if it were a throne in the center of the room and the other competitors clustered around her.

Emma allowed Blake to lead her to a small settee nestled in an alcove off to the side. Her pulse hadn't quite slowed from the shock of watching three guests suddenly evicted from the game without preamble or discernable reason. At any second she might find herself ejected from the game, jilted by Blake, and publicly mortified.

She would be worse off than before the letter was stolen and sent off to the newspaper.

Blake sat beside her on the settee, which was upholstered in a soft green velvet and rather small. Very small. So very small that she and Blake had no choice but to sit with an improper lack of space between them. Her thigh against his. His arm against hers. Their hands awkwardly almost touching, fingers intertwining . . . she folded her hands primly in her lap.

Emma fixed her gaze straight ahead and focused upon the performers.

But, oh, she was just so aware of Blake. It was impossible not to be. She kept stealing glances, still in disbelief that there was a man so handsome in this world. And that he was beside her in this dark corner on this minuscule settee.

He shifted beside her. The touch sent a surge of heat coursing through her. She clasped her hands so tightly together that her knuckles turned white.

Blake turned his head slightly toward her. She

stiffened, every nerve on alert, heart pounding. *If Benedict were here . . .* But he wasn't. Blake was and she was acutely aware of that fact and little else.

"You do look beautiful this evening, Emma," he murmured.

"That again?" She gave a little laugh. Like fairies or Father Christmas, she ached to believe it, but just couldn't.

If she were so beautiful, she wouldn't be a wallflower on her fourth season. If she were beautiful, surely *someone* would have noticed so by now.

"I think it's your eyes," he said thoughtfully. "Such a deep blue, like the Mediterranean Sea."

"Having never seen the Mediterranean Sea, I shall take your word for it," she said dismissively. But truly, her heart was beating with more vigor, as if accepting the compliment even if she wouldn't. He hadn't forgotten their conversation about complimenting her eyes in a manner which she preferred. He remembered what she wanted. And delivered. And no one could hear what he said or understand the significance.

Why? Just . . . why? Emma took a deep breath, trying to still her tumultuous thoughts.

And then the musical began.

The musical was horrendous.

After a few bars in which there was no notable improvement, Emma dared to comment to Blake.

"Is it just me, or is the pianoforte out of tune?" she whispered.

"It sounds as if it had been dunked in the bottom of the lake, then transported across a bumpy country road, and then *not* tuned," he answered with a grin and she stifled a giggle.

"Well at least Agatha is not squandering her fortune upon such trivial things as musical instrument maintenance," Emma remarked.

"I wouldn't call my hearing a trivial thing," Blake replied. "Clearly, the Fortune Games have taken a devious turn. Brace yourself, Emma, this could be a long evening."

Emma didn't pay attention to the music. She was too distracted by Blake, who pretended to stretch and then draped his arm across the back of the settee—and her shoulders. Such informality was appallingly forward, but no one was looking, and sitting up perfectly straight was so tedious, especially when she wanted to lean back into his warm embrace.

She was aware of his scent, clean and masculine, and something else she couldn't name. It was just *him* she supposed, and it was intoxicating, like a drug.

"Do you know Italian?" he whispered to her.

"No, do you?"

"A little," he said.

"All the bedroom words, I'd imagine," Emma remarked, unfortunately making her own self blush. Blake noticed and grinned. She felt a rush of pride for having amused him.

"Bedroom words?" he echoed with feigned innocence. "What, pray tell, might those be?"

"As an innocent young maiden I can assure you I have no idea," she said quite stiffly. Why, why,

why had she mentioned bedroom words? Honestly, no good could come of this conversation.

"You didn't read them in one of your books?"

"Apparently those books are not fit for ladies," she replied, with genuine sadness at the fact. She had been repeatedly rebuffed in her efforts to borrow those sorts of books from the circulating library.

"Pity, that. Well I had thought she was singing in Italian, but now I am not so sure."

"Is it French? I don't remember much from lessons at Finishing School."

Blake cocked his head to the side and listened intently for a moment. "I don't think it's actually a language, or even words at all," he said.

She laughed again, softly, then listened closely to the music. He was right, Angelica Scarlatti was singing utter nonsense. Still laughing, Emma glanced up at him and caught his eye. He, too, was amused.

She glanced around the room and saw that everyone was bored and tortured while she and Blake were cozy in this dark corner, trading quips and making jokes.

Then the violin made a particularly jarring, sawing noise and she tilted her head curiously.

"Is the violin playing the same song as the others?" she asked.

"Definitely not," Blake replied. "Not the same song, not even the same key."

"What an original concept," Emma said politely.

Blake smirked. "Do say so to Aunt Agatha."

Emma gasped, shocked. "I wouldn't dare," she said. But then the music ceased and a footman stepped forward bearing a tray, draped in velvet. Agatha was grinning wickedly, and when Emma saw . . .

She gave a little laugh and said, "However, I will give her my compliments on procuring a flute at such short notice."

BLAKE WAS ACTUALLY enjoying himself, which was strange, since he was sitting through the most god-awful music that had ever been performed in England. But Emma was warming to him and trading quips about this bizarre musical they were forced to endure. He discovered she was sly and funny. She didn't fawn and simper like other women tended to do around him; Blake found he liked her more for it.

But that all changed with the shiny silver flute that one of Aunt Agatha's footmen presented.

It went without saying that he had never played the flute. Had never even picked one up. Yet refusal was not an option. Not when rising to the challenge was an opportunity to impress and amuse both Emma and Agatha.

As if he had been dared to jump off the roof or swim across the Channel. He couldn't say no.

"Do you read music, at least?" Emma asked, adorably concerned for him *now*—though not when she had made the outrageously false declaration that led to this moment.

"Not in the slightest," he replied.

"Well you can't be any worse than what we just heard," she said, smiling sweetly.

"I'm flattered by your confidence in me," he replied.

"This musical just became even more entertaining," Emma remarked.

"For you," he said, and then she smiled so prettily that his breath hitched in his throat for a second.

"Ashbrooke, I'm not getting any younger," Aunt Agatha declared from the front of the room.

"You may not wish to live for this, dearest aunt," he replied as he strolled toward the makeshift stage and gamely picked up the flute.

"Oh I can assure you, I do," she said.

"The song we have selected is 'L'amore Misterioso,'" the opera singer said. "Do you know it?"

"I'm not familiar with it, no," he answered. It was the absolute truth.

"It is very simple. Just follow along with the music and you will be just fine," Angelica Scarlatti cooed. In another time, or place or evening, he might have planned an assignation with her, for she was a stunning woman: tall, honey-hued hair and a figure to die for. Not to mention a mouth that she held in a perfect "O" shape for quite some time. While singing, of course.

Blake found Emma in the audience, gave her a wink, and was rewarded with one of her adorably crooked smiles.

On the count of three, half the musicians began

to play. The rest waited a few more seconds. Blake felt ridiculous holding the tiny flute in his large hands but he endeavored to act as if he was an accomplished flautist and it was a perfectly masculine activity, like fencing, shooting, boxing, or some other violent endeavor.

From her perch in the front room, Agatha beamed at him. The others wore expressions of pain, vexation, or even anger. For Blake had been presented with a chance to fail spectacularly—no one believed that rubbish about his flute playing—but he was soldiering on to their disadvantage. But then his gaze settled upon Emma, smiling broadly and with something akin to affection in her eyes.

In spite of his absurd pose at the moment—pretending to play a delicate flute in front of a hostile audience—he felt a surge of pride. She had not been the slightest bit interested in him. She thought him a bore. She thought *nothing* of him. That is, until he had earned her admiration by brazenly risking humiliation in order to stick to their ruse. To do otherwise would have called her a liar. For better or for worse, in the Fortune Games they were united.

It was a new feeling, that. Having worked for something, especially a woman's affections. Imagine if she surrendered completely . . .

Chapter 9

I shall just sit back, ogle the opera singer and wait for everyone else to trip up. The fortune will be mine. . .

—Delusional fantasy of Lord Dudley

Immediately after Blake's performance, Lady Agatha departed and the evening became more interesting. Had she retired or merely visited the ladies' retiring room?

Many glanced at the tall grandfather clock, watching the minutes tick by as the horrendous cacophony droned on. Blake and Emma caught each other looking longingly at the clock and shared a private, knowing smile.

Five minutes passed, then ten. Fifteen minutes passed and then, finally, thirty minutes had elapsed from the moment Agatha had beckoned her footman and quietly slipped out of the drawing room.

Lord Pleshette was the first to make a move. When Angelica Scarlatti finished a song and everyone mustered polite applause, he took the opportunity to murmur, "Excuse me, but I have had enough this evening" to Lord Dudley as he stood and exited the room.

Everyone watched as he slowly approached the door, which was just slightly ajar. He slowly pushed it open, first one inch and then another and then:

"Aaarrrrgh!"

Pleshette emitted a truly bloodcurdling scream as a bucket of flour crashed from its precarious perch on the top of the door, knocking him on the head and—the worst of all possible fates—thoroughly plastering his fine wool coat in a shade he had proudly described as "pine forest at dusk," and which complimented his satin waistcoat in the precise shade of "fresh spring mint at dawn."

"No, oh no, not the coat," he said with a strangled cry of distress, dizzily stepping about and frantically trying to brush off the flour, which served only to ruin his fine kidskin gloves, in the perfect shade of buttery caramel, which only distressed him more.

The music screeched to a halt.

From the hall, a cackling was heard.

"Do you not like the musicians I have hired for this evening, Pleshette?" Lady Agatha asked. Everyone was quiet, the better to overhear the conversation that took place in the doorway.

"Miss Scarlatti and her players are magnificence personified," Pleshette answered obsequiously. "I merely needed to . . . answer the call of nature."

"Hogwash," Lady Agatha barked. "The musicians are awful."

"We were merely honoring the lady's wishes," Miss Scarlatti explained. "We do not usually play like this."

"This is madness," someone was overheard to say.

"This is the Fortune Games," Dudley said dryly.

"Shhh," Lady Bellande admonished.

"Do you know what I think, Lord Pleshette?" Lady Agatha inquired. He wisely kept quiet, as it was clearly not a question to be answered by him. "I think that you were going to retire for the evening, thus abandoning your fellow guests to this auditory torture. Or perhaps your daring escapade would have inspired a mass exodus, which would have traumatized the tender feelings of my musicians and gravely insulted the effort I went to in order to provide this entertainment."

"Lady Grey, my intentions were pure. My heart is good." Lord Pleshette dropped to his knees before her.

"Does anyone care to vouch for him?" Lady Agatha asked.

No one did. In London he might have been a friend or family member, but at the Fortune Games he was just one more person standing in the way of a ninety-thousand-pound inheritance.

"Instruct your valet to pack your things," she directed. "You and your staff shall leave at first light."

"Lady Grey, I implore you . . ." Lord Pleshette

made one last, desperate plea, hands clasped and pressed against his breast.

"Play on, Miss Scarlatti," Lady Agatha said with a wave of her hand. "The night is still young."

The music began anew, transformed from a horrific cacophony to the sweetest, most harmonious and soul-stirring sounds. The pianoforte had not been out of tune, the player had simply been striking the most discordant combination of keys possible. The violin now played the same song, and Miss Scarlatti had a voice like a lark, like sunshine, like gold, like a burbling brook.

The beauty of the music made one marvel all the more over the evening's events. There was only this moment, full of hope and possibility. Yet everything was a test, every step a potential trap, and disaster might befall one at any second.

One moment, Emma had been enjoying Blake's terrible performance on the flute, admiring the determination with which he seized the moment and accepted the challenge. The next, there was a stark reminder that Lady Agatha wasn't joking.

Emma's heart was still pounding.

This was a game, and one could be asked to leave at any moment, given her unknowable whims. Emma realized she ought to take care. No more jokes during the music or slipping away from the day's activities. Not if she wanted to win. She had to, for losing now would ruin her forever.

"She is definitely singing in Italian now," Blake murmured. Emma felt the vibrations of his voice tremble down her back. "Would you like me to translate it for you?"

"That would be lovely," she whispered. Emma wanted to know the words, to lose herself in the song and cease worrying about the Fortune Games and Benedict, who might not have her now if she lost.

But then Blake began to speak. His voice was low, so only she might hear. His arm was around the settee again, then around her shoulders, urging her close to him.

She was enveloped by his embrace, his scent, his presence, his warmth, his everything.

"Il pescatore è stato perso sul mare . . ."

He grinned wickedly and translated, murmuring the words so only she might hear. She wasn't sure if she should trust his translations—didn't *pescatore* mean fish?—but she couldn't help falling under the spell of his low, rich voice and the vibrations it cast upon her skin.

"I long to taste your kiss, your passion, your lips . . ."

Her lips parted. She closed her eyes to block out everything but this beautiful music and Blake's voice.

"Il pescatore ha cercato terra, terra asciutta!

"I hunger for the touch of your skin, soft, white, glowing in the moonlight . . ."

A heat began to steal over her, starting in her belly and spreading across her skin. Like a blush, like sunshine, like the warmth of a man's touch, or so she imagined. Lord above, did she imagine.

Even though she could have sworn *terra* meant earth and that Blake was lying. Couldn't she just pretend?

But it wasn't just any man's touch she imagined, caressing every inch of her bare skin. Where she fought to picture Benedict, her traitorous brain wouldn't allow it. Blake was all she saw, all she could think about.

"Il pescatore ha visto scure nubi tempestose. . .

"I dream of knowing you intimately . . ."

He couldn't possibly mean that. The words Angela Scarlatti sang couldn't mean that either. Nothing made sense. Not him . . . not her . . . But truth be told, she wanted to know him intimately, too. She was desperately curious about his kiss. His touch. His passion. His lips, on hers.

"Here," Blake whispered, tracing his fingertip from just below her earlobe down to her bare shoulder. She couldn't help it, she tilted her head to grant him more access. Traitorous self!

"I want to kiss you here," Blake said, pressing his fingertips to the delicate hollow of her throat, then he traced his fingertips lower, to her breasts. "Imagine it," he commanded.

Her eyes flew open and she turned to face him.

"Why?" Why should she imagine such a wicked, impossible thing? Why should he ask—nay, order—such a thing of her? Why was he attempting this . . . seduction?

"Why not?"

Gazing into his dark eyes, she did not have an answer for him.

Emma knew she was plain. She knew she was not the sort of woman who inspired wicked thoughts in men. She could not afford to believe otherwise.

Moreover, she did not possess the temperament to smile coyly, or glance smolderingly over her shoulder, or move seductively. No, she smiled to be nice, she glanced to see, and she moved to get from here to there, with zero intentions of seducing a man along the way.

And Ashbrooke asked her why she should *not* imagine that she possessed a body a man like him would want to kiss.

Think of Benedict. He respected her. He treated her well. He understood her completely, as she was. She was not the kind of woman the Duke of Ashbrooke found beautiful or alluring, or anything.

And yet . . .

"Perhaps I might feather kisses from here . . ." He pressed his mouth against her inner wrist, and she bit her lip. ". . . to here."

Here being up higher and higher until Emma panicked and jerked her arm away. The audacity of the man was breathtaking. Taking such liberties with her, when they were in a room full of people who saw them as enemies, along with an eccentric old woman who could banish them at any moment.

Emma considered all of that, but she also thought, *And then what will you do?*

She did not dare voice that question, so she kept the words to herself.

"Do you want to know where I would kiss you next?" Blake asked in a voice that was pure wickedness.

Her corset was suddenly too tight. She couldn't breathe.

"Not particularly," she answered, breathlessly.

"Here," and he pressed two fingers against the nape of her neck. Then he dared to trace a line down her spine to the small of her back. "Perhaps lower," he suggested.

Why are you doing this? The question echoed around and around her brain, doing battle with wanton imaginings and desperate pleas for Ashbrooke to touch her everywhere, anywhere.

But then she remembered that he was Ashbrooke and she was London's Least Likely, and he had resolved to woo her just to prove he could have any woman he wanted.

"This is highly inappropriate," she said, straightening her spine and stiffening her resolve. She would *not* be another conquest for him.

"Which is half the fun of it," he murmured, grinning devilishly. "The other half is imagining how it might feel if I kissed you, Emma, in all those places. Are you imagining it?"

"No. I am thinking of B—" She stopped herself because Benedict was *hers*. The minute she said his name aloud to Blake was the minute he became fodder.

"Ah, the other man. Your lover boy," Blake remarked dryly. For a second she thought he might be jealous, but she dismissed that thought as madness. If anything, Blake was just peeved that she saved herself for another man. "Did he ever kiss you like that? Or at all?"

"Your Grace," Emma said strictly, sounding for all the world like she was a Prim, Proper Matron of Impeccable Virtue. Like *she* was the one the ton called Prissy Missy. When just a moment ago she had been a young woman nearly swept away and seduced by a rogue.

Her heart yearned to be that girl, but her pride wouldn't allow it.

"I know, I know. My manners are appalling. I do apologize," Blake said.

The hauntingly beautiful music continued, and Blake tragically kept his hands to himself, along with his mouth and his compliments and his hints of seduction. Emma reminded herself of the world as she knew it and she planned it to be.

But she stole glances at the gorgeous man beside her and desperately missed those few moments when she quite nearly surrendered to him.

Chapter 10

"I am not so sure about Blake and that girl. It's all too convenient, and love rarely is."

—Aunt Agatha, to Angus

The next day
The Hunt

Blake watched as Agatha returned to the house on the arm of her handsome young footman and constant companion. This year she had devised a bizarre scavenger hunt that was sure to keep everyone out of doors all day. In other words, out of her way.

In previous years she had watched the games' activities with glee, marked by her cackling laugh and devious smile. Her loss of enthusiasm saddened him.

Blake turned away and strolled through the gardens with Emma until they found a secluded bench, offering privacy from their competitors.

"What does the list say?" Emma asked. He glanced at the sheet in his hand. Across the top of the page were the words: *The Fortune Games*

Scavenger Hunt. Then he skimmed the list of items they were required to find.

"Oh dear God," he muttered. "She must have gone mad."

Emma leaned to have a closer look, her breasts brushing against his arm. She did not stiffen—though he might have. For once she did not shun a sign of affection toward him. It only served to remind him how long it'd been since he'd had a woman. Days, at least. Perhaps even a week. Maybe longer.

"First on the list: 'a spark,'" Emma said.

"That is easy. I have matches," Blake suggested.

"What are those?" Emma asked, predictably. His obsession with the newest inventions meant he was often asked such questions.

"Matches are a new, slightly dangerous method of starting a fire, lighting a cigar, or illuminating the darkness for just a few fiery seconds," he explained. "They are the future. Much like the Difference Engine you all disdain."

The very future Aunt Agatha probably wouldn't give him the fortune to create. Had she known of his new obsession? Is that why she had not invited him?

"I don't disdain the Difference Engine," Emma said, and he lifted his head in surprise. "I think you should try to build it."

"Do you?"

"Yes. I think building a machine that will dramatically improve the world will be an excellent use of your half of the fortune," she said. And then, grinning, she added, "If you win it."

"My half?" *If he married her, he could have it all.*

"We had an agreement, Your Grace. I have plans for my share," Emma said. "Might I remind you that my services as faux fiancée are not free, nor are they cheap."

"'Your Grace'? Are we back to that?" Blake asked, forcing himself to hide a scowl of annoyance and another emotion he couldn't identify. He didn't want to be "Your Grace" to her, nor Duke, nor Ashbrooke.

Had he begun to confuse their forced intimacy with a genuine one? What a miss-ish thing to do.

She took the paper from his hands, her fingers brushing his, and began to read.

"What else is on the list?" he asked.

"Beauty. A Lady Grey rose will do nicely for that," Emma murmured, not lifting her eyes from the page.

He wanted her to look at him. Instead, he leaned close and glanced over her shoulder to read what else they would spend their day searching for. He also leaned over to be near, to inhale her scent, to possibly press a light kiss on her cheek . . .

"'The sound of music,'" Emma read. She didn't move away. But neither did she lean into him, catch his eye, or indicate that she was aware of him at all.

"That is easy. I shall play my flute."

"It says the sound of music, not auditory torture," Emma replied, but she was smiling. Teasing him. Women never teased him. They batted their eyelashes, pouted seductively, and took any opportunity to brush against him. They agreed with whatever he suggested.

The novelty of Emma's teasing and refusal to simper was intriguing. He didn't know what she would say next. He didn't know if she would agree, refuse, laugh, or change the subject. Blake found himself all the more attuned to her because of it.

"What are we to do for the feeling of love at first sight?" Emma asked. Aunt Agatha had outdone herself with the bizarre and impossible scavenger hunt tasks.

"My interpretation of this is highly inappropriate, as you would say."

"Love, not lust. Well, dearest fiancé," Emma said with a charmingly crooked smile. "How did you feel when you first met me?"

Blake burst out laughing. She did, too.

Miraculously, they could find humor in the situation now, even though the memory still provoked the same feelings of terror, as if he were suspended on a limb not knowing when or where it was about to break.

He recalled swaggering into her drawing room, only to be confronted by an audience of women with whom he was not acquainted—including the one to whom he was supposedly betrothed. Addressing the wrong woman would have ruined them both. Addressing the right one was impossible.

Then Emma had stood and offered her hand, saving them both from humiliation. He had been so relieved he could have kissed her. Then he noticed, with great relief and the stirrings of pleasure, that she was pretty. Which meant they might be able to pull this off.

Then he forgot her name.

"I felt relieved," he said. "Also, terrified. Along with a sense of urgency and a spark of opportunity."

"That is actually poetic, Blake," Emma said softly. "I think it feels like butterflies in your stomach. That's how I feel every time I see . . ."

Her voice trailed off. She had a daydreamy look about her, and Blake knew that even though she sat beside him—so close as to be touching and warmed by the same sunshine—in her heart and thought she was off with lover boy.

It rankled, that.

"Who is he? You still have not told me his name. I am beginning to suspect that he does not even exist."

"What purpose would telling you serve? I can't imagine any," Emma replied, still keeping her eyes firmly fixed upon the list in hand.

"Sating my curiosity," Blake suggested.

He was dying to know what man had bested him for the heart of this wallflower. It wasn't about winning his own wager either. After all of his calculated smiles, smoldering gazes, delicate touches, and tempting kisses . . . he was the one falling for her.

"Oddly enough, sating any feeling of yours is not high on my list of priorities," Emma said primly, and he made a sound somewhere between strangled laughter and a cough. Did she realize how that sounded? No, not this innocent. "Now let's see, what else is on this utterly mad list?"

"'Happily ever after'?" Blake read, skeptical how to find that in an afternoon.

"'The truth,'" Emma read grimly. "The truth about what?"

Blake read the next item on the list.

"'Eternity.' The woman put 'eternity' on a scavenger hunt," he remarked, leaning back, closing his eyes, a position of defeat.

"I think it's all remarkably clever. Certainly it is far more interesting than a rock, or a leaf, or a stick," Emma said. "Though I suppose you would prefer that, given that it requires far less ingenuity."

That caught his attention. That sly insult so lightly and primly remarked upon in a dulcet voice. As if he would hear her tone and not the words, and thus not comprehend that she had just called him an idiot.

"What makes you say that?" he asked coolly.

"I don't know. I am sorry—"

"Do you think me some half-wit, Emma? Some hulking ignoramus?" Blake focused his complete attention upon her and drew himself up to his full height. Being an orphan, he didn't have an example of haughty, overbearing ducalness to follow. He seemed to have inherited it, along with the name and title.

Typically, people began to cower and quiver when he stared them down. Grown men begged for his pardon. Women fluttered their lashes and cooed.

Emma just shrugged.

"It's just that you are so . . . handsome," she explained. "So you needn't be smart. You only have to smile and act rakishly charming to get what you want."

"I see. By that logic, you think you are plain, and therefore clever," he said.

"I *am* plain. And I am at least well read if not clever," she replied calmly.

"What if I don't find you plain?" Blake asked the question, and a truth revealed itself to him in the slight pause of his heartbeat.

He did not find her plain.

She wasn't the sort of beauty who stopped a man in his tracks from across a crowded ballroom, but the more he saw Emma, the more he knew her, the more he wanted to know her. Intimately. Completely.

"If you think me pretty, then I do think you are a half-wit," she said dryly.

"Your logic is interesting, Emma. In simple terms, if you are not plain, then you are not clever. Or perhaps you are pretty and clever."

"Not in any world I know," she muttered as she lowered her gaze, refusing to meet his eye.

It slayed him, that.

She and the rest of the world had labeled her Wallflower or London's Least Likely, and neither she nor the rest of the world ever reassessed that opinion. She took it to heart and let them ignore her. She didn't deserve that.

And yet here she was, on the arm of a duke and refusing his overtures.

As if she didn't believe he meant them.

Not being a complete idiot, Blake understood that if he wanted to seduce her, it would take more than a sensual touch, more than a passionate kiss. His pace quickened as it occurred to him that she might refuse him because she did not even believe him.

He would have to make her believe she was worthy of seduction.

"Emma, we are participating in Lady Agatha Grey's Fortune Games. We are not in any world anyone would recognize," he replied carefully. "Therefore any rules or previous 'truths' do not apply."

"I still want to win," she said, lifting her blue eyes to meet his. The wanting was unmistakable. Wanting for her lover boy and whatever daydream life they led. Blake gazed at her, knowing his eyes were also full of desire, and wanting.

"I as well," he said, and he was no longer speaking just of the games.

A spark

Blake and Emma spent the morning among the roses in the garden, capturing butterflies to contain in a glass jar, to approximate the feeling of love at first sight.

Next they wandered through the garden, searching for truth and eternity.

Blake heard footsteps crunching on the gravel—they were not alone. Should they be discovered in a compromising position, it would be an opportunity to allay any lingering suspicions that he and Emma weren't engaged as they claimed to be. With George having departed—that morning they'd heard the cannon fire indicating a contender's exit from Castle Hill and the Fortune Games—the one person who knew the truth was gone. But who knows what he might have said . . .

It was the sensible thing to be caught kissing his fiancée in the gardens. Blake would have laughed, for he usually endeavored *not* to be discovered thusly. Truly, though, he thought only of tasting Emma.

"Emma, come quick . . ." He reached out for her hand and led her off the path and into a grove of trees. Momentum sent her crashing against his chest, and he clasped her against him. His breath hitched. Certain parts of his anatomy hardened. She took only a small step back when he reluctantly loosened his embrace.

"What is it?" Of course she didn't trust him. She shouldn't. She really shouldn't. His intentions were utterly wicked.

"This," he said with a murmur, and pulled her close again.

Then he lowered his mouth to hers. Just for an

instant. Just enough to make it seem real, and romantic, and as if they were actually in love. Just enough to prove themselves to whomever was approaching.

"Really, Lord Copley, this is utter nonsense." Lady Copley's sharp voice sliced through the pleasant hum of the summer afternoon. "Trying to light a fire with your spectacles."

"You don't have a better idea, wife. Or any idea at all," Lord Copley countered.

"What are you doing?" Emma whispered against his kiss. But she didn't stop. Thank God, she did not stop.

He didn't know. He'd meant to allay suspicions of their false betrothal. He meant to seduce her—at first to confirm to his own pride that he could. But more and more he hungered for her warm looks, true smiles, her playful banter and her taste . . . like innocence and desire all at once. It wasn't just a game to him anymore.

The truth was, he wanted the same thing as Lord Copley out there—a spark.

"Just a kiss," he whispered. *Just a kiss. Just a spark.*

No, he wanted a wildfire. Burning hot and bright and leaving the world utterly changed.

A quick kiss wouldn't be enough. Blake nibbled on her lower lip and his hands skimmed along her back, coming to rest on her bottom. He felt her stiffen, then relax. He wanted her arms around him, to feel her breasts against his chest, to hear her sigh with pleasure.

"Lord Copley, how long must we persist in this foolishness?"

This was just pretend.

"Until we have a spark. A second after that we'll have a full blown fire."

Or was it becoming something else, something real?

"And burn down our inheritance in the process!"

"Mmm . . ." Had he murmured or was that Emma? He didn't know anything, except that her lips were soft and her kiss was so innocent, so curious, in spite of herself. If nothing else he would always know that he was the one with whom she learned to kiss. Not her lover boy.

"Look! It's starting to smoke!" Lady Copley exclaimed. Her husband only grunted in acknowledgment.

Slowly but surely Emma began to yield. Her lips parted and he slid in, tasting her at last. Had he expected to be her first? Expected that this would be new to her? She kissed him as if she'd had *some* experience—this set his blood simmering—but she kissed him as if she didn't have *much* experience.

From a deep, unthinking part of his brain came the overwhelming desire to be her *only* experience.

"Oh! The edges are starting to glow!" Lady Copley declared. "The leaf is smoldering now!"

Emma's skin was warm under his touch. He had dared to touch her bare arms and the soft skin left uncovered by her bodice. His own temperature was spiking and he wanted to rip off his jacket, tear off the cravat, waistcoat . . . everything, and lie down here, on the soft mossy ground and make love to this women who slowly but surely was starting to spark and then to smolder from his touch.

For a kiss that had been just an act, a decoy, part of the games, it had turned into something else entirely.

"Fire!" Lady Copley exclaimed.

Blake pulled back suddenly and looked away, but not before a glance at Emma. Her eyes, half closed in dreamy pleasure. Her mouth, redder from the heat and friction of their lips together.

Had something changed? It felt like something changed. Blake took a step back. Emma clasped the jar of little white butterflies to her chest.

"How long does the first feeling of love last?" he mused.

"I don't know," she answered.

The sound of music

Emma's heart was still racing as they crossed the gardens and strolled through the cool, dark rooms of the house until they came to the music room. Against her chest she held a jar of fluttering butterflies . . . much like the strange sensation in her belly. They had left behind the Copleys and the small fire they created with just a few dried leaves and the magnifying lens of his spectacles.

It was nothing compared to the fire smoldering within her.

Blake had kissed her.

It hadn't meant anything, of course, but tell that to her racing heart! She tried. It didn't listen. The cursed thing had a mind and desire of its own, quite at war with her wishes.

The Duke of Ashbrooke had kissed *her*—plain old wallflower Emma Avery. Not only that, but there were strong indications that she was not immune to the Ashbrooke Effect, as she had thought. Not in the slightest. Her lips still tingled.

To be fair, she hadn't had time to dodge his advances or to conjure up Benedict's face in her mind. Which didn't matter because the kiss meant nothing. It was all just part of the ruse. *But no one saw.*

Once in the music room, Blake searched for "his" flute. Overwhelmed by nervous energy, Emma sat down at the pianoforte and began to play. She started with "I Once Loved a Lass (the False Bride)," her solo performance that never was, and ought to have been were it not for the evil machinations of Lady Katherine Abernathy. It had always been her favorite.

It was a pretty song, with highs and lows rising in sweet repetition and a melody that was at once hopeful and slightly melancholy.

"You play well," Blake said, abandoning his search and coming to stand beside her. Her fingers found the chords, one after another, and flew over the keys. She hadn't played in years and she was pleasantly surprised that her hands still knew their way around the keyboard and that the song she'd spent hours diligently learning had stayed with her.

Blake took a seat beside her on the bench. Heat suffused her. Her fingers slowed, tripping to a stop.

"No, don't stop. I know that song," he said softly. "Keep playing. I shall sing along with you."

If only Lady Katherine would see me now, Emma thought, and not just because of the unfathomable sight of the duke of Ashbrooke beside her on the piano bench, but because of the warmth in his eyes when his gaze lifted from her fingers to her face.

Emma started over from the beginning, her fingers moving back to the first chords and keys, stumbling slightly here or there. It was one thing to play a song, quite another to do so with a handsome rogue beside her. Quite, quite another when he had just kissed her in the garden.

Blake began to sing in a low, rich baritone. His voice was rough in an appealing way. She pursed her lips in annoyance. Was there nothing he was bad at?

"'Oh, I loved a lass and I loved her so well,'" Blake sang. Then turning to Emma, he said, "You know the next line, don't you? Sing with me, Emma." Really, there was no way she could say no.

Shyly and softly, she sang the next line, "'I hated all others who spoke of her ill.'"

He sang the line that followed: "'But now she's rewarded me well for my love.'" Her heart, cursed thing, beat harder at the prospect. It had never occurred to her to imagine such a thing, until he sang the words to her on a quiet summer afternoon.

"'For she's gone and she's married another.'" It was her line, and her voice wavered. She planned to marry another, truly. But what if she stayed with Blake, rather than jilt him as they had agreed?

In perfect time and in perfect pitch, Blake sang, "'When I saw my love to the church go, I followed on with my heart full of woe.'"

She couldn't help but imagine it. As she did, her finger stumbled, missing a few notes until her fingers tangled and the song came tumbling to a halt.

"I always liked that song," he said softly.

"I was fond of it, too," she said.

"Perhaps we have something in common after all," he remarked, and she saw the hesitancy in his suggestion. It was just a song . . . but as they accumulated more common ground, would it be harder to part?

"Nothing like shared preference for the same music for a lifetime of matrimonial bliss," she remarked lightly.

She had to keep things light. Distant. Because that kiss had knocked her off balance, left her dizzy and breathless. If she wasn't careful, she could fall right in love with him.

"Please don't take this the wrong way, Blake . . ."

"That sounds like the prelude to a grave insult," he remarked with laughter in his voice. Emma smiled.

"Perhaps our chances of winning this game are greater if we perform this song," she said gently.

"Instead of my flute playing? What are you saying about my flute playing?" He feigned a wounded expression.

"To start, one could hardly call it playing," Emma said frankly.

"You speak so cruelly of my talents, my darling *Emily*." In spite of herself, she smiled.

"Talents?" Emma echoed. But then she started to laugh.

"Oh, I'll show you my talents," he murmured.

"Oh?" she questioned.

Blake dipped his head, seeking another kiss. She closed her eyes, waiting for the warmth of his lips upon hers. She would indulge, just for a second because she craved him. His lips touched hers. Another spark. Another shiver up and down her spine. *Benedict . . .* Or *this?*

A passion she had never imagined.

A desire she had never known.

A happiness she couldn't afford.

After but a moment—a dangerously sweet moment—Emma turned away from Blake. She had to, for her own good.

Eternity
Lady Agatha's private sitting room

Blake paused in his search for eternity to visit Agatha, hoping to find her alone. He knocked on the door to her private sitting room and strolled in without waiting for an answer, just as she had instructed him to do so many years ago.

She sat on her settee, indulging in the sacred ritual of afternoon tea and perusing a thick stack of gossip-laden correspondence and periodicals.

"My dearest Aunt Agatha," Blake said, settling into the seat opposite her. "How are you enjoying this year's Fortune Games?"

"Shouldn't you be participating in them?" Agatha inquired. "And where is your beloved fiancée?"

"She is seeking truth and I have come to you in search of eternity," Blake replied. He didn't add that they were taking a break because they needed to cool their heads and allow their pulses to subside to a normal pace. At least, he needed that. The woman affected him. When he was the one who usually did the . . . affecting.

"While I'm thrilled you have thought of me when you sought eternity, I must tell you an unfortunate truth: I won't live forever, Blake."

"It only seems like it," Blake said with one of his charming grins.

"You're so witty, aren't you? All the bloody time," she replied, with a roll of her eyes and a dismissive wave of her jewel-bedecked hand.

"How are you, truly, Agatha?" Blake asked, leaning forward.

"I'm tired," she confessed. "Bored. Very glad you showed up with that girl."

"Her name is Emma," he said. Not Emily, though he did love the appalled expression on her face when he called her that.

"I like her," Aunt Agatha said.

"She's nice," Blake said benignly, because his real impression of her was a tangled knot of feelings he didn't dare sort out.

"No she isn't," Agatha retorted. "She's blunt, outspoken, and too plain to get away with it. But she's exactly the woman you need if you ever stop thinking with your twig and bits and used your brain instead."

"I cannot believe you just referred to my intelligence as twig and bits," Blake replied.

"I raised you, boy," Agatha said, bracelets jangling as she shook her finger at him. "Also, I am old and don't give a damn about propriety anymore."

"One wonders if you ever did," Blake mused.

"Oh, of course I did, once upon a time," Agatha replied, lips pursed. "Sometimes, you must play by the rules. If only so one can break them more effectively. For example, showing up to a house party when one had not been invited."

"I have forgiven you for that lapse in etiquette," Blake said.

"Having said that, I am happy you are here," she said gruffly.

"Even though you didn't invite me?" He tried

to keep up his easy demeanor and speak in a carefree voice. He didn't want anyone to know how bothered he was that she hadn't invited him.

"I have learned the rules by which you operate, Blake. A lack of invitation was a surer way to have you come running than if I were to send you the same one as all the others."

"What does that mean?"

"You were born with looks, money, charm, wit . . . "

"Do go on," he drawled and she scowled at him.

"Those things have made life easy for you," she said, speaking softly, though her voice wasn't weak. "It's funny, you thrive on a challenge, and yet so rarely are you faced with any. Well, any that really matter. Stupid wagers and loose women don't count. I want you to know how sweet victory is when you have fought for it."

He wanted to ask *Why now?*, but he didn't want the answer. Was she dying? She must be dying. It was inevitable, given that the old broad had to be pushing eighty years of age. Possibly even ninety. Or one hundred. Blake took the opportunity to look out the window. More to the point, he couldn't quite meet Agatha's gaze.

She had a way of getting directly to the point.

Why did it matter, anyway, if he played her games for a fortune he burned to have, but didn't desperately need? Not the way George did, or Miss Dawkins, or even Emma.

Or did it only matter that he was *here* with *her* in the closest thing to a home and family that he had experienced? What did it say about him that the surest way to guarantee his attendance was a lack of invitation?

Or that the surest way to capture his attentions was to push him away? *Emma.*

"No one knows me like you do," he replied. He meant to sound flippant. He failed.

"Well that's really up to you now, isn't it?" Agatha replied.

Blake shifted uncomfortably in his chair and said, "I shall mull that over at another time. I have this ridiculous game to play. You would not believe what some batty old broad put on a scavenger hunt. Eternity!"

"How clever," Agatha said, grinning.

"Devious, more like it," Blake replied, standing. "Want to give a man a hint? Don't want to overexert my brain."

"If you'd actually apply your intellect to the list you would detect a theme, at which point eternity becomes completely obvious," Aunt Agatha said. She didn't need to say *you dolt*, but it was there in her tone.

"I'll ask Emma. She'll know," Blake said confidently.

He walked down the hall thinking of sparks, the feeling of love at first sight, beauty and truth, happily-ever-after, and eternity . . . and a theme . . .

"Well doesn't Aunt A have a romantic streak," Blake muttered to himself as he turned around and strode back to her sitting room. He barged in without knocking.

"Can I borrow a few of your wedding bands?" he asked with his most charming grin. "I know you must have at least half a dozen."

"Lord save us all from your sense of humor. There, over on the dressing table," Agatha said. "Put them to good use."

Happily ever after
In the library

This was no longer just a game. It wasn't just a song or just a kiss. Emma didn't recognize herself anymore. For she had quite easily slipped into being a girl who kissed a duke behind a tree in the garden, sang duets with him in the Music Room, and otherwise forgot about the man she'd loved for three seasons now.

She sought refuge in the library, a long room with windows overlooking the lawn, dark bookshelves stretching from floor to ceiling, sparkling chandeliers, and roaring fireplaces at either end. Alcoves were built into the shelf-lined walls, providing shadowed and intimate nooks.

Emma's pace slowed when she entered, wide-eyed with wonder at all the leather-bound volumes, taking in the familiar scent of books and the comforting silence of a library. Until this moment she fancied winning the games as a way to obtain the funds she needed to marry Benedict with their families' blessings. Now she fiercely wanted to win for this room alone.

She imagined hours, days, weeks, a lifetime here with Benedict. He would love this room as much as she. He would forgive her for the deception required to gain this room of wonders. They would be *happy* here.

Almost.

Her vision came with a prick to her conscience. This was Blake's *home.* It was clear by the easy way he strolled through the rooms, the corridors, and the gardens. As if he belonged. He had a story for every room, right down to the scratches on the banister.

"What are you looking for?" Blake's low voice rent through the silence. Emma gasped and spun around, not having heard him enter.

"Happily-ever-after. Do you know where the novels are shelved?"

"Not a clue," Blake replied, leaning against a bookshelf. He looked so bloody perfect. A duke in his palatial home, at ease in his fine, fitted clothing. His hair disheveled *just so.* His smile was ever so slight, but ever so effective at making her heart skip a beat.

How vexing.

"Do you not read?" she inquired. He scowled mightily at her, and she needed that normalcy. She was beginning to fear that her heart would never return to its regular pace again. Somewhere, between love at first sight and the sound of music, things had *changed* between them.

Kisses were dangerous. She'd had no idea.

"Of course I *read,* Emily," he retorted, and it was

her turn to scowl at him. "I just prefer to live my life rather than read about it."

"What is that supposed to mean?" she asked, already disliking his response.

"I could read about sword-fighting. Or I could actually sword fight," Blake stated. "I could read about Brighton, or I could just go there. I could read erotic literature or I could—"

"Your point is made, *Duke*. Easy for a man to say," she replied. "As a woman, I'm afraid my options are far more limited. So many experiences are only available to me in books."

"You just think they are," he replied, still leaning against the bookshelf.

"I'm certain my attempts at sword-fighting would be frowned upon," she said.

"You are far too concerned about what people think about you, Emma."

"Easy for a duke to say. You would care if you were a young woman named one of London's Least Likely," she said strongly. "You can afford not to care because you are a man, a high-ranking one at that. Plus you are charming, well-liked, handsome, intelligent and—"

"You think I'm handsome?" Blake asked with a lift of his brow.

"We both know you are and it's not a matter of opinion," she retorted. "But the point is, when people hold a favorable opinion, it's easier to—"

"You think I'm charming," he said, strolling toward her with a grin on his face and a swagger in his step.

"And yet I am not charmed by you," Emma mused.

"Are you saying that you are London's Least Likely to fall for me?" Blake asked, towering over her. She stepped back until the bookshelves dug into her back. Blake placed one hand on either side of her, effectively boxing her in.

"That is exactly what I am saying," she said. He was so arrogant. He set her nerves on edge. He played with her affections and her very grasp on reality. He made her heart race, and he made her crave kisses that drove her to dizzying heights of pleasure. With a gaze from his darkened eyes, he made her dare to believe that she was desirable.

"And yet some say I am a master of seduction," Blake replied in a low voice that sent a shiver shimmying up and down her spine.

"And yet here I am, hardly seduced," Emma replied. *Breathlessly*. Dammit.

"We can fix that," Blake murmured, tracing a fingertip along the edge of her bodice and along the swells of her breasts. She fought back a sigh and tried valiantly to recall why it was so imperative that she *not* be seduced.

Benedict. The Wager. The Fortune Games. Pride.

"No one is watching. Not George, nor Lady Bellande or anyone," Emma pointed out. "There is no need for this display."

"Even better that no one is around," he said. He gave her a look that positively smoldered. She felt sparks and shivers as he pressed kisses along the edge of her bodice. Her skin tingled from the warmth and pressure of his lips upon her bare skin.

She wanted to say: *Kiss me. Kiss me on my lips. Kiss me lower. Show me things I'm not supposed to know.*

None of those words crossed her lips.

"I am not like your other women," Emma said. He laughed, and she felt a rush of breath across her skin, like a caress.

"Trust me, I know," Blake murmured. "It's impossible to forget."

"Yes, so why—" But her protestations died on her lips when he slid his fingers through her hair, clasping her face gently in his big, strong hands. He closed the distance between them, pressing the long hard length of him against her. Just enough for her to know of his desire. Just enough to remind her that he was bigger, stronger, and had her trapped. His point was made: she was at his mercy. She only had to say *No* or *Let me go* and he would release this hold on her.

Emma lifted her eyes to his, not quite able to say *Yes* but with no desire to leave.

"I want you, Emma," he said, gazing at her. No one was around to see or hear those words—or what came next.

Blake claimed her mouth for a kiss. The scorching, devastating kind that was impossible to fight. One could only surrender. The warmth from his touch seemed to make her own temperature spike until she felt certain she'd melt.

If no one could see, what was the point of this?

If no one could see, what did this mean?

Against her better judgment, Emma closed her eyes and breathed him. She grabbed a fist of his linen shirt in her palms, holding on for dear life.

Benedict . . . She shouldn't do this. She shouldn't forget him. But it was so hard to keep him in mind when her every nerve was attuned to the expert seducer before her.

Blake leaned against her, and she felt his hard arousal pressing against the vee of her thighs. Her breasts were pressed against the muscled plane of his chest, the centers becoming stiff peaks. She craved his touch, there. This was more intimacy with a man than she had even dreamed . . . and it was not enough.

Blake cupped her breast in his palm. No, this was not enough.

The kiss deepened, and she didn't shy away from it.

But then she felt his smile against her lips and she feared that it wasn't a smile of happiness or pleasure, but of triumph. She could only imagine what he was thinking: *London's Least Likely to Be Seduced, Fallen in just one afternoon.*

Chapter 11

Of all the priceless art and heirloom jewels, one of the most valuable items in the Grey fortune is the Castle Hill urn. It alone is worth such a sum as to keep a family of twelve in style for a year.

—The Exhaustive History of the Ashbrooke Clan and Their Holdings

Destruction

Blake made Emma feel things she simply couldn't handle. It wasn't just the new, exhilarating sensations that made her gasp in pleasure. It wasn't just the newly awakened desire within her that howled for satisfaction. It was more than the fluttering of her pulse when he was near, or the way she felt warmed whenever his brown eyes gazed upon her.

She reminded herself about Blake's wager. She reminded herself that this was pretend. She reminded herself of *why* she flirted with such danger: Benedict.

Benedict didn't turn her world upside down with every encounter. He wasn't forever trying to kiss her or seduce her or lead her into all sorts of trouble. He was steady and constant and the kind of man she could be happily married to forever.

Of course she felt like a wretched traitor for the palpable, intense longing she felt for Blake. She wanted his touch. She wanted to taste him on her lips, run her fingers through his hair, feel his arousal against her. Her resolve was weakening.

Traitor. Weakling.

So she escaped Blake's embrace and fled before she drowned in regrets. She pushed open the library doors and dashed down the hall. She rushed headlong through the pink marble foyer, barely noticing Miss Dawkins, who awkwardly carried a large gold-framed painting.

Emma collided with Harriet Dawkins.

The ladies stumbled. In an effort to right each other and save the painting, they collided with the pedestal and the large porcelain urn perched upon it. Past tense.

The family heirloom fell, shattering on the pink marble floor.

Large, sharp shards and a million tiny pieces jutted out from the pile of ashes the urn had contained. Emma knew all about the urn, thanks to reading *The Exhaustive History of the Ashbrooke Clan and Their Holdings.* It had been a personal gift from the King. The hand-painted porcelain depicted Castle Hill through the seasons. The painter had been an infamous recluse who produced only four priceless pieces in his entire career.

"Oh no," she gasped.

"Oh dear," Harriet whispered. "I'm so sorry."

"No, I must apologize. It was my fault."

"No, mine. I'm so very sorry."

"Me, too," Emma said. Harriet's face paled. "Are those ashes?"

"Oh my God," Emma whispered. They had broken a priceless family heirloom and disturbed the dead. And lost the Fortune Games.

"We are wrecked," Harriet said. "Utterly and completely wrecked. I suppose we should alert a housemaid and then go pack our things."

Harriet sighed, as if watching all her hopes and dreams wash away, and she was powerless to stop it. Emma suspected they were the same dreams as hers: that winning the games would enhance her prospects and give her a chance for true love, or at least a measure of security in the world. But Harriet's swift surrender tugged at Emma's heart and conscience. She didn't deserve to lose because of something that was just as much her own fault, if not more.

A few others emerged from their card games in the drawing room to see what had happened.

"Emma!" Both she and Harriet turned to see Blake rushing into the foyer. "Oh bloody hell," he muttered, skidding to a stop when he saw the destruction.

"Harold!" At the sound of Lady Agatha's shout, the three turned and lifted their gazes to see her standing, with Angus for support, at the top of the stairs.

"Who is Harold?" Harriet asked in a whisper.

"He was Agatha's fourth husband," Emma

whispered back. The only one she liked. The one she had loved. There had been a whole chapter on their romance in *The Exhaustive History of the Ashbrooke Clan and Their Holdings.*

"And he is currently that pile of ashes upon the floor," Blake said grimly.

Lady Agatha glared at the scene below as she slowly descended the stairs.

Emma had never known what it was to cower in fear—she'd read about it, of course. But until this moment she hadn't truly known. This was it. This was the loss of all her hopes and dreams. All because of a foolish mistake. She ought to have stayed and kissed the rogue. Let that be a lesson to her!

"Who did this?" Agatha barked, now standing before them.

Harriet whimpered, and Emma knew she could let her take the blame. Harriet wouldn't protest, for in her heart had already presumed herself guilty and accepted her fate.

It occurred to Emma that if she were more ruthless, more heartless, more like Lady Katherine Abernathy, she would declare that Harriet in her haste hadn't seen where she was going. Harriet knocked it over. Harriet was to blame. It wasn't true, but Emma knew that no one would say otherwise.

But even though she didn't know Harriet Dawkins well, Emma recognized in her a kindred spirit. A girl who wasn't perfect, but was perfectly lovely. A girl who was *not quite* but was in fact quite wonderful, truly. Emma felt she didn't deserve to win any more than Harriet, and knew that the only way Harriet would have a chance was if she gave it to her.

"I did it," she said in a rush, before Harriet could interject. "I did this. It was a mistake and I am so very sorry."

"Emma . . ." Blake murmured, touching her arm. She'd just have to explain to him later that her sense of kindness and decency was worth more than ninety thousand pounds. She had already betrayed her loyalty to the man she loved in a misguided attempt to secure the funds they *thought* they needed. These wicked desires to win were causing all sorts of problems for her conscience. Perhaps it wasn't worth it.

"Good luck winning the games after that mistake, Lady Emma," Dudley remarked from where he stood near the drawing room door. He crossed his arms over his chest and sneered at her.

"Are you still here, Dudley?" Agatha asked, bored.

Dudley shuffled awkwardly, unsure of how to answer that.

"Be gone with you," Agatha said with a dismissive wave of her hands.

"But Lady Emma was the one to break this beautiful, priceless family heirloom and trample upon the ashes of your beloved third husband," Dudley protested.

"Fourth," Emma corrected. "Harold Henry Harrison. The vase had been a wedding gift to you both from the King."

"More Debrett's?" Lady Agatha inquired.

"Actually, it was in *The Exhaustive History of the Ashbrooke Clan and Their Holdings,*" Emma said.

"Interesting bit of knowledge to have at your fingertips, Lady Emma. And I'm glad to see that someone is enjoying the reading material I had so thoughtfully provided to all of my guests," Lady Agatha replied. "That's the thing, Dudley. I shall be interested to see if she is able to redeem herself after this tragedy. Whereas you will simply wait for others to fail and make snide but unclever remarks off to the side. How dull. Do go on."

"Lady Agatha . . ." Dudley shut his mouth when he saw it would be pointless to continue, for she had already turned to address a servant about cleaning up.

"Do take care, the rest of you. Wouldn't want to wreck everything before someone has a chance to inherit it."

Chapter 12

Can you hear that rustling? It's the sound of the haute ton frantically opening their invitations to the unexpected wedding between the Duke of Ashbrooke and Lady "Buxom Bluestocking" Emma Avery. While the duke and his intended vie for Lady Grey's fortune at her annual games, the bride's mother has begun planning the wedding of the season.

—"Fashionable Intelligence,"
The London Weekly

The last night of the Fortune Games

The collections from the day's romantically themed scavenger hunt were artfully displayed on tables lining the drawing room. For beauty, there were Lady Grey roses, mirrors, and paintings portraying the beautiful Sussex landscape. Blake and Emma's collection of butterflies in a jar fluttered as love at first sight. Candles flickered. Blake's matches were dismissed as "more newfangled trouble."

Agatha had slowly examined them all, with her Angus offering his arm for support. At her direction, he made notes in that red leather book he carried everywhere. To everyone's surprise, she did not send anyone home. While she seemed intrigued and pleased by the assortment of items, the group tensed in expectation of swift and sudden dismissals. Blake and Emma had pleased Agatha with most of their selections, thus earning back some points they had lost.

They were surprised again when Agatha announced there would be dancing and that the local gentry had been invited. Angelica Scarlatti and her players remained to play beautiful music. There was flirting and dancing. Young marriageable women sighed over Blake and lamented the news of his betrothal.

As she always did at balls, Emma sought refuge in the corner. Instead of fellow wallflowers for company, she had Lady Agatha.

Emma did not see Blake and she imagined all manner of trouble for him. There were quite a number of pretty young daughters of country squires. Lady Bellande was still on the prowl. He could be with any of them.

The world was returning to rights. Emma Avery, wallflower. The Duke of Ashbrooke, off to some debauchery.

"Did you enjoy the Fortune Games, Lady Emma?"

"Honestly, Lady Agatha, I did," Emma replied. "However, my expectations were quite low." Agatha gave a bark of laughter. "I had a marvelous time during today's scavenger hunt."

By marvelous she meant: wonderful, wicked,

tempting, maddening, and utterly lovely. It far surpassed her usual day's activity of sitting in her drawing room, without callers, feeling so very *not quite.*

"You would never have so much time alone with your betrothed in London," Agatha said, as if she could read Emma's mind as to *why* she had enjoyed the games so much. All those stolen moments when Blake made Emma dare to believe she was beautiful and desirable. Oh, she wasn't *convinced,* but she had considered it for the very first time.

"I've had very little time with Blake in London," she said, "and I expect we shall return to that." It was the truth, but she still felt like a liar.

"If the gossip is to be believed, you two only just became betrothed immediately before the party," Agatha said. Was there suspicion in her eyes? An accusation in her tone? Or was her guilty conscience just imagining it?

"Whirlwind courtship," she whispered, because it hurt to lie but she could not bring herself to confess the truth. Not on the last night of the Fortune Games.

"So tell me, Emma, what you would do with my fortune, should you win it? I never did get to hear your answer."

"Hopefully nothing, for I realize what must transpire for me to possess it," Emma said, and the moments the words were spoken, she knew them to be the truth.

Usually nothing extraordinary occurred in the

wallflower-spinster-dowager corners of the ballroom, but tonight something quietly remarkable happened. Emma realized that while she desperately wanted to win the games, possess the fortune, and live happily ever after, she did not want to pay the price.

Not when the price was Agatha's life, Harriet's possibly dowry, Blake's Difference Engine and all the people who would benefit from it, or even Lady Bellande's charity balls. Not when the price was her pride and decency.

"Hmmph. I won't live forever, you know," Lady Agatha said. "How would you spend ninety thousand pounds?"

"Like Miss Dawkins, I would use it to marry. And, honestly, some new dresses," Emma added, thinking of the critical glances she'd received at her plain and unfashionable gowns.

"And yet you have betrothed yourself to Blake, who has no need of my fortune. If I give the fortune to you, I am in effect giving it to him. Technically speaking."

"What if you didn't? That is to say, what if we didn't marry?" The words tumbled out.

"I would roll over in my grave and haunt you until the ends of the earth," Lady Agatha said. Emma laughed nervously.

"I'm not joking," Lady Agatha said flatly.

"I am aware," Emma said with a sigh.

"In truth, Emma, I shall be dead and won't care one whit about anything. But I shall give you this piece of advice, as someone who has been married more than a few times: *the heart wants what the heart wants."*

Startled, Emma's gaze flew to Agatha, and noted her expression was at once kind, shrewd, wise, and sharp. Emma could not make sense of it. Did she know? Was that permission to marry Benedict? Is that what she still wanted?

Out of the corner of her eye Emma saw Blake approaching. Rather, she saw the crowd melt apart, leaving a clear path for to him walk directly to her.

"Emma, darling, I have come to rescue you from Aunt Agatha's evil clutches," he said smoothly.

"I do not need rescuing," Emma protested.

"How kind of Your Rakishness to grace the wallflower and dowager corner with your charming presence," Agatha drawled. "Our hearts are all aflutter."

"I have recently discovered what treasures there are to be found in the darkest, most remote and uninviting corner of the ballroom," Blake said, and not in his usual, cavalier way. He looked not at Agatha, but at Emma.

"I think there is nothing more tragic than two young lovers in the first blush of romance spending time conversing with a chaperone looking on," Agatha declared. "Off with you both. Waltz at least thrice, and scandalously close together, if for no other reason than because you can."

"Would you care to waltz, darling Emma?" Blake offered his hand. Emma hesitated, stricken in an attack of her nerves. She'd hardly done much dancing during her seasons and had never danced with a duke. For all the intimacies she had shared with Blake today, he hadn't held her in his arms, swept her off her feet, whirled her around the room until she was dizzy from the thrill of it.

She'd never been the girl singled out to waltz with the most handsome man in the ballroom. She imagined that Prudence and Olivia were with her, whispering encouragement and nudging her in the back.

"Apparently, I would like nothing more," she replied, and it was the truth.

WALTZING IN BLAKE'S arms was everything she had dreamed it would be. Everything she, Prudence, and Olivia had discussed and imagined—all while pretending not to care, really. It was just a waltz. It was just a man. It was just another ball.

Except when it wasn't.

In Blake's arm she felt so petite and weightless. He was so sure in his every step, and she felt his certainty in the way he held her hand and whirled her around the ballroom. She breathed him in. Savored the warm pressure of his palm, scandalously low on her back. Dangerous as it was, she started to surrender and to trust him.

What if she really could trust him?

If they were to marry—which was ridiculous, because he hadn't asked and never would—would she be able to trust such a renowned rake to return home to her and only her? No, of course not. The reason he could waltz her around so perfectly and seduce her so expertly wasn't just because of all the practice he'd had, but because it was what he did.

Not that it was even worth considering.

"We won't win," Emma said, breaking the silence. A reminder that she oughtn't get swept away in this one, fleeting moment was definitely in order.

"Why do you say that?" Blake asked softly.

"Lady Agatha pointed out a legality that I had overlooked. What is mine becomes yours. And she despises your matches, your Difference Engine, your desire to change the whole world order. We won't win."

"I'm sorry," he said finally. He sounded genuine.

"Here we are waltzing and pretending to be in love when there is no point to this charade any longer," she mused. Emma caught *sadness* in her voice, as if she wanted this game to last longer, even though she had spent much of it steadying her nerves until the world returned to normal.

"Don't say that, Emma. Can we not just enjoy this for what it is? A perfect summer evening, fine music, a beautiful woman in my arms, although she is a deplorable dancer who keeps stepping on my toes."

"Well I haven't much practice," she protested. "And I can't imagine it hurts you very much to have me stepping on your boots."

"Emma," he said, his voice urgent as he pulled her closer. Ducking his head to murmur in her ear, he asked, "What would it take to make you truly surrender, Emma?"

"I couldn't say," she whispered. Her heart beat, *bump, bump, Benedict, Benedict.* But her gaze was drawn to Blake. Every nerve attuned to Blake.

"You don't seem to care for pretty compliments, though you do like when I kiss you."

She blushed and looked away. She saw Agatha watching them. Agatha would say the truth.

"I just can't believe you, Blake. I suspect all the romantic affections are part of the ruse. As for your compliments—if my eyes were so pretty, if I weren't so plain, wouldn't someone else have noticed by now? No one has. I am a wallflower of the first order."

"Was," Blake corrected. "After this you will be sought after. Men will praise your eyes, your crooked smile, and the adorable way you crinkle your nose when sherry is placed before you. They will notice because I shined the light on you," he said, and she opened her mouth to protest his vanity. Even though she had to admit there was truth to his words. Then he continued, taking her breath away, "But they will compliment you because it's true."

He saw her. Really saw her.

Blake saw beyond the horrid nicknames or her reputation. He saw the real girl who lived and breathed and loved. The girl who wasn't perfect, and he waltzed with her anyway.

He believed in her. The question was, could she believe in herself? As if Blake had lifted the veil over her eyes, Emma dared to consider *everything* in a new light. Had she perhaps put too much stock in the talk of the ton and started to believe that she wasn't remarkable or special? To even consider that was such a dramatic reversal of everything she'd ever thought and felt, Emma didn't think she could quite process it. Certainly not while Blake held her closer than was proper and slid his hand lower that he ought to.

Was it madness to put her heart and hopes in the hands of a known rogue? Probably.

In spite of all the thoughts and feelings jumbling within her, she couldn't think of a word to say, so she said, "I am speechless."

"Good. I was afraid I had lost my touch with the ladies," Blake said with his infamous heart-melting grin. It was the Ashbrooke Effect in full force—from his charming smile to his seductive touch to his masculine scent, which she inhaled deeply, only to crave more.

She was not immune. Not at all.

But she was Emma Wallflower, the one woman who didn't tumble right into his bed, and thus the one he was intent upon seducing. For the moment. She was not quite ready to surrender completely and risk losing him. She wasn't about to be just another one of his women either. Nor was she about to let him win his own wager.

"How endearing. How romantic," she said. "I am just another one of your ladies, to be seduced and discarded. To be notches on your bedpost or trophies on your wall. What a great honor. I cannot describe how special I feel."

"You overheard me at the inn," he said plainly.

"Yes, I did. But even if I hadn't, I still wouldn't have fallen for your efforts at seduction," Emma said. She took great pleasure in them, surely. But she didn't believe he meant them—not in any serious, lasting way. *But he thinks your crooked smile is charming.* He adored something she'd always been teased for.

"Because of your lover boy?" Blake asked with a questioning lift of his brow.

"Because it's you. And me. And this is naught but a ruse and we both know it," she said, though it became more difficult to determine where the game ended and the truth began.

"One should never do anything by halves, wouldn't you agree?" He didn't give her a chance to reply before carrying on. "Thus we should play our parts in this mad charade fully and completely. We should totally immerse ourselves in the roles of the beloved, besotted betrothed." That smile again. Her traitorous heart.

"Why?"

"Why not?"

"That's hardly an answer," she replied. *But what if he means it?* He'd planted the idea in her head that perhaps, just perhaps, she wasn't an unfortunate spinster, but still a lovable girl. *And if that were true?*

"Very well, Emma. I'll give you a complete and

honest answer. At first I was merely intrigued because you—and only you—refused my advances. You teased me, you challenged me, and you have shown me the pleasure of anticipation. But then I tempted and cajoled and tasted you, Emma. You tasted sweet, because it was *you* and the pleasure was all the more great because I earned your kiss. I have felt you, after hours of imagining a touch of the forbidden. And now I crave you because I have tasted and touched and I only want more. I'll make no promises, and you won't either—I know your heart is set on your lover boy. So here is yet another proposal for you: one kiss. Just for the pleasure of it."

BLAKE LED EMMA by the hand out of the ballroom and out to the garden and the warm summer night air. He'd meant every word he told her tonight. His eyes had been opened to her. The mask had been lifted. He wanted her. More than anything, he wished she would see herself the way he did.

She wasn't just another conquest.

This wasn't just another kiss.

His heart was pounding, hard, as if he were some randy schoolboy about to experience his first woman. It would be just one kiss. Not even a first kiss.

A *last* first kiss? He pushed that thought away and focused only on Emma's small hand in his. The moonlight was just right, the garden was deserted. He led her to a place where they were assured privacy: the small clearing around the pond where he had kissed her after the walk from the ruins.

"One kiss," Emma whispered, her voice almost lost in the gently rustling tree branches above. "Just one."

"One kiss," he promised, reaching out to cradle her face in his hands. He slowly brushed his thumb across her lips. There. He would kiss her there. It was a promise that would surely be broken before the night was through. He hoped she'd forgive him.

Blake lowered his mouth to hers, closing the distance between them. His heart beat hard and hardly steady as he felt her soft lips. Though he wanted to sink his hands into her hair, pull her flush against him and kiss her fiercely, he kept his touch light and kiss gentle. One kiss. If that were all they had, it wouldn't do to scare her off so soon.

Cautiously, Emma slid her arms around him, drawing their bodies closer together. Once again he underestimated her. Once again she surprised him. It seemed they were of one mind: one kiss had better be something else entirely.

With his tongue he traced the seam of her lips, and she parted them, letting him in and letting him taste her. He caught a sigh and a moan. Though tentative at first, she dared to taste him, too. Noble intentions of being gentle began to recede. Emma, sweet, maddening Emma, had refused and rebuffed and it only made him want her more.

He wanted to sink to his knees and drag her

down with him. She had made herself forbidden, untouchable, and impossible to possess. He could never resist a challenge. But what he thought would be some sort of victory—this kiss—was only an exquisite, torturous reminder that one kiss was not everything. There was the matter of her heart. And every last inch of her that he wanted, simply, to know.

The night was loud with a chorus of crickets and the heady rush of their breathing, turning frantic now, as this kiss took a turn for wicked. There was something just devastatingly sublime in knowing that for all their differences, she felt that same urgency, that same ever-building pressure threatening to explode, that same desperate need for more. Now.

He was hard, so hard. With one hand he clasped her bottom, pressing her against his arousal so she would know how she affected him. Emma wasn't just some plain wallflower. She was the one woman who challenged him, teased him, *seduced him*. She was the only one who occupied his thoughts. She was the one whose slightest caress, smile, or suggestion had him desperate for more.

To feel her, even through all of that damnable fabric, was torture. The way she moved against him made him want to growl, tighten his fist around her hair and pull her to the ground and bury himself deep inside her.

He kissed her hard. She kissed him back. Her tongue, tangling with his. Frantic breaths, hers and his. He couldn't breathe. His heart was pounding.

He couldn't taste her or touch her enough. This kiss . . . they would not stop with this kiss. There was not enough time in the world for this kiss. It would take a lifetime.

Blake jerked away and stepped back to put some distance between his desire and Emma, and to cool the insane thoughts of his overheated brain. *A lifetime.*

A lifetime. He, who often did not even stay to see the sunrise with a woman, wanted to see a lifetime's worth of sunrises with one woman. Which begged the question, why not have her here and now and marry her after all?

So much for just one kiss.

He was breathing hard.

Her eyes were large and dark. Even in the moonlight he could see her cheeks were flushed. Her mouth was a plump crimson pout; the mouth of a woman who had been thoroughly kissed. Like this, she was a stunning beauty.

He wanted to gaze upon her thusly for hours and days. He did not want anyone else to see.

"I need to cool off," he said. She nodded. "Wait here, but turn around."

"What are you doing?"

"Stopping at just one kiss," he said, glancing over his shoulder at her, only to see that she was glancing over her shoulder at him. He took off his boots and breeches, then stripped off his shirt, letting it fall carelessly to the ground.

And then, after a moment of silence, "I need help with my dress," she said softly.

He ogled her backside and eyed the buttons on the back of her gown the way a burglar might regard a lock protecting untold riches.

"I'm trying to keep my promise," he said. "You're not making it easy."

"Do you want me to go?"

"No," he said roughly. "No."

He swiftly undid the buttons of her dress and unlaced her corset while ordering himself to complete mathematic equations in his head. But 237 plus 189 equaled—*oh God, her skin was so soft*—and 17 multiplied by 12 equaled—*she is so beautiful*—47 plus 99 minus 32 added up to—*I have never wanted a woman so badly.*

Had anyone told him he'd be naked in the moonlight, panting with lust for London's Least Likely, he would have laughed. He wasn't laughing now.

"The chemise can stay," she said, though he soon discovered it hardly provided any coverage at all, especially once she followed him into the pond. He dove in, glad to have water shock his heated skin.

Emma gasped with each step as the cold water lapped at her ankles, then her knees, then the secret place he wanted to kiss. Slowly, she waded farther out, and was almost completely immersed before she ducked under completely.

Blake lunged for her, thinking she had slipped or stepped off into deeper water. He assumed she couldn't swim. His heart stopped and his chest tightened in the frantic moment before she surprised him by popping above the water's surface, splashing him playfully and laughing in the moonlight.

"I used to love swimming in the lake at our country house," she explained. "But Mother forbid it when it was time for me to become a Lady."

"When was that?"

"I was just ten. Instead of games and play, I memorized Debrett's and learned to mind my manners," Emma said.

"That sounds dreadful," he said. But it had been the same for him: at some point games and reckless adventures were forced aside for lessons in mathematics, Latin, botany, philosophy, and all that. Everything wild and reckless was fit into a formula.

"The reward is Being a Lady," she said with a laugh. "I must be a lady so I might marry well."

"Also, how dreadful," he said, but Emma seemed to be lost in a world of her own thoughts. As if this cool water truly woke her up, as if this wild, midnight adventure unlocked something in her. He watched and listened as this transformation occurred.

"Did you know, Blake, that following the rules is vastly overrated?"

"Yes," he said, not sure if he agreed with what she said or whatever wicked plan she was obviously considering. There was an unmistakably mischievous gleam in her eyes.

To his surprise, she swam toward him, wrapped her arms around him and pressed her lips against his.

There was no turning back after that.

SHE MUST HAVE gone mad, utterly mad.

Emma had agreed to *just one kiss,* not realizing that there could be no such thing. Not when a kiss quieted her mind so all she did was feel a pleasure so intense it was almost unbearable.

When Blake stepped back, she had taken a moment to catch her breath. But her corset felt far too confining. The silk of her dress stretched taut against her bodice. When he started to remove his clothing, she thought, *Me, too.* She wanted to feel free. She wanted to cool her heated skin. She wanted to indulge in this wicked, passionate midnight encounter, for tomorrow the games would be over and who knew her fate after that?

This might be her only chance.

While they were at the games, she would play the game. When tomorrow came, she would return to life as London's Least Likely to Misbehave. But tonight she would indulge in the unfathomable: that she was the woman who captivated a man like Ashbrooke.

Tonight he was even more handsome, impossibly so. His cheekbones seemed higher, and in the moonlight his eyes appeared darker. Her gaze dropped to his firm, sensual mouth.

Perhaps it was the wildness of her surroundings or the champagne she had drunk earlier. Perhaps his kisses had permanently altered her brain, but something just clicked for her. Playing by the rules had gotten her nowhere. Daring to break them had led her to follow him into the pond and to this moment. She didn't want it to end.

So she kissed him again.

He kissed her back, wet hair slicked back from his face, wrapped his arms around her and pulled her flush against his hard chest. Her nipples hardened, becoming exquisitely sensitive and aware of the thin, wet fabric of her chemise and, even better, Blake's warm skin against her own.

"Wrap your legs around me," he said gruffly. She did, oh she did. She felt him, hot, hard, and throbbing at the sensitive place between her legs.

Time passed. She sighed. He moaned. She threaded her fingers through his wet hair and he clasped her bottom with his strong hands. Their kiss had gone from just perfect to perfectly wicked. She ought to have been cold, but there was a heat starting in her belly, smoldering hotter and spreading through all her limbs.

Vaguely, she was aware of Blake carrying her toward the shore and laying her down upon his jacket, which had been thrown down on the mossy ground. A cool breeze stole across her skin just as his hot mouth closed around her nipple, drawing a sharp gasp from her lips. He teased her, tonguing circles around the dusky centers until they were stiff peaks.

Slowly, oh so slowly, he kissed his way down, across her belly. She writhed a little, nervous and suddenly aware of the twigs and sticks under the jacket, the late hour, and the absolutely mad thing she was doing. What was he doing? It was Ashbrooke, she rationalized; he must know what he was doing. His hands clasped around her thighs, urging her open to him. Her skin felt scorching—was it mortification or anticipation? And then he kissed her in the sensitive place between her legs, teasing her with slow lazy circles of his tongue.

Emma moaned from the heat and the strange, new, lovely sensations. She moaned and sighed because a pressure was slowly but surely building inside her. Her hips bucked when he slid one finger inside her. She was shocked by the pleasure of it. In and out, he stroked her surely but gently. Just a little touch was making her lose control. Breathing was hard. She couldn't focus. Her skin felt feverish. She felt slightly panicked and yet vaguely reassured because of all the men in the world, the infamous Duke of Ashbrooke would bring her to pleasure. Right?

"Blake," she gasped. "I can't breathe."

He didn't stop.

"I'm dizzy," she panted. Truly, she felt like she would faint. The world was spinning and her knees felt weak even though she was on her back, which was absolutely absurd but completely true. The Ashbrooke Effect, she thought, barely, before his touch became exceptionally wicked and she just . . . shattered. Cried out his name. Sucked in deep breaths of air and wondered what magical explosion had just happened.

Blake covered her body with his to keep her warm. Tenderly, he brushed away a strand of her hair. He gazed down at her, making her feel truly beautiful for the first time in her life. *Remember this.*

Idly she caressed his back with her fingertips, tracing them along the long, smooth expanse of skin. She felt his muscles tense and flex under her touch. She felt his arousal pressing against the vee in her thighs.

"Emma. I want you." His voice was a rough whisper. She wanted him, too, but couldn't manage to voice the words. Gently, he guided her hand to his cock. It was hot and hard. His hand closed around hers, showing her how to stroke him, up and down the length of his shaft.

Emma watched his eyes darken, then close. His lips parted, a moan escaping. She now recognized what he must be feeling: the same heat, the same tension. It pleased her tremendously to give him such pleasure. Especially since she was just a wallflower and he must have surely known accomplished women. His every sigh, his every groan, emboldened her.

Just one kiss . . .

Emma bit her lip, dwelling upon the wicked thought that had just occurred to her. Kissing him, there, as he had done to her. Could she? Should she? Tonight was for daring. So she adjusted her position and took him in her mouth.

"Oh God, Emma," he groaned. She took more of him in, reveling in his sharp gasps. She clasped the rest of him with her palm, moving up and down in time with her mouth. He murmured her name. His breathing became shallow and fast and then he quickly rolled away from her with a shout as he reached his climax.

"Just one kiss," he murmured, pulling her close against his chest.

"Just one kiss," she repeated, curling up in his warm embrace.

Chapter 13

"You should tell Emma the news about Benedict," said Prudence.

"Or you can," Olivia said.

"No, you can," Prudence countered.

"No, you," Olivia replied.

And so on and so forth.

The Fortune Games were over. All that remained was goodbye.

The others left immediately after breakfast, their departure marked by the explosion of cannons on the front lawn. Blake lingered; he wouldn't, couldn't, say goodbye, and wouldn't, couldn't, say why. It had something to do with the madness that happened last night, what awaited his return to London, and what he would leave behind today.

Blake linked his arm in Emma's and together they watched as Agatha slowly climbed the stairs whilst holding onto the arm of her ever faithful footman. Her solicitor, Eastwick, followed behind, ready to draft yet another version of her will. Blake hoped it wasn't her *last* will and testament, but perhaps second to last, or third, or more. He could get by without the fortune. He wasn't sure that he could get by without Agatha, the one person in the world who knew him and who didn't fuss preciously over him.

Agatha and her men paused for just a moment, a few stairs from the top.

Blake felt something tighten in his chest, as if a pugilist's fist clenched his heart and squeezed hard. He wanted to call out to her, had to tell her . . . Well, he didn't know what to tell her. His mind went blank. Any words died in his throat before he could give voice to them. But he knew that this moment was incomplete, and that if he got in the carriage and drove off now, he would regret it forevermore.

He dashed across the foyer and bound up the steps two at a time, meeting Agatha at the top. He pulled the frail old woman into his bearish embrace.

"Last ditch attempt to win the games," he said, stepping back. When of course it wasn't that at all. It was *Thank you* and *I love you* and *I will never forget you.*

"I am undone by your sentimentality," she said dryly. Of course, she meant *Thank you* and *I love you* and *I will never forget you.* He knew because he knew *her.* Also, he saw the slick sheen of tears in her eyes.

Afterward, in the carriage, Blake knocked hard on the roof, signaling it was time to go. The carriage jolted to life and rolled down the drive, away from his only family, Agatha, who was probably dying. Away from the only place he had called home, which would soon belong to someone else.

If he couldn't stay forever, then he wanted to leave immediately.

Emma sat across from him, dressed in a green traveling dress. Though her eyes were full of questions, she had the good sense to stay quiet and leave a man to his brooding.

Or so he thought.

"Is everything all right?" she asked in a small voice.

"Of course," he replied, settling his gaze out the window.

"We have survived the Fortune Games," she remarked.

"Survive is one way to put it," he said. But he didn't quite feel like he had. He glanced across the carriage at Emma. Plain, bluestocking, on the shelf wallflower who had thrown her arms around his neck and kissed him . . . in the water . . . in the moonlight. And it was a greater pleasure than he'd ever experienced. But he couldn't be falling for her. Not *him*, not *her*, as the lady herself would say.

Yet, the thought of her with lover boy tied him up in knots.

"Lady Agatha did not announce a winner. When do you think we might hear?" Emma asked, mercifully interrupting his thoughts. Did she ask only so she might know when she might jilt him? Why did that cause another sharp pang in the region of his heart?

"She has already made up her mind," Blake said. Hell, Agatha probably knew the first night. "We will only wait on how fast her secretary can write as she dictates. And the postal service, of course. She sends the same letter to everyone who participated. Then the gossiping starts."

"Let's hope we hear before the wedding," Emma said.

The wedding.

It hadn't occurred to him that the wedding date would arrive before Agatha's pronouncement. He'd heard vague rumblings around town about Emma's mother planning the wedding of the season, but dismissed them as something not to worry about and ceased to give it another thought. After all, one did not have a *real* wedding for a fake betrothal.

But what if the wedding date approached before Agatha made her choice known?

What if they did something drastic and irreparable—like marry, or jilt each other?

Blake looked out the window, seeking a distraction in the endless expanse of fields.

"Do you think we will win?" Emma asked.

"I have no idea. It is impossible to anticipate the inner workings of Aunt Agatha's brain. I have not yet been able to determine the formula by which she calculates the winner, for she forgoes any sort of logic or rationality that another person might recognize," Blake replied.

"You speak so harshly to her. I am still not used to it."

"That is how we are. For if we display a moment of softness, everything will be lost," he said.

"Whatever do you mean by that?"

Blake sighed and glanced longingly out the window. He foresaw hours of dodging Emma's honest, heartfelt, devastating questions, and he'd opened himself up too much already. But there was no avoiding those blue eyes, so he told her just enough.

"At the age of eight I was orphaned," he explained, sounding bored even to his own ears. "I trust you read Chapter Ten in that exhausting history book about the Ashbrookes."

"I did."

His parents had died in an accident because of a stupid miscalculation. A damn fool architect relied on faulty calculations from his reckoning book. There had been too much weight and the whole damn roof collapsed. Exactly the sort of thing his Difference Engine would prevent. He couldn't fix the roof, but he could make sure it never happened again. In the meantime, he'd keep everyone at a distance so he didn't experience that devastating loss again. Obviously.

One glance at Emma's blue eyes and he knew she had read between the lines of Chapter Ten and pieced together the truth. There was no need to explain more, for which he was grateful.

"After that, I stayed with a series of nervous, smothering aunts, cousins, and other overly emotive relatives. Then I went to live with Agatha," he said, smiling faintly at the memory of their first meeting. "She had just lost her fourth husband, Harold—the one she actually loved. We could have moped, the two of us."

"But instead you carried on as if everything were just fine," Emma said. "When my brother died, my parents tried to pretend it never happened. But his presence is still felt. I might not have to marry for money if he were still here."

Blake pocketed that information, finding that Emma made more sense now. The games were about lover boy, but even more. Money, she needed money. But she wanted love.

"But one always wonders what might have been," Blake said, and she smiled so sweetly, as if he had understood and said the right thing.

"Does it bother you that she holds the Fortune Games rather than just give the fortune to you, her favorite?"

"It's her fortune to do with as she wishes. Would possessing it make my life easier? Yes. But so would a more respectable reputation," he said with a shrug. He saw that now. If he possessed the money, he could build his damned engine himself. If he possessed a good reputation, he could solicit investors. Either way he needed Emma.

That was in addition to the raw, driving need for her taste, the sensation of feeling her soft hands on his chest, and the sound of her soft moans in his ear. That kiss had destroyed him. He never *needed* a woman before, and the prospect terrified him.

For if he needed her and craved her, it would be

impossible to maintain the distance with which he conducted all of his affairs. But then again, Emma had never been just another affair. *What did that make her?*

Too many questions he couldn't answer.

Besides, the answer didn't matter. She had her lover boy, whom she loved so much that she was willing to embark on a sham marriage in order to swindle a fortune from an aging old broad.

Or had things changed for her, too?

"What happens when we return to town, Blake?"

"You will go to your house. I shall return to mine. I will probably have a bath, and then a whiskey," he said, even though he knew she was not asking about logistics, but about fate, their future, the contents of his heart and his innermost thoughts and feelings.

He did not have an answer for her.

"No, you blockhead," she said with a delicate upturn of her lips. "With us. What happens if neither of us wins? What happens if one of us wins?"

"I shall prepare to appear desolate and inconsolable as you jilt me and run off with whatever his name is," Blake said, repeating their plan. If they stuck to the plan, then he need not examine his heart and feelings. He need not renege on every promise he'd ever made to himself. All because of just one kiss. Ridiculous. "Presumably lover boy will wait for you. Did you explain this charade to him?"

Across from him in the carriage Emma paled.

"Of course he'll wait for me," she whispered.

"You didn't tell him?" Blake lifted one brow.

"I couldn't," she whispered. "I couldn't get away to see him and I didn't dare put it in writing. The last time I— Never mind."

Blake watched her fingers anxiously gripping and releasing the fabric of her skirts.

"I'm sure he'll wait for you. How long has he been courting you?"

"Three seasons. Without proposing." There was a twinge of bitterness in her voice.

"Then it is highly unlikely that he has, upon a moment's notice, proposed to another woman," Blake said to console her. She looked so distraught that he wondered if they should pull the carriage over for her to be sick.

"He'll wait for me. He'll have seen through . . . all this . . . "

Blake murmured his agreement while privately thinking that if any man suddenly stole his woman, he'd follow them both to the ends of the earth. And lover boy had not followed them. Or fought for her. He declined to point this out to Emma. Truly, she looked devastated, and it killed him.

"I'm eager to have the matter settled," she said, tightly gripping her hands in her lap. He bit back questions of how or with whom.

"The fact is, it would be foolish to make a decision regarding our betrothal until we hear from Agatha about the outcome of the games," Blake said, adding a dose of practicality to a conversation that had been far too fraught with *feelings*. "We should maintain the ruse just a little bit longer."

Chapter 14

The most coveted invitation this season is the invitation to the wedding of the Duke of Ashbrooke and Lady Emma Avery. The big event is just days away.

—Miss Harlow's "Marriage in High Life," *The London Weekly*

Emma arrived to a home she hardly recognized. Every last inch of it was draped in silks and satins, wrapped in lace, and decked in all manner of wedding frippery. Servants scurried about with bolts of ribbon and sample bouquet arrangements. While Emma was at the Fortune Games, her home had been devoted to plans for her upcoming wedding.

Which was still on.

Presumably.

It hadn't been explicitly canceled. In fact, she quickly learned that the date had been set for a few days hence, on Saturday. In addition, invitations were sent and sketches for her gown were in the works. Her first fitting was scheduled for the following morning.

As far as her mother was concerned, The Wedding Was Happening.

Emma didn't have the heart to say otherwise.

Besides, she had a more pressing—and private—concern. Had Benedict waited for her? In spite of Blake's reassurances, she worried that Benedict had betrothed himself to another. Which was madness!

Except that her love for Benedict was now tempered by confusion from her ever-changing feelings for Blake. They'd only been parted for hours, but she hungered for his presence. She missed the dry remarks he would have made about the explosion of wedding things, and she missed the knowing glance they would have exchanged, for they shared a secret.

Yet what of his own intentions or feelings? He had said those devastatingly romantic things to her. That wasn't just a kiss they had shared under the moonlight. It was erotic, intimate, and intensely wonderful. Even he couldn't have experiences like that every night.

Their careful conversations in the carriage about *what would happen now* had only one conclusion: everything hinged upon the outcome of the Fortune Games, which could be announced at any moment.

It would be foolish to break the engagement too soon, but that did not mean they would indeed marry.

All this ambiguity was driving Emma mad.

She had half a mind to tuck into the sherry bottle, her nose crinkling as she considered it.

"What do you think of the guest list, darling?" her mother asked, fussing with an arrangement of peonies and roses. Emma took fortifying deep breaths and reviewed the list. Benedict's name was not on it.

"Lord Stanton?" Emma queried. "He has been introduced to me at least four times. He never remembers who I am."

"He will now, darling."

Emma read more of the list. "And Lady Abernathy?" she cried out. "You know she is my nemesis."

"I thought you would like to make her suffer by celebrating your high ranking and handsome husband," her mother said, bustling about with a bolt of satin and then a roll of tulle and a seventeen-page list of things to do for the wedding. "She can't possibly refuse the invitation, and it would be embarrassing for her to look put out during the ceremony. Therefore, she will attend and smile prettily while absolutely seething inside."

"Excellent point, Mother. Thank you."

"Only the best for my daughter duchess," she hummed merrily. Mostly, her mother vexed her. But then every once in a while she did just the right thing.

"Oh, there was something I wanted to tell you, Emma, town gossip . . . Oh, well. I'm sure I shall recollect in due time. Speaking of the time—oh my goodness!" her mother exclaimed, ceasing her bustling to note the time. "We must begin preparing for the ball tonight."

"It is one o'clock in the afternoon," Emma pointed out. "The ball is not for another eight hours."

In fact, Emma had hoped to pen a note to Benedict, perhaps even arrange a walk in the park where she might explain everything. Privately. She didn't dare put such incriminating information in writing. She had learned her lesson about *that*.

"You're right, darling. We should have tea first, for fortification. Then Madame Auteuil is coming 'round with a new gown for you. But then you know how long your hair takes to curl, and you must look absolutely perfect tonight. Everyone will be watching you."

"I am betrothed. Can I not let myself go?" Emma mused, imagining a life of never having to sit with a lethally hot iron pressed to her head for hours at a time. It was almost worth keeping up the betrothal for.

"Au contraire! Tonight is your debut in society with your fiancé. He's coming at nine o'clock to collect us."

But would they still be betrothed when the ball was over?

Chapter 15

No one has ever taken much notice of Lady Emma Avery, best known as the Buxom Bluestocking. But lud, has the ton taken note of her now! Potential heiress to a massive fortune and with a duke on her arm, how can anyone look away?

—"Fashionable Intelligence,"
The London Weekly

Life was different on the arm of a duke. For one thing, people stepped aside to allow them to pass, like the sea parting. Emma was not bumped and jostled and elbowed in the head by tall, oblivious gentlemen. No one stepped on her toes. Not once did someone exclaim, "Oh, Lady Emma! I didn't see you there!"

She was all the more self-conscious of her manners, her dress, the curl in her hair. She felt each glance that sought to discover what His Handsomeness, the Duke of Ashbrooke, saw in *her.* Every element was scrutinized, judged, and discarded until they shrugged and turned away from an unsolvable riddle.

Perhaps being a wallflower wasn't so terrible after all.

After the butler announced their entrance, a swarm of guests enveloped them. More specifically, a thick crowd gathered around Ashbrooke. Women cooed and fluttered and thrust their barely clad bosoms forward for his perusal, not at all dissuaded by the presence of his betrothed. She couldn't help but feel that if, say, Lady Katherine Abernathy were on his arm, no one would wonder why.

Blake clasped her hand, interlacing his fingers with hers. The crowd pushed and pulsed around them, eager to get close to the principal players in London's latest drama. Young bucks clapped him on the back in congratulations and called for celebratory drinks.

The surge of the crowd forced them apart, and rather than be tugged down and trampled, Emma let go of Blake's hand. She watched him being carried off in the direction of the card room in the midst of a boisterous and celebratory group.

Left on her own, she forced a smile to her lips and held her head high. She managed to politely acknowledge the kinder group who remained to take note of her. She had only one thought: to find her friends—and some solace in this madness—as soon as possible.

It took her far longer than usual to pass through the ballroom to the particular corner where the wallflowers gathered. It was near the dance floor—but not too close. It was adjacent to the lemonade table, so one might think they were simply parched, not desperately trying to be noticed and not noticed all at once.

Olivia was there, with Prudence. Both in white dresses trimmed with ribbon, lace, and flounces. They were occasionally chattering but mostly watching the dancers with expressions of thinly veiled envy.

"Emma! You have survived the games!" Olivia gushed when she spied her forcing her way through the crowd. "And now you have returned to London triumphantly!"

"And you still deign to recognize your humble wallflower friends even though you are soon to be a duchess," Prudence said, smiling and bowing with great exaggeration.

"Oh please, you two," Emma replied with a laugh, feeling a tension in her unwind now that she was back with familiar faces and people whom she could trust to view her as a friend and not competition. "I'm happy to be back with my friends."

"We are happy to have you," Olivia said. Then, very seriously, she said, "We are also very keen to meet your fiancé."

"Where is he?" Prudence asked, glancing around as if the duke were nearby and they might have missed him. Which was impossible.

"Oh, he is probably around having dalliances, winning wagers, and generally being overbearingly Ashbrooke," Emma said flippantly. She didn't know where he had gone. Already the world was returning to its normal order—the duke as the life of the party, she in the wallflower patch. She was vexed to have lost him already, making her all the more eager to find Benedict, with whom she felt content and safe and like she belonged.

Already the events of this evening's ball had shown her that a match between her and Ashbrooke would never survive even if a very small, minuscule, rebellious part of her heart had dared to consider it. After all, the wedding had not been canceled. Then again, neither had he proposed in truth.

This was where she belonged—with her friends, off to the side. Not on the arm of a dashing duke.

"Now tell me, what gossip have I missed in town?" Emma asked. Then, dropping her voice. "And most importantly, is there news of Benedict?"

Prue and Olivia looked at each other warily. Emma's gaze narrowed.

"Lady Millard had a baby. A girl. Mother and daughter are doing well," Olivia said. "Lord Millard is devastated not to have a son."

"And you would not believe the rumors about Lord Roxbury," Prudence gushed. "The ton is in an uproar."

"Mother hid the newspaper from me, for the gossip about him is, in the words of my mother, 'outrageously inappropriate for the innocent eyes of a young lady,' " Olivia added.

"I may have procured a copy," Prue said. She and Olivia grinned slyly.

Emma admitted an interest in the scandalous Lord Roxbury. But she was more preoccupied with her own dramas. With that small, rebellious bit of her heart crying for Ashbrooke, she wanted to see the man she had loved for years and whom she planned to marry.

"But what of Benedict?" she asked, anxiously voicing the question.

"Oh, look! There he is! Your fiancé," Prudence said proudly.

"Young ladies do not point," Olivia admonished, and Prue ignored her.

There he was, indeed.

Ashbrooke arrived and stood before them, exceedingly tall, broad-shouldered, and impeccably dressed in expensive, perfectly fitted evening black and white clothes that seem to cling lovingly to his every muscle. Much like most women did, given the chance.

Blake smiled, revealing a dimple in his cheek and a rakish gleam in his velvety brown eyes. It hinted of wicked secrets and naughty thoughts. Made a girl feel weak in the knees, that.

He was hopelessly handsome. And he was here, in the wallflower corner, for an unprecedented visit.

Collectively, all the girls in the wallflower patch sighed, Olivia and Prudence among them. One could practically hear hearts fluttering or feel a breeze from all the batting lashes.

Viewing him as the wallflowers did—with pure, lusty adoration and unconcealed longing—Emma felt her heart skip a beat and her breath catch. She had kissed this man. She had pressed her own lips to his, now curving in a seductive smile. She had bared her body to his. She had done all sorts of wicked, erotic things with him.

And as for their possible future together? He had told her, *We'll see.* He had said, *Maintain the ruse a little longer.* It was devastatingly vague, especially with her mother's wedding plans progressing at full force and Benedict, somewhere, in this ballroom.

She heard another wallflower murmur, "Never thought I'd see the likes of him approaching the likes of us."

"I told you, fairy tales do come true," the girl replied, poking her friend with her fan.

"Good evening, Ashbrooke," Emma said, finally finding her voice and her wits.

"My darling fiancée," he murmured, taking her politely outstretched hand and kissing her shamelessly on the intimate, delicate skin of her inner wrist. "I thought I'd lost you."

Behind her someone sighed. Emma bit back a groan.

"Please, may I introduce my friends?" she asked, gesturing at Olivia and Prue, who were blushing furiously and giggling uncontrollably. "Lady Olivia Archer and Miss Prudence Payton."

"It is a pleasure to meet you both, mademoiselles," Blake said, along with his most charming smile and a deep bow. He kissed the hand of each girl.

Olivia giggled. Prudence's cheeks went from pink to fuchsia.

Emma scowled.

"My apologies for interrupting your conversation," Blake said, ridiculously. Of course they welcomed all and any interruption from *him.* "Emma must have been telling you all about her brilliant performance at the Fortune Games."

"Actually, I was more interested in news from town. Particularly . . ." Emma's voice trailed off when it became abundantly clear that her friends only had eyes and ears for the dashing duke.

'Twas the Ashbrooke Effect in full force.

"How is your aunt? Was she in fine spirits for the games?" Olivia inquired kindly.

"She is well, and as devious as she's ever been," Blake replied. "It's very kind of you to inquire."

Olivia blushed at the compliment.

"Has a winner been announced yet, Your Grace?" Prudence asked, ever concerned with practical matters.

"While I'm sure my batty Aunt Agatha has made up her mind, the letters announcing the news have yet to arrive in town. She had taken quite a liking to Emma. But then again, how could she not?"

Blake smiled at her, and Emma felt her lips tug up involuntarily. It was impossible to resist him, even when he was vexing her. She wondered, fleetingly, what it might be like if she didn't have to resist his flirtations all the time.

"Blake—"

"My dearest fiancée—"

"Stop trying to woo my friends."

"No, we are happy to be wooed," Olivia replied. "Never mind her."

"Woo away," Prudence declared with a wave of her hand. "We shan't stop you."

Blake gave Emma a smug look.

"Traitors," she muttered.

"I had come over not just to meet your dear friends," Blake said, "but also to request the honor of a waltz. Darling."

She supposed they ought to, for appearances. But appearances did not make her heart quicken at the thought of finding herself in his arms once again. A slight smile on her lips, she held out her dance card.

He started to write his name by a certain waltz.

"No, not the third one!" Emma cried, snatching back the card. Prudence and Olivia looked on, dismayed with her, when they knew very well what the third waltz meant to her. And to Benedict.

Blake regarded her thoughtfully for a moment, before deadpanning, "I can't imagine why. The fourth, then," he said, and wrote *"Ashbrooke"* on her card. It stood out among the other empty dances.

After that he claimed waltzes from both Olivia and Prudence. They blushed and giggled and enthusiastically agreed.

"I shall let you all catch up on gossip," Blake said, showing his understanding of women. "Till then, Emma," he murmured, before strolling off through the crowd.

"Your fiancé, Emma! He's dreamy and utterly charming," Olivia gushed.

"You two, of all people, should not fall for his flattery or his looks," Emma told them. "You know how this came about. You know it means nothing."

"I think he does mean it," Olivia said thoughtfully. "You can see the way he looks at you. His gaze sparkles."

"No, I'd say it was more of a smolder," Prudence said. "He seemed to be thinking wicked things about you. Didn't you feel warmed in his presence? I felt . . . warmed."

"I do feel warm," Olivia said.

Emma also felt warmed. Smoldering. Craving. Oh, they couldn't truly know until they kissed him in the moonlight! But some female had to keep her wits and her virtue around Ashbrooke. Clearly, it should be her.

Which wasn't to say she wasn't tempted. She was.

Her thoughts strayed constantly to the last night of the games. She found her fingertips pressing her lips, in memory of him. But it all depended upon the outcome of the games . . .

Blake hadn't said, *"Marry me anyway."*

He hadn't said, *"Forget your lover boy."*

His exact words were, "We should keep up the ruse a little longer."

"You probably feel warm because this ballroom

is excessively crowded," Emma said, growing impatient. "Now tell, what is the news of Benedict?"

She ached to find him and console him, for he must have been devastated by the news of her sudden betrothal. If she could just explain what she had done, and why, then all would be well. They could elope tonight!

Prudence opened her mouth, though no sound emerged. Olivia's eyes widened considerably and she barely managed to point behind Emma—even though ladies did not point. Emma whirled around, coming face-to-face with the man himself.

Benedict looked just as she had last seen him: the same soft brown tussled hair, the same inquisitive bright blue eyes, the same full mouth that had once brushed against hers for what she now knew was a sweet innocent kiss.

Nothing like the devastatingly wicked kisses with Blake, the thought of which made her cheeks redden considerably.

"Hello, Emma," Benedict said softly.

"Benedict!" she exclaimed, a rush of pleasure coursing through her. It faded swiftly when she saw that his smile was merely polite. On his arm was Emma's worst nightmare: a tall, blond, beautiful woman dressed in an expensive gown in the latest fashion. "And . . . Lady Katherine," Emma said in a hollow, tinny voice.

She felt her heartbeat slow to the slowest pace possible while still keeping her alive. Her lungs, too, seemed to function at a glacial pace. She couldn't breathe.

Lady Katherine Abernathy and Benedict?

She was the cruel, beautiful darling of every party. There had been great expectations for her marriage to someone like Ashbrooke.

Emma loved Benedict, but he wasn't quite a catch, being a second son of an impoverished earl. He was the kind of man for a girl like her.

A match between Lady Katherine and Benedict was as unexpected as . . . a match between herself and the Duke of Ashbrooke. And yet, she clung to Benedict's arm like ivy on an old monument.

"Hello, Emma," Lady Katherine cooed. "Welcome back to town after the games! You must be the last to hear the news!"

Prudence and Olivia stood awkwardly beside her. Benedict stood, wooden, before her. Emma felt a premonition of doom.

Katherine beamed up at Benedict and nudged him gently. Tell her, darling."

"Emma, Lady Katherine and I are betrothed," Benedict said stiffly. The floor seemed to collapse under her feet. Emma fought, and failed, to keep a smile on her face. This was shock. This was betrayal. Had it been anyone else . . .

But the seasons had ticked by and . . . She sucked in her breath as it began to make sense. Heartless though she might be, Lady Katherine must have felt the same pressure to have a husband by the time of Lady Penelope's ball. *Any* husband.

"You're not the only one having a whirlwind romance," Lady Katherine said with a perfect, lilting laugh, a flip of her golden blond hair, a smile that wasn't crooked and a dowry that was enormous. "It's quite the thing! Perhaps you, Olivia, will be the next one to surprise us. Or not. You are London's Least Likely to Cause a Scandal."

Lady Katherine found her own wit hilarious. No one else did.

"For four years running," Olivia said gamely.

But Lady Katherine wasn't paying attention. "Oh, look! There is Miss Peters," she said. "I haven't shown her my betrothal ring yet. Come, Benedict . . . "

But Benedict stayed, blue eyes fixated upon Emma. She should have told him the truth. He should have had faith in her, waited for her. Why, she hadn't been gone three days! He couldn't possibly love Katherine, beautiful and vivacious though she might be. But she had pots of money.

Emma wanted to reach out and touch him, to make sure this was real and not a bitter dream. She had to say something, for this could not be the end of the only love she had known. The one man who understood her when no one else ever did.

All Emma thought to say was, "I saved the third waltz for you."

But that said everything, really. With those few words she was able to convey that she had waited for him, that she still wanted him and that she had faith in him. Benedict nodded in acknowledgment before walking off in the direction of his fiancée, leaving Emma unsure if he would return to her.

What, oh what, had she done?

Later that night

According to the betting book at White's—and others around town—the Duke of Ashbrooke and his fiancée are favored to win the Fortune Games.

—"The Man About Town,"
The London Times

In the third waltz, Benedict did not disappoint. Emma accepted his hand with a shy smile. No words were necessary. Even though he smiled, she saw the sadness in his eyes.

He swept her into his arms. The music began to play and they began to move in time to the orchestra. His hold on her was not as firm as Blake's, his steps not as determined, his hand not as indecently low on her back. But she breathed him in and fell back into the easy, comfortable feeling of his arms. Like home.

Even though her heart traitorously yearned for the adventure that was Blake.

"It appears we are both betrothed," Emma began. There was no point in avoiding the topic.

"Rather suddenly," Benedict replied.

"To whom one would not expect," she added. Her heart throbbed because in spite of everything they easily returned to finishing each other's sentences.

"Some would say it's a whirlwind romance," he said pointedly.

"Or perhaps there is more to the story," she suggested. "One would certainly hope so."

"Inquiring minds would like to know," Benedict added.

"Me, too," she replied, giving up the pretense and allowing the questions to tumble out. "I thought you would wait for me," she said softly. As she said the words aloud, it sounded so silly that she would ask him to wait for her when she'd run off with a *duke.* But it all seemed so implausible and everyone else found it suspicious. Why not Benedict?

"You were betrothed," he said flatly. "There was nothing I could do."

Ask me why. Follow me. Fight for me.

"How long have you been . . . when did you . . . what happened?" she asked.

"I had to, Emma. I understand, I suppose. It is Ashbrooke. And you know my family requires that I make an advantageous match. Katherine and I . . ." Emma winced at the familiar address, for it suggested a genuine intimacy. She cringed because she was in no place to judge or claim him. Not anymore.

Funny, how he could feel like home and utterly foreign all at once.

Funny, how her efforts for them to be together had driven them so far apart. Except it wasn't funny at all.

"Is your heart engaged?" she dared to ask. Somehow, the answer mattered, crucially. If it was a matter of money, she could understand. She would still be heartbroken, but logic would console her. But if he had never loved her, or if he had fallen in love with Katherine in less than a week's time—that would be devastating.

Benedict leaned close to whisper in her ear. She closed her eyes and took a deep breath.

"My heart is engaged. But not to my fiancée," he said softly, whispering a secret truth for her to hold close. Emma kept her eyes closed as they waltzed and whispered. He still loved her. Perhaps they still had a chance.

Opening her eyes, she peered up at Benedict.

"If I win the Fortune Games I shall be an heiress," she said. The words were plain, the implications profound.

Benedict paused.

Her heartbeat did, too.

And then the corner of his mouth quirked up in a smile—she loved to see him smile—and she leaned in close, desperate for what he might say.

"You might purchase a quaint London townhouse," he suggested.

"With a library," Emma added.

"With windows overlooking a garden," he said. "Where children might play."

"I wouldn't want to be lonely in this townhouse," she whispered. But it was Blake's muddy boots she imagined in the hall. It was Blake's jacket thrown carelessly over a chair, and the servants were addressing her as Your Grace and not Mrs. Chase.

Mrs. Emma Chase. Would she never exist?

But Benedict knew nothing of her traitorous

thoughts. He smiled, his bright blue eyes sparkled and old habits died hard. She melted, a little.

"Emma you could still have this," Benedict whispered urgently. He pulled her closer. Held her hand tighter. "*We* could still have this."

Benedict leaned closer and kept his mouth close to her ear while he whispered a plan that was madness, pure madness, but exactly the sort of thing young lovers did when fortune and society conspired against them, when they were determined to triumph and live happily ever after, no matter what. Not even if—

BLAKE WATCHED THE couples dancing—one couple in particular—with a mighty scowl. It didn't take a genius to deduct the identity of Emma's lover boy. Any fool could see her feelings of tortured love plainly on her beautiful face.

He took the liberty of interrupting his cousin's conversation with renowned gossip Lady Somerset.

"George, who is my fiancée dancing with?" It took an unseemly amount of control to modulate his tone from overbearing, violent, and possessive caveman to mildly curious gentleman. The question he did not dare ask aloud was, why does the sight of her in the arms of another man burn like cheap whiskey?

George squinted, tilted his head. Then he produced an answer.

"Benedict Chase. Rossmore's second son."

"Isn't he the one who lost his fortune in the 'Change?" The man couldn't resist an investment; unfortunately he couldn't determine the good from the bad.

"Yes, and his sons have all been instructed to procure heiresses. Chase seems to have done a bang-up job. He just recently announced his betrothal to Lady Katherine Abernathy. Her parents are livid because it was not the match they'd hoped for."

Of course not. Chase was an impoverished second son and she could have had anyone. Almost anyone. She'd been one of the debutantes to foolishly set her cap for him and sought him out at every opportunity for years. He'd taken care to avoid her, not wanting to find himself ensnared in an "accidentally" compromising position.

"How recently were they betrothed?"

"While you were off at the Fortune Games with your *own* fiancée," George said. Blake experienced an uncomfortable feeling, like heartache, for Emma. She played the Fortune Games for a man who, in her absence, immediately betrothed himself to another woman. It was all rather tragic, really. Even if it suited him.

"What do you know of his character?" Blake inquired, and George choked on his brandy, which Blake pretended not to notice.

"You're awfully intrigued, suddenly, about an impoverished second son. I can't imagine why," George mused in a provoking way that made

Blake want to punch something. But he forced a neutral expression as he replied.

"The man is waltzing with my fiancée."

"To whom you did not actually propose," George said a touch too loudly for Blake's comfort. No one seemed to hear, though Lady Somerset was lingering in the vicinity.

"I find that detail to be irrelevant," Blake replied offhandedly, only to discover that the words were true. At some point, amongst all the faux proposals and pretend affection, he'd started to feel connected to and possessive of her.

Though they'd only parted earlier today, Blake keenly felt the absence of her sly glances that suggested she wanted him in spite of her stiff resolve to refuse him. He missed the quips and teases, her crooked smile. And the kisses. He definitely missed that.

"Did you ever discover who had sent the letter to the newspaper?" George asked. "I'm dying to know who in town has such a devious imagination. I should not want to cross them again."

Come to think of it . . .

"No, and I hadn't considered it," Blake said honestly. He had originally dismissed it as a prank—but a deuced helpful one at that. He had focused only on how to convince everyone it was the truth, when in fact there was someone out there who knew their engagement was fake. Such potentially damaging information, in the hands of God only knew whom.

It was also a prank conveniently timed to coincide with the Fortune Games. Emma had mentioned needing to marry for money . . .

"What is done is done," Blake said, though without much confidence. A troubling thought, that.

George smiled smugly and asked, "Dare I inquire if His Grace has fallen for her?" And then, jesting, "Is my position as heir becoming uncertain?"

Blake dared not ask or answer that question. But the truth was proving impossible to ignore. His Grace was indeed in the midst of falling for her. Unexpectedly.

If he married her, there would be heirs and George would be out of luck. Presently, Blake was not concerned in the slightest.

"Excuse me, I owe my fiancée a waltz," Blake said before stalking off through the crowded ballroom, his eyes fixed upon Emma and her lover boy.

"Your Grace!" Someone called out to him, but Blake ignored the distraction.

Who was this man who had captured Emma's heart so completely that she refused *him*, a renowned lover, a wealthy man, a duke? Anyone would say that he was the better catch, the better man. Everyone except for *her.* He stifled a roar.

As he made his way through the crowd, Blake took a long look at his rival. The man was slight and plain-featured, with fashionably tussled hair and a painfully earnest expression. Blake rolled his eyes.

"Ashbrooke! Congrat—"

Blake moved forward, his attentions ever fixed upon Emma and lover boy. As she spun around in the waltz, he caught glances of Emma's adoring expression. How could this lover boy have such a hold on her? More to the point, could Blake captivate her thusly?

What if he were the one she loved so obviously and so completely? A sharp intake of breath. A quick kick of his heart. One word: *want*. One word: *need*.

Had the brandy he'd drunk earlier gone to his head? No, this wasn't like any intoxication he'd ever experienced.

"Blake!" Emma seemed surprised to see him interrupt her waltz with lover boy. That struck him as wrong. A faint flush crept across her cheeks as if she were embarrassed. Or guilty.

Jealousy had a firm grip around his heart. She was *his* as far as anyone knew, and he wanted that to be true. He definitely could not lose her to him.

"I have come for our waltz," he said flatly, the famous Ashbrooke charm having deserted him. It was plain that he was intruding upon a private, tender moment between lovers. It burned, that.

"But I promised you the fourth," she explained impatiently. "This is still the third."

As if he—an acclaimed mathematician—couldn't count. He designed a bloody machine that could count automatically. But he understood, perfectly. He was *bothering* her.

She was refusing him, the Duke of Ashbrooke, her fiancé, in front of the ton.

Blake rocked back on his heels. Waltzing couples nearly crashed into him and gave irritated looks—until they saw with whom they had collided and then they one-two-three-ed away at a greater pace than set by the orchestra.

One thing seemed plain to him: Emma could not have sent that letter. Not when she spent her every breath fighting him. Not when she was trying to dismiss him so she could dance with a short and impoverished bloke whom he could easily knock unconscious to the ground with one half-hearted blow.

He had half a mind to do it. And it wouldn't be halfhearted at all.

"Are you not going to introduce me to your lov—" Blake began as Emma reddened and cut him off.

"Your Grace, may I present Mr. Benedict Chase," she said.

"It's a honor to make your acquaintance, Your Grace," Benedict said.

"I understand congratulations are in order," Blake said. "My felicitations on your own betrothal. Lady Abernathy is a lovely young woman. Though I daresay she cannot compare to Emma."

"No," Benedict said, so softly, so genuinely, that both Blake and Emma turned to him in wonderment. Both men knew that in all the ways that truly mattered, Lady Katherine didn't hold a candle to Emma.

"Have you set a date?" Blake inquired. Emma's attentions were still fixed on Benedict, but her soft, dreamy expression had hardened.

She bit her lip when Benedict answered, "A fortnight from Saturday."

Even later that night . . .

Benedict mumbled his excuses at the end of the third waltz. Blake watched Emma watching him stroll through the crowds, presumably on his way to reunite with Lady Abernathy. Before the orchestra even began the next song, Blake pulled her into arms.

He held her far closer than was proper, but it was not close enough. He pressed his hand scandalously low on her back and it took all of his self-control not to slide his hand lower, clasp her bottom and press her against him.

"You drive me mad," Emma hissed.

"Mad with desire?" he murmured. She scowled at him. Blake wisely elected not to tell her that she looked lovely when angry, with her rosy cheeks, fiery blue eyes, and her mouth in the most naughty pout. Attempting to kiss her would be perilous; he wanted to anyway.

"You didn't have to meddle like that," she said dismissively. No one ever spoke to him dismissively.

"I wanted to meet the man I'll be jilted for. And the man who will soon possess my beloved aunt's fortune." And because Blake was under the influence of the hot flares of jealousy, he said, "I want to know who will own the only place I've called home."

"We had a deal," Emma replied, struggling to keep her voice down. "I thought you were a man of your word. We split it, should we win and should, God forbid, Agatha pass on this year. Do you realize what an impossible situation we are all in?"

"It's not impossible," Blake protested.

"Benedict and I are in love, but engaged to other people," Emma explained. "You and I stand to win a fortune, but at what cost to a truly spectacular woman?"

Very well, the situation was impossible. He needed the fortune, or he needed a permanent alliance with a well-behaved woman like Emma. Yet it was becoming harder to avoid a difficult conclusion: he needed her in other ways, too.

He needed her to gaze lovingly at him, the way she did with Benedict.

He needed her to tease him, as she did.

He needed her to treat him just like a man, not a duke.

He needed her to challenge him. She made him a better man.

He'd go mad if he didn't taste her soon or feel her soft skin against his. He needed Emma for the sake of his sanity.

He had to go and fall for London's Least Likely to Love Him.

Finally, she exhaled impatiently, shook her head and muttered, "I should have never—"

"Never what?" he asked. When she did not reply, when she would not look at him, he asked again in a firmer voice, "Never what, Emma?"

"Just know this," she said, looking him squarely in the eye. "I did not send that letter."

That letter, that letter . . .

Who had sent it, then? Did she know who did? Did it even matter anymore? Someone had written it and sent it to the newspaper. And *everyone* had read it. The damage was already done. There was no way to undo it and almost no point in knowing who had caused it. Difficulties like Benedict's own sudden betrothal or Blake's tangled feelings could not have been foreseen. The only thing to do was push forward.

"Yet you agreed to this," he said, pointing out one critical detail.

"I did not agree to this!"

Her eyes flashed with true anger. His heart stilled. Her cheeks flushed an angry pink. Her curls shook because she was *trembling* with rage. He couldn't breathe.

"You did—I proposed and you—"

"You kissed me with everyone else looking on," Emma cried, struggling to keep her voice from being overheard by couples waltzing around them. "I did refuse. But you did not accept it."

Neither his breath nor heartbeat resumed. Even in that addled state, he paled at the memory.

That day in the garden, she had said "no" eight

different ways, but he, being a delusional thick-skulled egotist, did not for a second think that a woman would—could—refuse him. He hadn't even heard her.

She had agreed in the end, reluctantly, when he gave her no other option. He had cajoled and *kissed* her in the garden, with London's biggest gossips looking on. She never had a choice in the matter. He had forced his will upon her.

Blake thought he might be sick.

The truth was, he had barred her from her beloved.

The truth was, Benedict still claimed her heart, while he was falling for her swiftly, surely. Damn near completely.

The truth was, he hadn't given her a choice before.

Now he wanted her to choose him.

Chapter 16

"The Duke of Ashbrooke, reformed?" gasped one matron. "I never thought I'd live to see the day!"

"By all accounts, you have," the gentleman replied dryly.

"Pity, that," she murmured.

White's Gentlemen's Club
A private room

"THANK YOU FOR meeting me, gentlemen." Blake addressed the round, distinguished faces of the peers assembled before him. They leaned back in thickly stuffed leather chairs before a polished oak table bearing glasses of French brandy. In their thick fingers, burning cigars sent smoke curling up toward the ceiling.

That they were even present was a testament to Emma's restorative powers to his reputation. A wild, wicked rogue bachelor was not to be trusted. But a man betrothed to a sensible women with an impeccable reputation could be considered upstanding, reasonable, and trustworthy.

Nevertheless, they were *here,* and he was going to take full advantage.

"As you are aware, I've made changes in my personal life and the way I conduct my . . . business," Blake said. He stood before them, projecting a confidence that ebbed and flowed but always rose to the challenge. There was no wager, challenge, or dare that he did not attempt to conquer. He was Ashbrooke. He always won.

Losing was not an option. Especially when winning had never mattered more.

"Knowing this was a concern that influenced your decision to invest, and given the changes I've made," he went on, "I thought you would like the opportunity to reevaluate that choice."

Lady Emma's bedchamber

Emma had a choice to make.

Benedict had made the most scandalous suggestion at the ball: elopement. A mad dash to Gretna Green. Happily-ever-after with the man whom she had loved steadfastly for three seasons was just within reach.

Then there was Blake.

A mad wild adventure that would likely end in a heartbreaking disaster of epic proportions. Blake made her feel new, lovely, terrifying, sensual, maddening things. Could she live with her pulse constantly racing? And what of the nervousness when he was not around and the anguish she felt as she wondered who he was with?

She imagined long, passionate nights with him—in exquisite detail—but she feared a rake like him would tire of her and seek his pleasures elsewhere. She imagined a cold bed, a broken heart, and the whispers from the ton . . . *We always wondered what he saw in her. Never expected the match. No one thought it would last.* She'd be a duchess, yes, but a lonely one.

Emma could picture a different life with Benedict—one of serene contentment with a reliable man. She could count on Benedict not to stray, for he seemed to lack the appetite for such passion. *She wouldn't miss the passion, would she?*

This wretched business with Lady Katherine was simply because he was driven to such desperate measures by his father's urgent need for money. *Shouldn't he have fought for her more?*

Emma pushed aside her doubts and considered logic. Reason. Values. Odds. Her odds of happiness were greater with Benedict because there was less of a chance that he would act disreputably and ruin everything. There was also the fact that she had loved him for three years already, and had embarked on this whole scheme in order to win the fortune they needed to marry. She could not give up on him now.

Even if Blake tempted her tremendously.

Blake whom, she noted, had not actually proposed to her for real. At all. Ever.

Until the winner of the Fortune Games was announced, she had choices. If she were *not* named the winner, Benedict couldn't marry her for lack of funds. And Blake, who had never really proposed, would have no incentive to.

She had to make her decision—and soon.

Emma announced her choice to her fellow wallflowers.

"I am going to elope with Benedict."

She expected they would be shocked, complete with dropped jaws, raised brows, and an utter inability to speak. Olivia and Prudence provided exactly that reaction.

Emma had not anticipated the way her stomach would churn violently in their awkward silence, broken only by the sounds of hammering and shouts from the laborers working on a mysterious construction project in the garden.

It was Prudence who spoke first—after a few false starts and deep breaths. "You could be the future Duchess of Ashbrooke, Emma. But you will scandalously elope with second son Benedict?"

"I'm marrying the man, not the title," she answered, a touch haughtily. Truly, she had given the matter much thought. She considered the tug of her heart, the feeling of her gut, and logically considered both men and the life she might lead. But it really came down to one thing.

She didn't believe that she could keep the duke interested in her for very long.

There was also the not insignificant lack of an actual proposal from Blake.

"Are you mad?" Olivia quite exploded. "You cannot elope! And you cannot jilt the duke for . . . for . . . Benedict!"

"Shhhhh," Emma cautioned. If her mother caught wind of this, she would be locked up, and let out only for strictly supervised wedding dress fittings and for the big day itself, which was rapidly approaching—just a few days away now. It was the talk of the town, and it seemed only she dreaded it. "I thought you liked Benedict," she said.

"We did. We do. But that was before you met the duke," Olivia said. Oh, it was always *the duke, the duke, the duke!*

"Might I remind you that our engagement is a sham?" Emma pointed out with some irritation. Her friends had not steeled their hearts to his devastating smiles and the wink of his eyes. Thus, they forgot the truth of the matter. *It was all pretend.*

Even she had momentary lapses where she believed.

For all she knew, Blake would jilt her once the winner was announced. She ought to flee with Benedict while she had the chance. Logic, that.

"You were hardly gone two days before Benedict was betrothed again," Prudence said. "Doesn't that seem suspicious?"

"And what will Agatha think if it turns out you win her fortune, only to give it to another man when you marry?" Olivia asked.

"She told me 'The heart wants what the heart wants.' Besides, she may live for another year of Fortune Games," Emma said. "Whereas I will be bound for life to whomever I marry."

"But why are you even considering this? The duke seems to love you," Prudence said. As if that were the end-all, be-all. Then she frowned, considering something unpleasant. "And there's something about Benedict . . ."

"What about Benedict? Is it because he needs a rich bride? I know that, and I have always known," Emma replied strongly. "That is why I embarked on this whole charade! Blake and I made an agreement that we would split the fortune if we won. So I played the part, all for Benedict."

"But he betrothed himself to Lady Katherine within days," Prudence said. "He did not wait for your return—possibly triumphant and rich—nor did he ask us why you suddenly made another match. Shouldn't he save himself for true love?"

"Blake, on the other hand—" Olivia said dreamily.

"Is a known rake, rogue, and debauched soul," Emma replied succinctly. He was a notorious charmer and seducer of beautiful women. He loved hard and left at first light. "It is unfathomable that he should fancy *me*."

"But he obviously does," Olivia sighed.

"But for how long?" Emma said, and there was anguish in her voice. "Until a pretty opera singer catches his eye, or a merry widow seduces him, or a housemaid bats her eyelashes at him? He will embarrass me with his infidelities. How long can I trust him?"

White's Gentlemen's Club

"While we are impressed with your sensible betrothal, we can't help but wonder for how long this good behavior will last. Have you reformed for good, or until certain temptations arise again?" Lord Doyle's gray brows arched questioningly.

Blake's temperature spiked. He fought the urge to loosen the cravat his valet had tied too tightly around his neck. He knew the temptations Doyle alluded to—the man's mistress, for example. But these days and nights, Blake was only interested in Emma.

"Will you miss sessions of Parliament when they are discussing our proposals because you have been waylaid by an opera singer?" Archibald McCracken demanded.

It had happened before, when Blake had arrived late to an interview with the wealthy shipping magnate. He'd come straight from the bed of a woman, after a long night of smoking, drinking, gambling, and wenching. He'd been in no condition to convince a man to part with his money.

"Or will you arrive stinking of booze and hung over after having drunk someone's excellent and expensive vintage brandy on a dare?" Lord

Norton questioned bitterly. Blake made a note to replace the man's vintage collection of rare wines and brandies that had been devoured at Blake's urging at one hell of a house party.

"Or will you find yourself locked in a wine cellar with a man's innocent twin daughters?" Tarleton hollered, face red and eyes bulging.

"While we are glad to see you turn your life around and start acting like a gentleman, we are concerned about how long this will last," Doyle said moderately.

"Speak for yourself," Tarleton said in a furious huff, obviously still mad about his *innocent* twins.

The gents didn't believe him. They couldn't hand over their money or their faith in him and his machine when this "reformation" could just be this week's folly.

Just as Emma couldn't love him if she doubted his devotion to her—or lacked the confidence in herself to believe him.

"Fifty thousand pounds," Blake said. "Building the machine will require fifty thousand pounds in finished designs, manufacturing, and assembling of parts. But then all the reckoning books in the world will need to be reprinted. Other industries will prosper because of it. Subsequent iterations of the machine could produce unfathomable innovations. All you need to do is have faith in this future. All you need to do is say yes."

Lady Emma's bedchamber

"Emma, you stand to win ninety thousand pounds," Prudence said in a reverential gasp. Ninety thousand pounds was an unfathomable sum.

"*If* I win and *if* Lady Agatha dies within the year, which I wholeheartedly hope she does not. There are so many *ifs* . . . " Emma said. "There are too many variables to consider. Too many possible outcomes; some of which are great, some of which are disastrous. I ought to hedge my bets and accept the first reasonable offer. Benedict's elopement."

"But if you win," Olivia said.

"And if you inherit," Prudence added.

"If you learn of your possible inheritance before your wedding day," Olivia clarified.

"Which wedding day?" Prudence asked with a challenging lift of her brow.

"The wedding my mother has planned is scheduled for two days after Benedict suggests we elope. He said we should go on Thursday, at midnight . . ." Emma's voice trailed off. "We have been too long on the shelf. We have done *nothing* for too long. Now is my chance to seize my surest path to happiness and I want you both to understand."

"But Blake . . . " Olivia protested.

"Has not actually proposed," said Emma, which was truly the crux of the matter. "I cannot consider him a real suitor if he has not actually asked me to marry him in truth."

"And yet," Prudence countered, "with ninety thousand pounds on the line, how can he not?"

White's Gentlemen's Club

Fifty thousand pounds. The words still hung in the air, much like the thick gray smoke of the gentlemen's cigars. *If, if, if* . . . there were so many things in that number: securing the necessary support from the government, securing the necessary funds to construct the engine, demonstrating that this new venture signaled a future to be embraced, not the devil to be scorned. All depended upon Blake's ability to convince them to trust him.

Lord Ferguson cleared his throat. "With all due respect to your calculations, we still have concerns—"

"You have six daughters, do you not?" Blake interrupted. Norton's eyes flashed.

"Aye, and I'll thank you to stay away from every one of them," he growled.

"Fear not, I am devoted to my fiancée," Blake said truthfully. "But have you thought to dower them, while considering the cost of upkeep to an estate like Berkley Park," he asked, referring to Norton's crumbling ancestral home. With land rents declining and such expenses looming, Norton had to do something drastic or face bankrupting his family. Blake knew this, but would Norton acknowledge it?

"We must face facts," he went on. "Land-based wealth is going away and our ancestral homes are damned drafty and in need of upkeep. I know; I have seven of them. You could marry one of those title-grubbing American heiresses . . . "

Those Americans disturbed the Englishmen's gentlemanly sensibilities. He now knew he needed to appeal to them as a gentleman himself.

He knew from Emma that they wouldn't just take his word as a known rake and infamous rogue, prone to debauchery with different company each night. Just as he must seduce her, he must persuade these gentlemen to bet their futures on him.

"My cousin, Lord Winwood, married one of those Americans," Lord Doyle said quietly. "Her father suspected him a fortune hunter and tied up her dowry so much that Winwood was forced to beg for funds to make even minor repairs to the estate, like fix a leaking roof. His wife even refused to pay his club membership."

"Cut off from your club. Begging from Americans. Dependent upon your wife. Is this really the fate you choose for yourselves, gentlemen?"

Lady Emma's bedchamber

"Would it really be so horrid being married to Blake?" Prudence asked. "You would be a fabulously wealthy duchess dressed in the most stylish gowns."

"No more languishing in the wallflower corner," Olivia sighed.

Emma didn't think it would be horrid at all. Not when he kissed like the devil and held her close like his life depended upon her. Not when a wink of his eye or a hint of his wicked grin made her warm all over. Not when he showed her a pleasure she had never imagined.

What would be horrid was losing his affection. Losing him, while having to turn a blind eye to his infidelities as her heart was breaking. Being a duchess—and all the lovely things that came with it—would not be consolation enough.

Where her friends saw a glamorous life, Emma saw lonely nights in a large house, wondering with whom her rakish husband cavorted. She didn't believe that she, London's Least Likely, could keep such a wicked, roguish man enthralled from now until death do they part.

He was intent upon seducing her now, but what happened when she said yes?

She could win big, or lose everything. She was not a betting kind of woman. She had made her choice. Better never to lose him now, before she lost her heart. Better to marry Benedict.

White's Gentlemen's Club

"You have a choice, gentlemen. You could walk away now and hope things work out in your favor: that your rents increase, that your daughters marry men plump in the pocket, that rich American brides leave gaping holes in the wedding contracts. Or you could take a chance with me. Either way, you are wagering on your future."

"How do we know you won't drink the lot of our money?"

"Or spend it on baubles for other men's mistresses?" Doyle inquired.

"Or compromise our daughters," Tarleton said, his voice quiet with rage.

"Even your own aunt doesn't trust you with her fortune, else she would have invited you to the Fortune Games," McCracken said cuttingly. Blake's breath caught from the sting. "Why should we trust you with what fortune we have left?"

"You're asking us to take a damn big risk, Ashbrooke."

"And I'm asking you to trust me," he said softly, the truth of it occurring to him as he spoke the words. "Every force possesses an equal and opposite reaction. My aunt didn't invite me to the games, for it was the most certain way to ensure my attendance. My previously outrageous behavior rightfully caused you to withdraw your support from my project. True to the equation, I have responded with an equal and opposite reaction: I have reformed. Where I was once a drunken wastrel, I have become sober. Where I was once an unconscionable and unfaithful rogue, I have now become hopelessly infatuated with and devoted to my fiancée."

Who keeps pushing me away. Like Agatha. Like the

investors. None of whom believe . . . until an equal and opposite force is presented.

"All these forces are part of a single reaction; one does not exist without the other."

"What's your point, Ashbrooke?"

"Only one question remains: Are you willing to take the risk with me?"

Chapter 17

"Have you seen the news about the duke and Lady Emma? I say, I had been suspicious from the start . . ."

—Everyone in London, practically

The Drawing Room, Avery House

On a gray afternoon, Emma curled up on the settee before the fire in the drawing room with the hope that the romantic dilemmas of Tessa Tidwell in the novel *The Terrifying Travails of the Temptation of Tessa Tidwell* would distract her from her own.

Benedict—the sure thing?

Or Blake—the rogue in every way?

She had made a decision, but tell that to her traitorous thoughts, which kept straying to the smoldering pleasure of Blake's kiss and the wonderfully wicked sensation of their bodies pressed close together, limbs intertwined.

When Blake appeared in the drawing room but a moment later, catching her woolgathering with the book open on her lap, Emma thought him a vision she conjured up.

But no, he was really here. She knew because her skin tingled in anticipation of his touch.

"Blake, what brings you here?"

"Can a man not visit with his beloved intended?" He sat beside her on the settee. She risked temptation and remained. Even worse, she took a deep inhalation to breathe in his intoxicating scent. She glanced at the drawing room doors and was vexed to see they were open.

"Of course one can. I just thought there might be a reason," she said. Like, oh, calling off the engagement because the winner had been announced. She half expected it, half feared it.

The winner, as far as she knew, had *not* been announced. Alas.

"How about this for a reason: your sparkling conversation. Or your entrancing crooked smile. Or," he said, dropping his voice to a murmur, "the pleasure of your kiss."

"Of my just one kiss," she corrected. That one kiss could be the only one. She wouldn't survive another.

"We'll see about that," he said wickedly.

"Whatev—"

"As it happens, I do have a reason," Blake said. "But first, there is something I have to do." He dipped his head toward hers. His mouth claimed her lips, already parted in surprise.

Outside, a rumble of thunder. Inside, the snap and crackle of the fire. Beside her, Blake kissing her gently in the drawing room as if . . . as if he were a real suitor desperate for a stolen moment of pleasure.

She couldn't help it, she threaded her fingers

through his hair as she'd just been imagining as he rasped her name, "Emma." He cradled her face in his palms and she felt positively cherished. "Fetch your bonnet. And your smelling salts. We are going out."

"It's about to rain," she pointed out. Indeed, there was another ominous rumble of thunder.

"Perfect," Blake murmured, clasping her hand and leading her to the foyer, where she could see his carriage waiting outside.

"I need a chaperone," Emma said, stupidly. She could just imagine Olivia and Prudence screeching at her: *Now is not the time for propriety!*

"I'll pretend I didn't hear that," Blake replied. He waited impatiently while the butler handed Emma her bonnet, a spencer, and gloves.

"You are something else," she murmured as she dressed for an unanticipated outing. In the rain. Unchaperoned.

"It's the Ashbrooke Effect, isn't it? Are you suffering terribly?" he asked as he helped her into the carriage. "I told you to fetch the smelling salts." She took her seat facing forward, and when he got in to sit opposite her, all the air in the carriage seemed to dissipate with his arrival. She felt lightheaded.

"Do you really believe all that nonsense?" she asked.

"Yes. I make myself swoon with an alarming frequency," Blake replied. Then he scoffed. "Of course I don't believe it. I can tell you don't either, which is one of the things I like about you."

"You like that I am completely unmoved by your legendary charms, your impossibly good looks, and utterly impervious to your attempts at seduction?"

Even as she spoke the words, Emma knew they were lies—all lies—but ones she clung to as if her future happiness depended upon them. Blake only gave her that grin—indeed, she felt a now familiar heat unfurling in her belly.

"It makes your inevitable surrender all the more pleasurable for us both."

The Drawing Room of Lady Olivia Archer

Prudence arrived with her cheeks flushed, sucking in huge, heaving breaths of air. She had obviously exerted herself in her haste to deliver The News.

Olivia came to the drawing room at once. "Tea?"

Wordlessly—for she had still not caught her breath—Prue handed over her copy of that morning's issue of *The London Weekly,* opened to "Fashionable Intelligence."

Intrigued, Olivia began to read. Her blue eyes widened considerably as she scanned the words.

"How devastating. Absolutely devastating," she gasped.

"Do you think she has seen it yet?"

"Who would share such inflammatory accusations?" Olivia questioned.

"More to the point," Prue said urgently. *"Who else knows?"*

Blake's carriage

"Where are you taking me, anyway?" Emma inquired. She glanced nervously out the window, seeing only familiar London streets.

"It's a surprise," Blake said. But it was more than that.

It was a grand gesture.

It was a declaration of his *feelings*.

It was madness.

He wanted it to be perfect, right down to the looming thunderstorm. He offered a prayer of thanks for the reliability of dreary English weather. He also prayed that this mad gesture of love would convince her of the truth of his feelings before she had even more reason to doubt them.

Blake had a dwindling amount of time to prove that he wanted their faux engagement to be a real love. Any moment now Agatha's announcement of the winner would arrive, and if Emma won and he begged for her hand, she would forever doubt his intentions . . . if she even said yes.

It was imperative that she not doubt his intentions.

The carriage sped along, turning into Hyde Park and traveling briskly to a remote corner amongst the trees.

"Are you going to ravish and murder me in the woods?" Emma asked, eyes wide with either terror or intrigue. He wasn't quite sure. "Have you received word from Lady Agatha? Is this a plot to dispose of me and keep the money for yourself?"

"You should read more lurid gothic novels," Blake told her. "Your imagination is sorely lacking."

"So you *are* going to ravish and murder me in the woods in order to keep the fortune for yourself. I knew it." She settled back against the velvet seats with a smirk of satisfaction.

"I promise that I will not murder you in the woods," Blake vowed, punctuated by an ominous rumble of thunder.

"Or *anywhere,*" Emma corrected. Then, with an adorable tilt of her head, she asked, "And what about ravishment?"

"I'm not in the habit of making promises I have no intention of keeping."

The Drawing Room of Lady Katherine Abernathy

"Of course I'm not surprised in the slightest," Lady Katherine told Ladies Crawford, Mulberry, Falmouth, and Montague. A copy of *The London Weekly* lay open between them. Like gossipy women all over town, they had immediately convened to discuss the latest revelation in "Fashionable Intelligence" concerning the most unfathomable alliance since . . . well, ever.

"Who would do such a thing?" Miss Falmouth wondered.

"Someone who is desperate," Lady Katherine said, fussing with her already perfect blond curls. "It all makes sense now."

"What are you going to do?"

Lady Katherine applied a hint of red paint to her lips. "We are going to pay a call, of course," she said with a smile.

A secluded corner of Hyde Park

Blake held Emma's hand as she stepped out of the carriage. He watched her expression as her gaze settled upon the ruins of an old gazebo nestled within a small clearing surrounded by gnarled old trees. A mist rose around it and long strands of ivy twined around the balustrade and crept up the columns.

"Blake . . ." Emma said his name cautiously, softly. "What is this?"

Proof. Love. Madness. More specifically: the ruins of an "ancient" gazebo that he'd had illegally constructed upon public lands, in the span of just three days, all at his great expense. When Blake had visited the day before, the stone appeared too new. So coal fires had burnt at his feet, blackening the stone. Mounds of ivy and huge branches of wisteria had been dug up and replanted.

The effect was perfect: the ruins of an ancient gazebo miraculously left undiscovered in Hyde Park. A tribute to a love story.

But Emma would know the truth. She would know that this monument had never existed until she imagined it and made it the setting of their dramatic and romantic first meeting.

Like their engagement. Their love. Their story. He wanted it to be real

"Why, look at that. It's the ruins of an ancient gazebo," he remarked lightly because, for all that he was a practiced seducer of women, words of real love were not often uttered. They didn't roll off his tongue like pretty compliments; they stuck in his throat and made it hard to breathe.

"I'm quite certain that wasn't here last week," Emma said cautiously. "I wonder who would build a deliberately old and crumbling gazebo?"

"A man mad with love?" Blake ventured.

"Or with money to burn," Emma murmured.

"Emma," Blake said, clasping her hands and facing her. She lifted her blue eyes to his, searching for answers. And he had them. His heart pounded hard, but hopefully.

"Emma I did this to show my love for you," he said. But there was a terrific crack of lightning, like the very heavens being ripped and banged open. His words were lost.

"I can't hear you!"

"Never mind," he muttered, tugging her hand and making a mad dash for the shelter of the gazebo.

White's Gentlemen's Club

The gentlemen of White's were discussing only one thing while they wagered fortunes, puffed deeply on cigars, and consumed copious quantities of wine and brandy: the rumor about Ashbrooke that had appeared in *The London Weekly's* gossip column, "Fashionable Intelligence."

"Shocking, isn't it?" George said noncommittally to the group when their attentions fixed upon him. Surely the heir to the scandalous man in question would have *some* intelligence on the matter. "When it comes to my cousin, the duke," he went on, addressing the group, "one scarcely knows what to believe. His reckless romantic streak is well known."

This was truth. Equally true: one well-placed remark had called *everything* into question.

At the gazebo

After a mad dash through a sudden deluge, Blake and Emma arrived breathless and wet under the cover of the gazebo.

It had to be noted that Blake looked impossibly handsome when wet. Not that Emma was surprised by it. Still, she thought it tremendously unfair that his hair curled just so, and wonderfully ridiculous that raindrops delicately clung to his long lashes. She knew how she looked after being caught in the rain, and it was rather like a drowned kitten.

But she didn't dwell on that. Her heart understood what this gazebo meant.

This is a grand romantic gesture.

This is what men do when they are in love and lack the vocabulary to express their feelings.

However, her brain shut down operations entirely as it tried to process surprising facts that added up to an unfathomable conclusion: *he* wanted *her.* So much that he went to expensive and possibly illegal lengths to prove it. Emma had read the gossip columns devoted to his previous romantic exploits; none had compared to this.

"Don't you remember, Emma? This is how we first met," Blake said softly.

"The letters," she said softly. She felt slightly off balance.

"The letters," he whispered. His gaze was steady upon her.

Those love letters they had stayed up all night writing. The love story they had bickered over. The disbelief that such an infamous rogue was in her bed and composing wickedly romantic letters to her.

She had never truly imagined this love might be real. Reluctantly she had accepted that he was not that kind of man, she was not that kind of girl, and they didn't live in that kind of world.

Or did they? The marble was cool and wet under her touch. *Real.* She wound a strand of ivy around her finger. *Real.* She turned to face Blake. His expression was serious for once: no devastating grin or mischievous spark in his eyes. His gaze was heavy upon her, as if seeking to ascertain how she felt from a flash in her eyes or a breath caught in her throat.

"You built all this for our story?"

"I built it for you, Emma."

The slowly dawning truth defied all of her expectations about Blake, about herself, and about love.

"I am speechless," she said. Because she had to say something—the moment seemed to call for it. And she did not know what to say. No one had ever romanced her, and certainly not so extravagantly—yet plainly—as this. It was terrifying, that.

The rain fell in sheets. In buckets. He could not possibly have planned that portion, and yet this moment was unfolding perfectly, just as she had imagined it. Unfortunately, she hadn't written any dialogue for herself—never believing this romantic moment would actually happen.

"Allow me to explain," he said, raking his fingers through his wet hair. "I would like our story to be real. That is to say, perhaps we might . . ." Blake scowled. She clung to every word, hoping, wondering, daring to believe . . . He quit his pacing, turned to face her and grasped her hands.

"Dammit, woman, I am falling for you. This is my attempt at bloody wooing you."

Emma laughed from nerves—this was happening!—and relief that even in this moment she and Blake maintained their banter. She was sure that a legendary seducer such as he had never, in a moment of desperation, uttered the words, *"Dammit woman I'm bloody trying to woo you."*

The imperfect language. The frustration. The throbbing of her heart. The taste of his lips. His warm hands holding on tight to hers. All these things told her this moment was real.

This love is real. The story is real.

"It's not the fortune, I swear to you," Blake said. "It is because I want you to look at me the way you look at Benedict. Because I want someone who will challenge me at every turn. I constantly crave your kiss. And I want someone who drives me utterly mad in all the best and worst ways. That someone is you."

It was not the love confession of a practiced seducer, for it lacked poetry and pretty compliments and murmured promises. No, this was the rough, imperfect, heartfelt statement of truth of a man in love. And it left Emma absolutely, utterly speechless.

She could scarcely breathe, which made her light-headed, which made thoughts impossible. She could only feel. She feared she might burst from the combination of shock, desire, and a nagging fear this was all a dream.

"It would be far less agonizing if you would say something, Emma," Blake said, his mouth tipping up into a grin. "Preferably something about your undying love for me and how you've been dreaming that I would confess my innermost feelings of everlasting love for you. Say something, even if it's 'Shut up,' or 'Get out,' or 'This farce of an engagement is over.' Say anything."

There was only one thing to say, really.

"Kiss me, Blake."

The Drawing Room, Avery House

Lord Avery burst into the drawing room in what his wife would politely describe as "a state." Lady Avery remained calm in the face of his blustering.

"Wife, what is this nonsense I'm hearing at the club about our daughter's engagement?"

"Hmm?" Lady Avery looked up from her embroidery. "What gossip?"

"Just returned from my club. They are saying the engagement between Emma and Blake is a sham. It's in the papers! Have you any idea why anyone would say such a thing?"

"None whatsoever," she replied, looking away and focusing intently upon the intertwining initials she delicately stitched onto the fabric: E & B. The "B" was not for Benedict—if she had her way.

"We haven't yet signed the contracts. Ashbrooke thought it'd be most efficient to wait until after the Fortune Games to see if they won the fortune." Lord Avery fretted, now pacing before the fire. "We stand to be devastated by this, if the rumors are true. Who will marry her then? How will we pay for the blasted wedding you are planning? We'll be bankrupt!"

"Ahem." The butler cleared his throat. He held

out a tray with a letter. "There are callers. Many, many callers. Are you at home to visitors, my lady?"

At the gazebo

He kissed her. It was simple: his mouth claiming hers. But what brought them to this moment had been anything but simple. In spite of all the deception, this kiss was real.

Emma felt herself grow bold.

The stones beneath her feet were proof.

The roof over her head: proof.

The wisteria and ivy entwined: proof.

Blake's arms wrapped around her: proof.

His tongue tasting and tangling so intimately with hers: proof.

The warmth unfurling in her belly, the flush stealing across her skin—all in spite of the downpour—was proof that Blake desired her. She grasped a handful of his linen shirt, holding on as if afraid she might be swept away in the rain.

Blake nibbled gently upon her lower lip before pressing kisses along the sensitive skin of her neck, drawing a gasp from her lips. Emma tilted her head as if to say, *More.* Her hands roamed and explored the silky strands of his hair, the smooth line of his jaw, the wide expanse of muscles across his shoulders and chest. Every touch told her this was real, which was possibly the most seductive part of all.

Blake tugged down her bodice and pressed a kiss upon her breast. Such a sensation in such a place shocked her. That they might be seen, oddly increased her arousal. She was surprised to discover such wanton desire in herself. Blake's mouth was hot upon the dusky center of her breast. The wind blew a cool breeze over her warm, exposed skin. Her knees buckled and he caught her. His touch *literally* made her weak in the knees.

The Ashbrooke Effect was real. She was not immune. Not at all.

"Damn," Blake swore softly. "I forgot a bench. I want to lie you down," he said, kissing her. "I want to feel you beneath me, on top of me . . . I meant to have a bench." His voice was hoarse and his hands exploring.

"You really did have an ancient looking gazebo constructed just for me," she whispered, needing to say it aloud for the truth to sink in. "For us."

Blake grinned and said, "If I'm going to seduce a woman, I'm going to do it properly. Or improperly, rather."

Then he kissed her again.

Then he swept her off her feet. Literally.

Blake lifted her as if she were weightless and set her on the balustrade. Still, she clung to him, not wanting anything to separate them. She needed to feel him so she might know, beyond a shadow of a doubt, that this moment was truly happening, that it was not some wicked fantasy.

Blake pushed up her skirts and urged her legs apart so he could settle between them. The pressure of his hard arousal against her made Emma gasp with wanting. She moved her hips, exploring the pressure, only for it to intensify with every touch. She wrapped her legs around him, urging him harder against her entrance, and he groaned. The sound thrilled her like nothing else. She, little Emma Wallflower, made the notorious Duke of Ashbrooke groan with pleasure from her touch. She made him hard. *He desired her.*

"Oh, Emma. You're so beautiful." Any protestations she might have uttered were silenced when he claimed her mouth for another kiss. Truth be told, she dared to believe him, just a little bit. She certainly *felt* beautiful right now. He, and only he, had ever made her feel that way.

He tugged down her bodice and she warmed under his appreciative gaze.

Even with her dress hardly covering her, Emma was not cold. No, she was warmed by his loving, desiring gaze. She was warmed by his hands, cupping her breasts. She was warmed from his hot mouth closing around the dusky centers of her breasts, which had been begging for his attention. The heat she felt burned within, making her almost intolerably hot.

But still she clung to fistfuls of his linen shirt and wool jacket. If she didn't hold on, she would surely fall, tumbling backward out into the newly planted shrubbery and muddy ground.

She did not want to fall.

She wanted to stay in Blake's embrace.

What if this were forever? What if he wouldn't

tire of her, or find himself entranced with a girl who was taller, with beautiful blond hair, the ability to bat her eyelashes, to flirt and act seductively? The idea that he could fall in love with her and only her made her heart start racing. If that could happen . . . if she could believe it . . .

Well then, she'd fall right in love with him.

Why couldn't she believe it?

"Touch me, Emma." The roughness in his voice thrilled her.

"I don't want to fall," she whispered.

"I will hold you. Trust me. Touch me."

Emma flattened her palms over his firm chest. She undid a few buttons and slipped her bare palms against his hot skin. The wicked idea of treating him to the same exquisite torture crossed her mind; she tentatively explored his nipples with her tongue, licking and kissing.

"Oh God, Emma," he hissed, his fingers threading through her hair, then grasping tight. She gave a satisfied smile.

She explored the wide expanse, feeling the taut ridges of his abdomen and the muscles across his chest with her hands. With her mouth. She breathed him in. Tasted him.

He was strong. He could hold her forever, if he wanted. She reached up and felt the strong line of his jaw, smooth. His hair was starting to dry, and it was soft.

"Emma . . ."

He pressed closer to her, and she felt his desire for her pressing hard against her. She didn't just imagine him inside of her, she craved it with an intensity that shocked her. She didn't know . . . and yet she needed him.

Blake's hand rested on her ankle before beginning a long, slow caress of her leg, up her stockings, past the garters, layers of skirts pushed aside. Their gazes locked.

"Tell me to stop," he whispered.

"Oh no," she murmured. Then she gasped in shock as he pressed his fingers upon the sweet place between her legs. She closed her eyes, bit her lip and gave in, moving with the slow, lazy circling rhythm of his hand. That pressure: it was building. That heat: it was impossible. She couldn't breathe now. She could only feel.

More, she needed more. Or she would explode. Blake, she needed Blake. Or she would die.

As if he just knew, Blake's mouth crashed against hers for a passionate kiss. The pressure of his touch intensified upon her, and she writhed in time to his rhythm. She moaned softly as she clung to him desperately. And then she could hold back no longer.

Emma cried his name as the pleasure shattered over her. When the lovely, amazing feeling started to subside, she collapsed into his arms, resting her cheek on his firm chest. His heart beat hard, like hers. His breath caught. She could hear it, and she could feel it.

She felt, too, that Blake was still hard. His arousal was pressed against the vee of her thighs.

"What about you?" she whispered, and he gave

a strangled sigh that sounded a little bit like, "Oh Emma" and a little bit like, "Oh God."

"I want to feel you," she said, peering up at him.

"I would *never* refuse you," Blake murmured, and they laughed together. *That* was the moment she felt such a powerful connection to him and the sort of intimacy that had never before occurred to her. It was one thing to indulge in all these wickedly sensual activities with him; it was quite another to laugh together in the midst of it. Try as she might, Emma couldn't picture sharing such a moment with Benedict. He was awfully serious.

She didn't try very hard to picture herself with him, though. Not when she had this intimate time with Blake, whom she wanted to please the way he had pleased her. There was a selfish aspect to her desire to bring him to satisfaction, too. Every time Blake gasped from her touch, or groaned with desire as they kissed, she felt a surge of pride and power. *She*, the Buxom Bluestocking and London's Least Likely, brought such pleasure to such a rogue.

Emma dared to think that *maybe* . . . maybe they could last forever in satisfied bliss.

But there were more pressing matters requiring her attention at the moment. Together, she and Blake fumbled with the buttons on his breeches until his arousal sprung free. She took him in her hand, marveling at the feel of him: hard and throbbing, but the skin soft and warm.

Blake's large hand closed over hers. Together they began to move up and down the long, hot, hard length of his shaft.

"Kiss me," he whispered. She kissed him slowly and tenderly until his breaths became shorter and sharper. Until his hand on hers moved harder, faster. Emma knew that same pressure was building within him, that same intolerable heat, that same need for more, more, more. She kissed him hard and rocked her hips in the same rhythm until he called out her name in a hoarse shout, until his teeth sank down on her shoulder, until he was spent after a few last determined thrusts.

They leaned against each other for support, then, with her cheek pressed against his chest, listening to his pounding heart. Blake threaded his fingers through her hair and soothingly caressed her back. They remained like that as their breathing returned to normal and their heads began to clear.

The rain had eased from the torrential downpour to a steady drizzle. A fog rolled in amongst the trees. They had just this moment blissfully alone before they had to return home, where not one but two weddings awaited her.

Chapter 18

This author has it on excellent authority that His Grace, the Duke of Ashbrooke did not propose to Lady Emma Avery. The lady herself did not buck convention and ask for the duke's hand. Thus, the question remains, how did this shocking proposal come about? It was The Weekly's own Mr. Knightly who received the announcement, which this author was able to peruse. 'Tis written in very ladylike handwriting, which is all the more intriguing because it was not a lady who relayed a certain outrageous tidbit to me: the engagement is a sham and they have no intention of marrying each other.

—"Fashionable Intelligence,"
The London Weekly

The Drawing Room, Avery House

In retrospect, Emma thought she ought to have brazenly strolled into the drawing room in her sodden dress and disheveled hair. She never should have snuck up the servants' stairs to her room to change her dress to restore her appearance to rights.

She had thought of propriety and the embarrassing if not impossible task of explaining why she looked as if she'd just been ravished in a park in a rainstorm without quite admitting to being nearly ravished in the park in a rainstorm.

In this instance, the *right* thing was very much the *wrong* thing. Appearing like a debauched maiden—especially with Blake on her arm—would have put the rumors to rest. Immediately.

But no. Oh no. Blake pressed a gentle good-bye kiss upon her lips when he saw her safely to the servants' entrance. He promised to see her again soon.

"But—" So many questions burned on her lips. *What does this mean? Are we betrothed in truth? What of the fortune and our fate? Did Blake love her? Dare she let herself fall in love with him?* But she was suffering terribly from the Ashbrooke Effect, and instead kissed him until her mind was utterly, deliciously blank.

Having heard the high-pitched buzz from the drawing room that informed Emma of callers, she thought it best to fix herself up. She changed into a clean dress, brushed her hair, and pulled it into a simple knot at the nape of her neck. Her appearance restored, she descended to the drawing room to face the vultures. Lud, did they crowd into the drawing room, perched upon every chair and settee. Some even stood, crowded into every available space.

At least Olivia and Prudence were here—with concerned expressions that made Emma feel queasy. She felt an intense pang of longing for afternoons free of callers, spent in blissful (if lonely) solitude with a book before the fire.

Her mother stood and pushed her way through the guests to clasp Emma's hands. "Where is the duke? Were you not with him?"

Emma sighed. Of course, they were only interested in the duke.

"We enjoyed a walk in the park," she replied.

"Just now?" Lady Montague inquired, with a wary look toward the window. A steady drizzle fell from thick gray clouds.

"You went out in the rain?" A woman Emma didn't even know was aghast at the notion. Who was she? And what on earth brought her here? It could only be one thing, Emma concluded: the announcement of the Fortune Games winner. But if that were the case, why did everyone care so much about her walk in the park in the rain with the duke?

"You do not look as if you had been in the rain," Lady Katherine remarked sharply. She gave a pointed look at Emma's fresh dress, and Emma wished desperately she had arrived through the front door, with Blake, in her ripped and wet gown, her hair a tussled mess.

"We did not see you return," her mother said. "Where is the duke now?"

"I believe he returned to his residence," Emma said with a slight shrug. "Or perhaps he went to his club."

She had been too busy kissing him in the most

indecent, wanton way to ask such mundane questions as to his whereabouts. She debated saying just that, for it would silence them all, when Lady Katherine heaved a sigh and said, "Pity, that. I would just so love to hear his comments on the rumors. Of course, *you* could also put the matter to rest, Emma," she added with a devious smile. Emma's heart lodged in her throat. "Is it true your engagement is a sham?"

AFTER RETURNING EMMA safely to the house via the discreet servant's entrance, Blake hummed a happy tune—*their* song—as he strolled back to his carriage parked in the mews. He chatted amiably with the groomsman for a few moments and flipped him a coin for his discretion.

Emma, God, Emma . . . he'd left her only moments ago and already he missed her. He had always loved women, stumbled head over heels for brief but intense affairs. He'd fancied himself infatuated before. But it had never felt like this. She made him want to be a better man. She made him want to prove his love for her.

Yes, love.

Blake braced himself for a wave of terror or panic to envelop him. None came. That had to mean something significant. He wanted to tell her that.

The investors were returning, too. His betrothal to a respectable woman had helped. Their appearance at the ball the other night made many believe the news that had been a "surprise to everyone."

Everything he wanted was just within reach.

He climbed into the carriage and started on his way home. On Emma's street he encountered an unusually large number of parked carriages, idle drivers and horses standing about snuffing and pawing impatiently. Well-dressed ladies hustled toward the Avery house. He slowed his horses from a trot to a walk. It had to be noted that no one seemed to depart.

Obviously there had been news—the winner of the Fortune Games, most likely.

Once he stepped into the drawing room, he realized it was something else entirely.

Lady Abernathy had that deceptively sweet smile of hers as she asked Emma, standing alone amongst the lot of gossiping birds, "Of course, *you* could also put the matter to rest, Emma. Is it true your engagement is a sham?"

In an instant he took it all in. The ferociously inquisitive faces of so many misses and matrons keen to know if they ought to celebrate or cut Emma. All too clearly he could see them hanging onto the hope that this bachelor would remain eligible on the marriage mart. *If it were anyone else* they would politely, but glumly, offer their congratulations. But because it was *he* and *her*. . .

Blake also detected the rampant desire for A Scene with which they might regale their acquaintances for weeks if not months. He had half a mind to provide it.

Emma's gaze anxiously fixed upon him. When he looked into her blue eyes, he saw her uncertainty. *Was their engagement a sham?* But he did not know the right reply and she provided no answer. He wanted only to please her.

Blake hesitated. The vultures leaned in closer.

Was he to claim her now, further cementing their bond and thus making it more impossible to break?

Or did she wish for him to make it easy for her and lover boy to be together?

She had wanted a choice—and here he was, in a position to decide for them both.

How was he supposed to think when the vultures clucked and circled? His heart pounded hard, like a kick drum. He felt a cold sweat on the back of his neck. Someone had betrayed him—or her. Who knew for certain that he had not proposed? His idiot friend Salem, his heir George, Emma, whoever had mailed the letter . . .

And above all, why did he continually find himself in the Avery drawing room, pressed to make life-altering decisions in front of a pack of gossips? The first time, the answer had been easy. Find the girl. Kiss the girl. Hold onto the girl.

He glanced again at Emma's blue eyes, which implored him to say something for God's sakes! The last time he let her speak for them, she'd told everyone he played the flute.

Blake treated everyone to a flash of the infamous Ashbrooke grin, known to melt hearts and make knees buckle.

"Sorry to dash your hopes and dreams, ladies," he replied. He slid his arm around Emma's waist. "But I'm afraid my heart is spoken for."

But even that would not deter Lady Katherine, who gave a little laugh and remarked, "That is, until the winner of the Fortune Games has been announced."

"Yes, about that . . ." Lady Avery murmured, and all heads swiveled to focus on her. "Emma, a letter arrived for you. From Lady Grey."

Emma tentatively reached out to accept the sheet of folded vellum from her mother's eagerly outstretched hand.

"Mother, this letter is opened already."

Indeed, the red wax seal had been broken. Blake narrowed his eyes and focused on Lady Avery. She quickly glanced away and gave a little laugh.

"I could hardly restrain myself," she replied, glancing around the room, seeking agreement from her guests. "Go on, read it!"

Emma slowed unfolded the sheet. Blake peered over her shoulder to read the letter that declared their fate. Lady Avery clasped her hands together and smiled with glee. The guests all leaned forward, nearly spilling off their chairs.

Emma gave a sharp intake of breath. So did Blake.

Chapter 19

Dear Lady Emma,

It is my pleasure to declare you the winner of the Twentieth Annual Fortune Games and thus the heiress to my enormous fortune. Though you made some missteps, I was impressed by your determination to play the game fairly. Lady Emma, I was witness to the entire disastrous scene involving you, Miss Dawkins, the priceless urn, and the remains of my beloved Harold. That you took sole credit for an accident involving multiple parties, and thus protecting Miss Dawkins, showed me that your kindness and dignity are worth more than my money. That you were obviously the only one to have read the history of the Ashbrookes that I provided showed me you will be a good steward of the family legacy. And to think, I had suspected you a fortune hunter when you arrived on the arm of that rascal. I no longer do. And I am never wrong.

Lady Agatha Grey

EMMA READ THE letter once, twice, thrice, and still could not quite believe the elegantly written words swimming before her eyes. The crisp vellum sheet wavered in her hands.

Blake's gaze confirmed the truth. It was there in the polite nod of acknowledgment and the strained smile that did not reach his eyes. Moments before, she'd felt so connected to him that she had been about to call off her planned elopement with Benedict. He had built her the gazebo! Shown her such pleasure! Saved her from yet another drawing room disaster!

But now, though they had stood a foot apart in her drawing room, she felt worlds of distance between them. Could everyone see the way he withdrew from her?

At the soiree later that evening the truth was undeniable when her arrival was announced. A hush descended over the four hundred guests, when no one had ever marked her arrival in a ballroom before. Now that she was Lady Grey's heiress, the ton took notice of her, and they did so with a vengeance.

Emma slowly pushed through the crowd, hoping to seek refuge with the other wallflowers. The mob followed her; a swarm of silks and satins, a hiss of whispers, and a low hum of fevered conversation.

"Lady Emma, congratulations on winning this year's Fortune Games! You must be thrilled." This, from Lord Stanton, who had been introduced to her thrice and each time said, "Nice to make your acquaintance."

"Tha—" Emma started to say, but was cut off.

"I daresay, the news was quite a shock," a orange-haired matron said, fanning herself vigorously. "In fact, one might say you were London's Least Likely to Win!"

A wave of laughter rippled through the crowd. Emma just smiled tightly. Apparently not even ninety thousand pounds was enough to make one forget her unfortunate pet name.

"Where is your *fiancé?*" someone asked, with such emphasis on the word and such a comically skeptical expression to demonstrate that though she stood to inherit a fortune, it wouldn't quiet the wretched rumors that had surfaced in the newspapers that afternoon.

In fact, many gentlemen seemed to take the rumors as an opportunity to flirt with her, possibly court her. This, of course, was the crux of the matter with Blake's affection and why she couldn't trust anyone: For so long she had been present, just as she was now, and no one noticed her. Thus she knew it was the fortune—or the possibility of it—that people saw now.

"A lemonade for you, Lady Emma. You must be parched." A gentleman with whom she was not acquainted bowed deeply and offered her a glass of lemonade. It was the fourth she'd been given this evening.

"Your eyes alone are a fortune," a dandified buck said, issuing an odd compliment. She was reminded of Blake scoffing at comparisons of her blue eyes to various bodies of water. He said her gaze was intelligent. That was far better.

Beside her, Prudence snorted, and Emma bit

back her own laughter amidst a flurry of questions from people who'd had every opportunity to converse with her over the years but had not even bid her good evening at a ball.

""However will you spend all that money?"

"Will you live at Grey Manor?"

"What will you do with the fleet of ships?"

"Did you really inherit a fleet of ships?" Olivia asked. "If you did, I hope it's a fleet of pirate ships. With pirates."

"Aye, matey," Prudence said under her breath, and they all giggled.

"I have no idea what I stand to inherit," Emma replied. "In fact, I hope I do not. I am rather fond of Lady Agatha. Here, take this lemonade, I see more coming."

"Of course, Lady Emma may not come into the fortune," Mr. Parks reminded the group.

Blake's cousin George was more charming. He smiled, and beside Emma, Prudence sucked in her breath.

"Congratulations, Lady Emma," George said. "It was a pleasure to compete with you, and I daresay you do deserve to win."

"It is kind of you to say so. I enjoyed making your acquaintance as well. When you told me about the games, you did not warn me of all this madness."

"It does get worse every year," George said with a laugh.

"George, you must have had a hunch that she

would win," Mr. Parks said. "Given that you wagered ten thousand pounds on the outcome and now you're a rich blighter!"

More guests approached and the mob surged forward. Emma, Olivia, and Prudence now stood with their backs against the wall. More young suitors arrived as well, with insipid compliments and tepid lemonade.

Emma regretted ever complaining about not being a diamond of the first water.

"Lady Emma, your gown is so becoming."

It was from last season, hastily mended this afternoon to appear more fashionable.

"Your curls are perfection."

They were the result of hours of effort with a hot iron.

"I see the heavens in your eyes."

"Your nose, Lady Emma, is a dream."

Emma just sighed.

Prudence and Olivia stood beside her all the while, awed into silence at the dramatic change in their circumstances. Usually they watched the swarm of suitors fawn over other girls. Never had they been so close themselves.

"I have never drunk so much lemonade in my life," Prudence muttered. "I may be sick, right into this potted palm."

"I am thinking now of all the balls in which I was parched but not one gentleman brought me a drink," Olivia replied. "I feared I would perish of thirst."

"Be careful what we wish for," Prudence said.

"If only someone would bring us champagne, at least," Emma said.

"Well, look who has a taste for the finer things, now that she is an heiress!"

"If you prefer this tart, warm lemonade, Olivia . . ."

"Champagne would be lovely," Olivia replied. "However, my mother says that it is not appropriate for me. I might forget myself. Whatever that means."

"Nothing fun is appropriate," Prudence remarked. "Young ladies have such limited options for entertainment."

"I never thought I'd say this," Emma said, "but I do miss the quiet of our wallflower days."

"I don't know why they even bother fawning. You are betrothed," Prudence pointed out.

"There is that," Emma said. But was she?

Blake had not *actually* proposed—and their wedding was to take place in just two days' time! For all she knew, he still planned to jilt her, or be jilted. For all she knew, none of that mattered since *someone* had mentioned to the newspapers that their engagement was a sham. She wasn't surprised, but her curiosity was piqued: who had sent the darned letter? And who else knew about it?

No matter . . . she would escape it all when she eloped with Benedict. Tonight.

EMMA HAD WON the Fortune Games. The declaration was not unexpected, but still Blake felt his equilibrium disturbed by the news. Even hours later, lost in the crowds at the soiree, he felt off balance, though that might be attributed to all the brandy he'd drunk since he read the letter over Emma's shoulder earlier that afternoon.

Given that the fortune he'd sought, the favor he'd craved, and his childhood home were essentially deeded to London's Least Likely to Love Him, a drink had been in order.

The thought of her living in Grey Manor with *Benedict* meant another drink was required. The thought of Emma married to Benedict and making love in the master bedroom, meant a few more brandies were utterly necessary.

Oh, and the rumor mill had exploded because someone had confided their suspicions to A Lady of Distinction that his betrothal with Emma had been a sham all along. Not exactly the sort of news that helped a man woo and seduce a reluctant woman.

Blake was achingly aware that he had fallen in love with her and that her heart was set upon that fool Benedict, and now there was nothing—*nothing*—stopping her from marrying him, leaving him a heartbroken mess. Unless at some point their fake romance developed into true feelings of love.

If he could only speak to her. If he could only touch her hand. If he could only kiss her.

But the mob of fawning, obsequious fortune hunters thronged around her and it was damn near impossible to get close.

His gut knotted as he watched George bend over Emma's outstretched hand, kissing it. If everyone thought her engagement was fake, it logically followed that they thought her a potential bride. Blake's hands balled into fists as she smiled prettily up at George.

It also logically followed that one of those two was a traitor, for who else knew of the deception?

Had Emma schemed from the start? Who had sent that letter, anyway?

Who had dared to suggest that his love was not real?

Only one thing mattered: that their love would be true. He had explicit instructions on how to woo her, and he would follow them to the letter.

Starting tonight.

EMMA HAD WON the Fortune Games, and if all went according to plan, Benedict knew he would ultimately be the one to win. After all, he had fallen in love with Emma *before* she was an heiress, *before* the ton took note of her. Already he missed the days when he could still claim her for a waltz. Tonight an absurd throng of guests surrounded her and he could not get close.

All he wanted was to marry Emma and live happily in their little townhouse with the library, the garden, and the children in the nursery upstairs. The enormous pressure his father had exerted had made Benedict buckle, but not break.

Marry an heiress, marry an heiress . . .

But the heart wanted what the heart wanted, and by God did he luck out when the woman of his heart's desire stood to inherit ninety thousand pounds. Unfortunately, she did so just a few days too late. Inconvenient, that.

He and Emma could still have their dreams come true. He'd planned everything for their elopement: his carriage was refurbished, the horses readied. Bricks would be warmed, soft blankets, a hamper of wine and foodstuffs tucked away. He had determined their route and identified the best inns along the way. He'd packed everything necessary, including his late mother's wedding band.

All he needed was his bride.

Benedict jostled with the mob, trying to get close to London's newest heiress, when suddenly there was a surge as the crowd parted, making way for His Grace, the Duke of Ashbrooke.

Behind him trailed a footman with a tray bearing not one, but three glasses of chilled champagne. Benedict looked over at Emma and her friends—there was no mistaking the stars in their eyes or the dreamy smiles of women utterly charmed, impressed, and practically seduced.

Tonight. Benedict would claim her tonight. He had loved Emma when no one noticed her. He knew Emma like no one else did. They shared the same dreams. He would be Emma's future happiness, not the duke. And he would prove it. Tonight.

"I LOVE HIM," Olivia sighed as Blake appeared, with a footman bearing glasses of champagne.

"He has his benefits," Prudence conceded. "I hope you keep him," she said to Emma.

"Good evening, ladies," Blake said with that swoon-inducing smile of his. Emma was not immune. She thought of how his mouth felt upon her skin. She thought of how he tasted. She thought of how he expertly touched her, taunting and teasing, until he brought her to dizzying heights of pleasure.

"Why are you blushing?" Prudence asked quietly.

"I could not say," Emma said, immediately taking a sip of her champagne. Truly, she could not put it into words.

"Cheers," Olivia said cheerily, and the three girls clinked their champagne classes together. The footman, kindly, had removed at least seven glasses of lemonade.

Seeing that they were taken care of, Blake turned to address the mob. They quieted immediately when he set his gaze upon them. Amazing, that.

"The lady is spoken for," he said calmly, and cool as you please.

The mob dispersed.

"Tell me that didn't make your knees a little weak," Olivia asked. Emma's heart leapt and she trembled as she brought the glass to her lips.

"It did," she whispered. Oh, it did. The question was, would he still act thusly a year from now, when a different winner was named? Or would he, too, be dragged away from her by some conniving siren? Was that just to put rumors to rest or simply a barbaric display of dominance and possessiveness?

Her gaze settled on Benedict, gazing at her shyly from a distance. He mouthed two words that made her pulse race: *Midnight. Tonight.*

Chapter 20

"Emma, will you marry me?"

"Emma, will you make me the happiest of men?"

"Emma, I feel most ardently for you. Will you consent to be my wife?"

—PROPOSALS CONSIDERED BUT NEVER DELIVERED BY A VERY INDECISIVE BUT DEVOTED MR. BENEDICT CHASE

Almost midnight . . .

EMMA HAD MADE her choice. She had declared her choice. Yet certainty eluded her. She paced around her bedchamber as if each step would strengthen her resolve.

An empty valise lay open upon the bed. Whatever did one pack for an elopement? The frothy lace, silk, and pearl-trimmed gown that her mother had ordered for her official wedding to Blake—which was scheduled for two days hence—would not do. All the ruffles and a delicate lace trim was a bit *much* for Gretna Green.

Emma added a hairbrush to the valise. She would certainly need that if she embarked on this mad trip.

If . . .

Doubts. They snuck up on a girl when she was trying to decide what to pack for an elopement adventure. After all, it was far easier to fret over this dress or that instead of This Fate or That Fate.

I have given Benedict my word, Emma thought. But that was *before* Blake confessed his feelings to her in the gazebo. She had not had a chance to tell Benedict otherwise.

Emma did not doubt Benedict's love for her—even in spite of his betrothal to Katherine, which she dismissed as a momentary aberration, a forced arrangement that had nothing to do with his heart. She and Benedict shared the same dreams, discussed at length over a three-year courtship. They would be happy. And he would be arriving within a quarter of an hour.

She added two dresses to her valise.

Her mind drifted to Blake. Maddening, impossible Blake. He made her feel beautiful, powerful, and alive. He listened to her and challenged her. He built a monument for her. Blake made his feelings plain.

Benedict had made his feelings plain, as well—and over the course of three years in which he could be relied upon for the third waltz, a conversation about books, a warm smile from across the ballroom.

But Benedict had never broken the law and spent an inordinate amount of money to dramatically and romantically realize a fictional first meeting.

In light of that, Olivia and Prudence would scream that she was UTTERLY ABSOLUTELY MAD to even consider anyone but Blake.

I'm not mad, Emma thought. I'm just . . . scared. *I'm not sure of myself.*

She had captivated Blake for *now*—but for how long? Yet how many other women had he fallen for and built monuments for? None. She would have heard about it.

The problem was that the vicious voices of the ton that were a steady buzz in her ear:

What is such a plain, nothing, nobody girl doing with a handsome man like the duke?

They drowned out the voice in her heart.

Her intrigued but terrified, yearning, and cowardly heart.

Emma added a night rail to the valise and wished it were more alluring, instead of perfectly appropriate for an unmarried woman too long on the marriage mart.

London's Least Likely. Wallflower of the first water.

What does the Duke of Ashbrooke *see in* her?

Emma abandoned her packing altogether.

Gathering all the candles in her room—given her penchant for reading late into the night, there were many—she lit each one and placed them all on her dressing table. She sat before the mirror, awash in a warm glow.

Having usually avoided her reflection, she sought to give herself a good, long look now. She wanted to stop seeing herself as the haute ton did and start seeing herself as Blake did.

Her hair was not the long, lustrous, golden locks of Lady Katherine Abernathy, which reflected candlelight so well and inspired all sorts of rubbish poetry. Her own hair was dark and glossy; though it couldn't hold a curl for long, it eventually softened into nice waves.

Emma frankly appraised her features. They were the prim, plain, unremarkable features of a lovely English girl. Her eyes were almond-shaped and her eyelashes, while not breathtakingly long and full, did flare up nicely at the outer edges.

Her nose was not pert, buttonlike, or adorable . . . but neither was it overly large or unshapely. Her nose was perfectly fine.

In this moment, when she ceased despairing over her lack of a full, sensuous mouth, she saw her own was nicely shaped. Perhaps even slightly like a bow. Emma ventured a smile at her reflection. She always hated her crooked smile, but Blake was entranced and intrigued by it. So maybe, perhaps, her smile was lovely after all.

She thought of all those hours when she did not smile. When she bowed her head in a book rather than assess her appearance. When she felt so unpretty that she didn't bother to *act* prettily.

Blake made her feel beautiful because of the light in his eyes when he gazed at her. Because of the way he always sought to touch her and to kiss her. Because of the way they were able to spar and banter and laugh together.

As Emma looked at herself now, she dared to

believe that she was beautiful. The mean voices of the ton started to sound a bit distant.

Who does she think she is? Lady Emma Avery, London's Least Likely . . . and yet also the Duke of Ashbrooke's fiancée and heiress to a massive fortune.

Oh, the wallflower? The undiscovered treasure.

What is she doing with him? All sorts of naughty, wicked, wonderful things.

He'll tire of her eventually . . . He might. But perhaps he won't.

A lifetime of not believing in herself did not quite vanish after one good, long look in the mirror. And it certainly wasn't helped by the relentless ticking of the clock, which annoyingly reminded her that any minute now, Benedict would arrive, intent upon a midnight elopement.

She had a decision to make.

Marry the man who loved her for three seasons when no one else did. It was a safe and sensible choice.

Marry the man who'd never had an affair longer than a fortnight, who possibly loved her *now*. But did she dare risk FOREVER with him?

That damned clock tick-tocked loudly on the mantel. She stuffed it in the valise along with nearly all of her clothing, which she hoped would muffle the sound.

Emma sat upon the valise, forcing it closed. Taking a deep breath, she closed her eyes and *listened* to the voice in her heart. She could hear it now, above the voices of fear and mockery that always called her London's Least Likely.

Blake had fallen for her and there was no denying it. He had told her in words and shown her in his actions.

There was also no denying that she had fallen for him, too. She wanted to see herself the way he saw her. She wanted to live knowing the passion he had shown her. She *wanted* to be so certain of their love that nothing could shake her confidence.

She wasn't there just yet. Her nerves were in an advanced state of agitation, given the choice she was going to make tonight. Her heart was already racing. With fear? Anticipation? If only she had more time!

Standing, she walked to her bedroom window. There, in the mews, was the small glow of a lantern, which was Benedict's signal that he had arrived. She was to sneak out of the house and meet him at the carriage.

That was the plan.

Until Blake climbed in through the bedroom window.

IT WASN'T THE first time that Blake had climbed a trellis in order to sneak into a woman's bedroom at some ungodly hour of the night. But it was the first time his heart raced while he climbed—not with fear that he would be caught or that he would fall, but fear that he would be too late.

It was also the first time that he wasn't sure if

the woman would be happy to see him. Emma was a lot of firsts for him: the first time a woman rebuffed him and the first time he confessed his love to a woman.

Given that she was not expecting him, it was to be expected that she stifled a shriek when he climbed into her bedroom.

"Blake! What are you doing here?"

It was a fair question. Given the situation, only the truth would suffice. After all, he could not claim to have been strolling in the neighborhood and thought to drop by.

"I missed you," he said plainly. He could only barely see her expression—even though she had a ridiculous number of candles lit on her dressing table—but he could not discern her feelings from the half smile upon her lips.

Though he had seen her since the end of the Fortune Games, he missed their sparring together at Aunt Agatha's, missed their banter, missed long gazes full of knowing that they shared a secret. More recently, he missed her soft cries of pleasure, the feel of her bare skin under his palm, and her crooked smile.

"You must have missed me very badly to venture into my bedroom at midnight. You couldn't wait for calling hours?"

The lady was not moved by his dramatic and romantic gesture of climbing into her bedroom. Yet.

This was Emma, the one woman who did not throw herself at his feet, which was why she was the one woman for him.

Blake glanced around her room. His gaze settled on a suitcase resting at her feet. He detected the soft, thin muslin of a chemise peeking out.

"Going somewhere?" he asked casually. Given what he'd glimpsed in the mews, he suspected he knew her answer.

"As a matter of fact, I was planning on it," she said, her voice wavering. He noticed that her hands were desperately grasping the fabric of her skirt. She was nervous about something.

"Oh? Where might a young lady be going at this late hour?"

"I have plans to elope with Benedict," she said.

His heart stopped beating. His lungs ceased to function. His stomach churned. His brain ceased to work, save for one thought: *No.*

Her voice had wavered. There was hope. He clung to it.

Blake took a moment to will his heart into beating, his lungs into breathing, to quell the revolt in his stomach. His future happiness depended upon the next few moments, and his only coherent thought was that she looked so pretty in the moonlight.

Emma bit her lip, uncertain. She gazed up at him. He ached to take her in his arms and make her absolutely, positively certain of the happiness and pleasure they could have together. Forever.

Instead, he leaned against the window frame and said, "That explains why he's waiting in the mews."

"What are you doing here, Blake?" she asked

again. There was no disguising the anguish in her voice. "Have you come to stop me? Is this because of the fortune?"

"I told you, I missed you," he said. Fortunately, he happened to miss her so much just when he might thwart her elopement. If that wasn't luck, he didn't know what was.

"How did you climb up here?"

Blake grinned.

"I had a trellis installed," he said. She pushed past him, brushing against his chest so that she might peer out the window to confirm that yes, he had embarked on construction projects to her own house.

"But this is not your house," she protested.

"Your parents just adore me," Blake said. Also, parents of daughters betrothed to wealthy dukes did not quibble about installing trellises to her bedroom window. Anything to ensure the match.

"They are deluded," she muttered. "You are impossible."

"That's what I adore about you, Emma. A man goes through all the bother of orchestrating a devastatingly romantic encounter and you call him impossible. At least you didn't swoon."

"Please," she retorted. "As if I would do anything so miss-ish as that."

She picked up her suitcase. The woman obviously overthought the venture and packed excessively. Either that or she was bringing her entire trousseau.

"Would you like help with that?" he inquired politely.

"I can manage, thank you," she said. Faintly. The suitcase was obviously quite heavy. She would have to carry it through the hall, down the servants' stairs, through the garden and out to the mews. Silently.

Made one wonder about Benedict. She was willing to go all the way to Scotland to marry him, and he couldn't meet her at the back door to help carry her suitcase? Disgraceful.

"It is midnight," Blake said coolly, even though his heart was pounding. She could not walk out on him. Not now. But he didn't say that. He was not a man who begged or pleaded. Instead, he said, "You had better be going if you want to catch him. Or do you plan to leave him waiting? A measure of his love for you, perhaps. How long do you think he'll keep the carriage parked in the mews? A quarter of an hour? An hour? Until dawn?"

"I don't know. I just don't know," she cried so passionately he had to believe she wasn't just replying to what he'd said.

"Do you think he will try to come to your window?" Blake wondered, looking out and down at the empty garden below. "Lord knows I've made it easy for him. What with having a trellis installed."

"I am undone by your consideration and charity," she grumbled as she tried to lug the valise toward the door.

"Tell me, did he weep when he proposed to you

at midnight at our gazebo? Did he fight off a band of armed street children to protect your honor? Did he steal into your bedroom for a passionate encounter? Will he even come to the door to help you with your suitcase?"

"It's just like the letters," she said. She set down the suitcase.

"It's all just like the letters," he said. "Emma, do you want to know the real reason I am here?"

"Yes, curse you," she muttered.

"I want our story to be real," he said softly.

"It's the competition, isn't it? Or is it the fortune?"

She was so suspicious. She did not have any confidence. She didn't know what she did to him. If he were patient, and lucky, he would be able to show her and to make her know that she was beautiful and wonderful and worthy of love. Even if she ended up running off with lover boy, at least she would know that she was an amazing woman.

"The chase certainly has my heart pounding," he said. "But it's not the competition or the fortune."

"If I had just thrown myself at you, fallen right at your feet gasping 'Oh, Duke, 'have your way with me,' you wouldn't be here," she said plainly, and it was God's honest truth.

Every step of the way she had refused and he had persisted. So he could not fault her for the logical question that followed.

"So what happens, Blake, if I say yes?"

She peered up at him, expectant.

His heart was in his throat.

He didn't know what would happen if she said yes. Correction: He knew exactly what would happen—they would make love, it would be exquisite—but he didn't know what would happen after that. Not being the idiot people often assumed he was, he knew this was the *after* she was asking about.

"You'll just have faith, Emma, that my intentions are good and that I want you, and only you."

"I want to, but I cannot. But Benedict—"

She picked up her valise, gripping it hard with both hands. If she left tonight, he would be wrecked, forever. No other woman would do.

When he spoke next, it was from the heart, from his gut, from his head. It was uncensored. It was the truth.

"You are used to being overlooked," he said, and she paused. He rushed on. "It's because we live in a world that values simpering instead of intelligence in a woman, and blondes instead of dark beauties, belles of the ball instead of the lovely wallflowers. But they are wrong, Emma, not you," he said earnestly. "You think you aren't quite enough, but you *are*."

She set the suitcase down.

Since she was not yet in his arms, he kept talking.

"I love your eyes," he said. "They're pretty and all, but there is an intelligence in your gaze. You see right through me, past all the trappings and posturing. It terrifies me but I crave it all the same. I saw the way you looked at Benedict, and I'll do anything for you to look at me that way. Like you love me. Like you believe in me."

It was the truth. She *had* to believe him.

He stepped away from the window, stepped closer to her. She did not move.

"I have known a lot of women. But I have never known a woman like you. I'm done, Emma. You are it for me. You are the one."

He lowered himself to one knee and clasped her hands. She gave a little start and her breath hitched in her throat. This was not like the last time he proposed, when they had an audience and it was all for show.

This moment was theirs, and theirs alone.

Emma bit her lip, trying not to cry. Gad, he didn't want to make her cry. He wanted to make her happy.

"Will you marry me for real, Emma? Marry me because you love me, or because you could. Marry me because you want to. Not because of our charade . . . just because of you, and just because of me . . ." The words tumbled out inelegantly but honestly.

She squeezed his hand. He dared to hope.

"I believe in the original letter, that you wept as you proposed," she said, but there was a catch in her voice and a smile on her lips.

"And I believe in the original letter, that you said yes."

ONE THING WAS certain: She would not be eloping tonight. Emma knew it by the wave of relief that hit her when Blake—not Benedict—climbed in through her window. She knew by how glad she was to set down that blasted suitcase. She knew by the urge to launch herself into Blake's arms. Oh, she still was plagued with doubts and uncertainties, and his handsomeness didn't help her think clearly at all.

But the word *Yes* caught in her throat, held back by a swarm of fears. Would he be faithful to her? What would everyone say? She could hear the vicious rumors already: *We were suspicious from the start.*

Did she prefer the quiet life of a wallflower or could she learn to gracefully manage the role of fabulously wealthy duchess? If tonight's ball were any indication, she was just not the right woman for that formidable role.

Would she be able to keep a man like Blake satisfied? Would he not become bored with her? She knew that he was a strong, intelligent man and that he knew his own mind and would not propose marriage lightly. The real question was: Did she believe she was interesting and loving enough? Could she, lifelong wallflower, London's Least Likely and the Buxom Bluestocking, believe in herself enough to say yes?

Quite possibly . . .

In spite of the messy fears and feelings, there was no question about her desire. Emma knew one thing truly and completely: She wanted him. Kissing him was inevitable. Everything else was inevitable, too.

She clasped his beautiful face in her palms and pressed her lips to his. In an instant a sweet kiss turned wild. Blake growled and pulled her close and together they went tumbling down to the carpet in a glorious tangle of limbs.

He ran his fingers through her hair, kissing her deeply. She tugged off his cravat and pulled at the buttons just enough so she could slip her hands under his shirt to feel his hot skin and the determined thud of his heartbeat. She lightly flicked her fingertip over his nipple and caught his sharp intake of breath.

Perhaps she could please him.

His hands skimmed up, up, up from her ankles and higher. She sighed. Blake's hands skimmed up, up, up her waist to her breasts. She moaned. Blake's fingertips began working at the blasted buttons on the back of her dress, then the lacings of her corset. Emma yanked at his coat; he shrugged it off. She swiftly unbuttoned his waistcoat.

She wanted him. She wanted this. Of that, there were no questions.

He wanted her, too. Of that there was no question. She could feel his rock hard arousal pressing against the vee of her thighs, demanding entry. Her skin now covered, barely, in her chemise, she felt the carpet rubbing roughly against her skin, never letting her forget this was real. This was happening.

"We should slow down," he whispered, while still managing to kiss her and hold her tightly to him.

Young ladies waited until marriage.

Young ladies probably did not act indecently with known rogues on the carpet.

"I don't want to wait," she whispered back.

"Oh God, Emma," he rasped, before he kissed her deeply again. His tongue tangled and teased with hers. She nibbled his lower lip, he sucked upon hers. Once again he clasped her ankle, roughly caressing her, and as his hand skimmed higher until he found that magical place, stroking slowly and gently back and forth and round and round.

She felt that warmth. A spark where their lips had first met. A fire, smoldering hotter with his every touch, and threatening to burst into flame at any second. She could hardly breathe. She could scarcely keep her cries and moans quiet.

"I want to be inside you," he whispered.

"I want you to be."

But he just kept teasing her, tormenting her, urging that heat and fire to burn hotter and hotter. With his fingers brushing through her hair, he tightened his fist and dragged his mouth down to her breasts, where he did the most wicked things that sent her spiraling over the edge. He caught her cries with his kiss.

He held her tight against his chest as her pulse slowed and her breathing returned to something like normal. Then he untangled himself and stood.

"Where are you going?" He was not leaving her already! All those fears came roaring back to the forefront of her mind.

"The bed. Unless you prefer the floor?"

"You're not leaving?

"We're not finished yet, *Emily*," he murmured with that wicked, heart-melting grin of his. Then he scooped her up in his arms, as if she were a princess. Then he tossed her on the bed.

"You're right," she said, smiling coyly and reaching for his arousal. Remembering that night in the moonlight, she took him in her mouth.

"That wasn't what I meant," he murmured. Then he gasped and she took even more of him. He lightly threaded his fingers through her hair as she explored him with her mouth, her tongue. "But don't let me stop you," he murmured. Emma reveled in giving him the same pleasure he had given her until he desperately urged her to stop.

She gazed up at him. Blake's own gaze was dark and questioning.

"Emma . . ." He brushed a wayward strand of her hair aside. She reached out for his hand, urging him to join her on the bed. He covered her body with his, inch after inch of hot skin and the exquisite sensation of his weight upon her.

Blake's kiss now was gentle, and she understood that for all their frantic passion, this was something to savor. It was a moment to remember. After this there would be no turning back.

She arched her back slightly, feeling his hard arousal seeking entry. Blake caressed her face, kissed her deeply, and whispered, "Tell me to stop."

"I want you, Blake," she whispered back. She

did. There was no doubt about that. She wanted him because he *saw* her. And he didn't just see her as she saw herself, but he saw a more beautiful, clever, and daring version than she ever gave herself credit for. He made her feel all kinds of warm, wonderful things from his every touch to the way he made her feel about herself. Lovable. *Perhaps this could work . . .*

The more he kissed her, sweetly, deeply, the more she got lost in the sensations, the more those thoughts went away and she indulged completely in this moment.

Blake pressed against Emma's entrance, wanting to thrust in completely and bury himself inside her. She gasped and he slowed. This was her first time. It was their first time. She arched her back, and he clasped her hand, entwining his fingers with hers and pressing it against the mattress.

His gaze locked with her dark blue eyes. He saw her fears. And her trust. And maybe something like love. Words failed him now but he wanted, needed, her to know that this meant *everything* to him. That he wouldn't disappoint her. Claiming her mouth for a kiss, he slowly eased in, inch by inch until he no longer knew where she ended and he began.

He began to thrust, slowly at first, until they found their rhythm. She was so wet for him it nearly killed him to go slow. She was so tight he forced himself to hold back. *Her first time.* But then she tightened her legs around him, dragged her fingertips down his back and kissed him hard. *But she was quite a minx.*

Blake lost himself completely in feeling her, tasting her, exploring her. Her every sigh, her every moan, spurred him on. His heart was pounding like the devil. He breathed hard, feeling the tension build until he couldn't take it anymore. He wanted her so much and he wanted her to know that he loved her.

Thoughts went away after that, he could only feel. And knowing he loved her, that this *had* to be forever, made him insanely aware of every last sensation. Her fingers stroking his skin, her mouth kissing him, him breathing her in, all of her curves beneath him . . . he moved in and out and in and out in rough but perfect rhythm until he buried his face in her neck and cried out her name as he came.

Chapter 21

Now that Lady Grey has named Lady Emma Avery her heiress, few people doubt that the marriage between her and the Duke of Ashbrooke will take place. Throughout Mayfair, marriage-minded Mamas and ambitious maidens despair.

—"FASHIONABLE INTELLIGENCE,"
THE LONDON WEEKLY

Ashbrooke Residence
The following morning

THE LETTER ARRIVED at breakfast. The crisp sheet of pristine ivory vellum was presented to His Grace in a silver tray polished to such a high shine that he could see his reflection in it. He looked happy. He looked, for the very first time, like a man in love. He'd left Emma just hours ago, at first light, and already he counted the minutes until he could see her again.

Blake unthinkingly picked up the letter and broke the red wax seal with no particular care. As if it were any other letter.

As if it were any other morning.

Last night he had made love to Emma. He had

also successfully prevented her elopement, at least for one night. He dared to believe that he had shown her that they belonged together.

Last night, in Emma's arms, he discovered he'd been making love all wrong before—or perhaps it hadn't been right, or *something*. It had never been that good, that great. With Emma, it had not just been a union of a man and woman. He would have sworn their souls connected. It was terrifying. Exhilarating. He wanted to do it again and again and again.

He had been lost and now found.

Thus he was *happy* when he opened the letter, which was perhaps the cruelest part of all.

Blake skimmed until he saw a name, a certain name. Then he slowed and went back to the start, reading slowly now, feeling each and every word like hot daggers piercing his vital organs. *I regret to inform you . . .* Then the words became blurry. Later, he would realize it wasn't poor handwriting, but a hot sheen of tears threatening to fall. He would not let them.

Avery House

Emma had seen Blake's carriage arrive. Then she fussed about with her hair (her perfectly lovely hair!) while waiting for a servant to knock on her door and inquire if she was at home. While waiting, she practiced a smile (a perfectly lovely smile!). She thought about pinching her cheeks, but they were already flushed pink. Her eyes were bright and her mouth . . . she touched her lips with her fingertips.

Blake.

Last night. Making love. There was no going back now, and she belonged to him body, mind, soul. She was nervous that he wouldn't return but her heart surged with joy and relief when the Ashbrooke carriage came into view—not that she had been watching from the window. Very well, she had done just that whilst in a wickedly wonderful reverie, reliving each and every moment from last night.

She was desperate to see him and desperate to tell him YES, yes, *yes.*

But then the knock on her bedchamber door didn't come, which was deuced odd. She knew, because she glanced at that clock—which had been replaced to its perch upon the mantel—with its ever so loud and cruel *tick tock tick tock.* How long did it take for him to hand his hat to the butler and for a servant to come upstairs and say, "The duke is here to see you"? Surely it did not take ten minutes!

He must be speaking with her parents. If he was telling them what had happened—Oh! That would be forcing her hand, and she wanted none of that. She had a choice now, and she wanted him to know that she chose him.

No, her mother had probably dragged him off to ascertain his opinion on different colors of tea roses or eggshell satin versus a pure snowy white.

That didn't make sense either. Her mother had barely asked her opinion on any matters pertaining to the wedding. Why on earth would she ask a man? Besides, *the wedding was scheduled for tomorrow.* There was nothing left to decide—other than if it would actually happen.

Emma looked at the clock: another four minutes had elapsed, and she now had to face a wretched possibility. Now that Blake had *won* her, was he leaving her? Dear God, he could be jilting her right now—just when she had decided *yes.*

No, she mustn't assume the worst. She ought to have faith. And confidence.

But she could tolerate the suspense no longer.

She would go downstairs. There was no reason she could not walk downstairs in her home and perhaps encounter him. Or press her ear against a closed door. Anyone would.

When she was just about at the bottom stair, Emma saw Blake emerge from her father's study. Immediately she knew something was wrong, for his expression was grave and his movements were tense. Behind him, her mother clung to her father's arm. Mother's eyes were red, as if she'd been crying, and her father just looked gray and deflated.

Emma experienced an unsettling ache in her belly. Something bad had happened; immediately she wished to go back in time just moments ago when she was fussing with her hair and eagerly awaiting a moment with Blake.

Blake looked up and his eyes met hers. He did

not smile. She rather thought he *could* not smile. The dynamic, commanding man she knew was gone.

"Emma." He said her name in a flat voice.

"Blake." She said his name softly, tentatively, questioningly.

"If I might have a word with you," he said. She glanced at her parents and they nodded and retreated into her father's study and closed the door, providing an unprecedented amount of privacy.

Emma felt, in equal measures, desperate to know what had happened and an utter dread of the moment when she knew.

Blake followed her into the drawing room and completely shut the door behind them. Not even an inch for the sake of propriety.

He reached for her hand. His felt so cold in hers, and she knew, just knew.

"Emma," he said in a rough whisper, "Agatha died."

"No," Emma said. Or perhaps she merely moved her lips. "No."

"I just received word this morning."

"Blake, I am so sorry."

"I have spoken with your parents. I thought she would have waited . . . I thought this was what she wanted, so she wouldn't . . . but we have no control over when our time is up, do we?"

She thought she was not expected to answer that.

Instead, she slid her arms around him, resting her cheek on his chest. He pulled her close and held her fiercely, burying his face in her hair. She felt a peculiar rise and fall of his chest. Breathing was hard for him. She felt his heart beating under her cheek. The rhythm was slow and irregular, as if his heart wasn't sure if it wanted to carry on or not.

"What happens now?"

"We will have to cancel the wedding," he said flatly.

Cancel? Or did he mean reschedule for a later date? Emma opened her mouth to ask, but Blake carried on, so deep in his sorrow that he didn't seem to notice her.

"I will go to Grey Manor. A funeral will have to be arranged."

"I will go with you," she said impulsively.

He continued as if she hadn't spoken. "Someone will need to manage the execution of her will and oversee affairs. It is official. It is yours, Emma. All of it."

Chapter 22

"Your Grace, I am loath to disturb you at this sensitive time but I have come into some information I feel strongly you would like to know."

"What is it, Jepson?" Blake wearily asked his valet.

"I know who sent the letter to the newspaper announcing your betrothal," Jepson said anxiously. "I have learned the news belowstairs. From Lady Emma's maid."

BLAKE DID NOT know which was worse: enduring Agatha's funeral or suffering through it without the solace afforded by Emma's hand in his.

He had left London immediately for Castle Hill to ensure that Agatha's explicit wishes for her funeral were carried out, right down to her stipulation that she—or her coffin, rather—arrived fifteen minutes late. One was never too dead for a grand entrance.

He mourned the loss of his beloved aunt. He mourned the loss of his beloved Emma. The wedding had been canceled—it should have been occurring this very moment if Lady Avery had her way and if Agatha hadn't died. Given the news

Jepson related, perhaps this tragic turn of events was for the best.

Blake could feel Emma's eyes on him, searching for a clue or an opportunity to speak. Did she note his hooded gaze, his clenched jaws, his hands balled into fists? No one else did. They fussed over him as if he were an eight-year-old orphan all over again. Except Agatha wasn't there to fix everything with her brisk efficiency and her utter lack of sentimentality.

"Go on, cry then," she had told him then. "Get all those tears out so we can move on with our lives. There is candy and it won't eat itself."

Blake didn't know what she would say now. Except, perhaps, there is brandy and it won't drink itself.

The Library at Castle Hill

When he strolled into the library, Blake's mood was black: like coal, like midnight, like a dungeon, like death itself. His last experience in this room had been nearly ravishing Emma up against the bookcase.

Today they gathered for the Reading of the Will.

Along with Eastwick, Aunt Agatha's lifelong solicitor, Blake recognized many of his former competitors in the Fortune Games, including London's Least Likely, who had defied all their expectations. She now stood to inherit *everything*.

He had lost Agatha, and now he would lose everything else. Was it just days ago that he had been poised to attain more than he'd ever dreamt? It was cruel how fast and far he'd fallen.

He could marry her. Claim it all for himself.

But could he really, given what he had learned? Was he really surprised? Everything had been pretend from the start.

Except at some point he had actually fallen in love with her.

Perhaps Agatha's death—and the cancellation of the wedding—was a gift, given that he now had doubts about marrying her. If they never rescheduled the wedding, everyone would believe she had jilted him. She could marry whomever she wanted. She could be happy.

Isn't that what he wanted?

Eastwick began by clearing his throat. Everyone's attention was already fixated upon him, particularly the sheaf of documents that rustled in his hand.

"As you are all aware, Lady Agatha revised her will every year. This one was written just after the conclusion of this year's Fortune Games. I can attest that she was of sound mind and body at that time. I shall now read the pertinent parts."

"To Lady Bellande, a donation to the Ladies Committee Benefiting War Widows and Orphans has been made in your name, which shall secure you a position on their board so that you may assist in their charitable endeavors." Lady Bellande fixed a polite, if patently false, smile upon her face. Eastwick looked up from the papers and said, grimly, to her: "You should be aware that committee members are required to give a donation of fifty pounds per annum. Appointment is for life."

To her credit, Lady Bellande's smile did not waver, though her complexion certainly paled.

Blake's mood lightened from black to dark gray, like thunderclouds, or the cold slate color of the sea on a dark day. But it plummeted back into darkness because he wanted to share a smile with Emma over this and couldn't bring himself to do so.

"Miss Dawkins," Eastwick declared, and the poor girl peered up at him nervously. "Lady Agatha has fixed a dowry of five thousand pounds upon you. That is in addition to whatever else your family will have provided. She has also gifted you her seaside cottage in Brighton."

Harriet Dawkins blinked back tears, then gave up. They rolled down her cheeks because that measure of security would make a world of difference to a girl like her—shy, quiet, few prospects, largely unnoticed. But Agatha had noticed, and Agatha had ensured that she would be taken care of, whether she married or remained a spinster. From the look on her face, Blake deduced that no one had ever considered her welfare before.

He felt the loss of Agatha all over again, for she had known how to give a girl like Harriet a chance and hope for a future. Above all, now that Miss Dawkins was financially secure she was able to marry whomever she chose and to marry for love.

Like Emma.

The realization struck him sharply. Agatha had bequeathed not just money, but the freedom of *choice.* Without Agatha's gift, their prospects were dim, uncertain, and bleak. Now the whole world was theirs to claim.

That old broad was a smart one. A romantic, too.

Blake missed her so much it hurt.

"I did not know we had a seaside cottage in the family," Lady Copley sniffed, utterly missing the monumental and priceless gift Agatha had bestowed.

"What you will find, Lady Copley, is that Lady Agatha's holdings were vast indeed," Eastwick droned. "Which means we have much more to get through. For you, Lady Copley, Lady Agatha wishes you to have her china set, since you complimented it."

Blake bit back laughter at Lady Copley's expression. She had loathed the china set, obviously, and only complimented it as part of the games. But Agatha had known how to discern the truth from the lies.

She must have known about him and Emma. She hadn't been fooled She had to have known their relationship was a sham. And yet, she still declared Emma the winner, which was maddeningly curious.

If she gifted Emma with the freedom to choose . . .

"There are other provisions made for her loyal

servants, particularly Angus," Eastwick went on. "She has left provisions for the village, etcetera. But the bulk of her remaining fortune, as you all know, will go to Lady Emma."

All gazes settled upon Emma, who lowered her eyes. She was not family. She was possibly not even betrothed to Blake. Unlike Agatha, those rumors did not die. Instead it was remarked upon how Lady Emma had taken the ton by surprise; instead of a retiring wallflower, she turned out to be scheming minx. She had been transformed from the girl no one ever noticed to the object of scandal and scorn, favor and flattery.

"Lady Emma's holdings now include the bulk of Lady Agatha's wealth, which includes ninety thousand pounds . . ." Eastwick paused to allow for the collective gasp. "She also will receive a large portion of the Castle Hill estate. As for the house itself, its contents, and the five hundred acres that immediately surround it, those are for, and I quote, " 'Blake, who has no need for another house, but who does need a home.' " She has also allotted up to ten thousand pounds to match funds the duke raises toward his Difference Engine."

Blake didn't breathe. His heart didn't beat.

Agatha had remembered him. She had left him the one thing he truly wanted. A home. Their home and all the happy memories it contained. And with her gift toward the engine, she had given him her approval for the endeavor.

Above all, *she had made it completely unnecessary for him to marry Emma.*

Which meant they could marry for love. *If* they married. They no longer needed each other for fortune or reformation.

Now, thanks to Agatha, they had a *choice.*

Blake's mood turned from gray to a dark smoky charcoal, or the ominous shade of dark violet before a storm at dusk.

He knew what he had to do. Even if it felt like hell—choking on the flames, fire burning his heart and the mocking laughter of the devil himself.

"What good is a house without the income generating lands?" Lord Copley asked, displaying his misunderstanding of the situation. While the last thing Blake needed was another house, he did want a *home.*

"That is all moot, for they are to marry and everything that is Lady Emma's will become his," Lady Copley replied.

"Is that so?" Lady Bellande said, smiling through her painted red lips. "The wedding has been canceled, and I have not heard that it will be rescheduled."

Later that afternoon . . .

Emma slipped her hand in Blake's, yearning for connection with him. They had barely spoken since the night they made love; there hadn't been a chance. Days and nights had been a whirlwind of funeral plans, tears, and tedious travel along deeply rutted roads in an enclosed carriage with her parents. There was so much she wanted to tell him and even more that she wanted to ask. But he seemed so distant, even as he clasped her hand and walked by her side.

Butterflies fluttered through the garden, landing on the plump, fragrant Lady Grey roses and sucking up the sweet nectar and the warm sunshine. Butterflies in her belly, like the feeling of love at first sight. Like how she felt now, with Blake.

She loved him.

When it happened, or how, she knew not. It might have been when he strolled into her drawing room after the announcement was posted. He could have mocked her, exposed her, or destroyed her. Instead, he transformed her circumstances so drastically she still hadn't quite found her footing.

Now, with her hand in his she finally felt a measure of security. Her doubts were not entirely assuaged, she wasn't certain of their future—other than that she couldn't be separated from him and still be happy.

More than anything, she wanted to be the woman he saw when he looked at her. Thanks to him and his stubborn insistence on wooing her, she was starting to be that woman and see herself as worthy of his love.

The gardens were silent except for the crunching sound of their footsteps on gravel and the low hum of insects on a hot summer day. He led her to the bench where they had spent many a happy hour, where she might have started to fall in love with him as they sought for love at first sight, or a spark.

When he climbed into her window the other night, she had been wavering over her fate. She knew then that she had fallen irrevocably in love with him. Only one man was going to love her like that: enough to venture into her bedroom at midnight and spend the hours until dawn demonstrating the dizzying heights of pleasure they could attain together.

She didn't know how long Benedict might have waited in the mews. He never seemed to pull through at the critical moment—to take those extra steps to the back door, to ask her to marry him even before his need for a fortune became plain. He did *just enough* to keep her, but nothing more.

Blake had swept her off her feet and carried her off into the sunset.

Emma glanced up at him now and felt a rock of ice in her belly when he wouldn't quite meet her gaze. His jaw was set. She wanted to tell him *yes*. The words were on her lips, ready, and then—

Blake's heart rebelled, but logic and reason won the day. His heart—and to be honest, other parts of him—loved Emma intensely, relentlessly. Yet his brain wasn't so clouded by lust and deluded by love as to miss the facts.

If he wanted Emma to take a risk on him, then he had to take a risk on her love for him.

For better or for worse, the stipulations of Agatha's will had ensured that they need only marry for love.

Given the scheme she had enacted that led to this moment, he knew the devilishly difficult thing he had to do. He had to give them a chance to start anew—without any schemes or deceptions.

"I know about the letter, Emma." As they sat next to each other on the bench, Blake watched her reaction carefully, hoping it would reveal the news to be a lie. He badly wanted it to be a lie. "Your maid appears to have informed my valet. Belowstairs gossip is always worse than ton gossip. My trustworthy valet informed me."

Emma had once told him a carefully crafted lie of omission: *Know that I did not send the letter.* But she had written it, with an acknowledgment of how ridiculous it was: *To the surprise of everyone . . .*

And now this scheming miss had managed to inherit ninety thousand pounds of what should have been his inheritance. Never, never underestimate the Wallflowers. Never ever give your heart to one—they'll trample all over it, like the most practiced and coldhearted courtesan.

"I did not write it," she said evenly. "I protested. I wanted to burn it."

"And yet the news appeared in print in the most popular newspaper in town. And now you have inherited a fortune. Well done."

"Who sent it?" she asked, oddly curious, considering. "You must know who sent it."

Blake laughed bitterly. "You and your mother, in league with the most audacious scheme that has succeeded beyond anyone's wildest dreams."

"My mother?" Emma stood and stomped away, before whirling around and returning to plunk herself back down on the bench. She muttered angrily under her breath.

"A girl with no prospects, a family in need of money," Blake said. "Why not announce your betrothal to a duke and rely on my honor to see it through? Were the Fortune Games part of the plan, or one hell of a boon?"

"Blake, I had no part in this!"

"Other than to protest," he said, reminding her of her own story.

"My friends wrote it. I had forgotten about it until it was too late!"

"The point is, Emma, we have made the best of a ridiculous situation. But now there is no longer a need to pretend. It's time for our betrothal—or whatever it has been—to come to an end." The words tasted like ashes to him. "Given the circumstances, we should be able to part without much drama. No one needs to be jilted. No reputations will be ruined."

"But you are jilting me now."

"I'm setting you free. The Fortune Games are over. You have won. You can now marry whomever you wish. Whomever you love."

He loved her. He ached to pull her close and

try to forget how he'd been a pawn in her game. Still, he wanted Emma to be happy. They had been given an opportunity to choose each other; it had to be seized. Even if this severing hurt now, the pain could not compare to a lifetime in which they both felt trapped and conned into marriage.

"Are you trying to do me some sort of *favor*?" Emma asked incredulously.

"I'm trying to do the honorable thing. When I left in the morning, Benedict was still there in the mews, waiting. I'm sure that he will still have you," Blake said.

His word and honor as a gentleman compelled him to ensure she knew that.

"But we made love," she whispered. "I am ruined for anyone else now!"

"You are an heiress, Emma. I'm sure most gentlemen will not be too concerned with your virtue."

"It's not just that. I thought you wanted me," she whispered.

I do, dear God, I do. He wanted her more than anything, but not on these terms, not by default, not like this. Though this was killing him, he was certain it was the right thing to do.

"You made me love you," she whispered. He nearly dropped to his knees, wanting to take back all the revelations and cruel words he'd spoken. But it was too late. "I gave myself to you," she said, her voice low. "My innocence, my word, my heart. And I held back because of this. I was so afraid of this. It was just a dream, wasn't it?" Then she laughed and said, "To think the great Duke of Ashbrooke would bother with a plain little wallflower like me."

Chapter 23

To the surprise of Lady Emma, she had fallen madly in love with the Duke of Ashbrooke.

—EMMA'S INNERMOST THOUGHTS

Emma's bedchamber

ONCE UPON A time nothing much happened to her. That was before The Letter. Emma stood and turned in a slow circle around her bedroom where The Letter had been written and lost. Where she had debated whom to marry, where she had given herself completely to Blake, and where she stood now, weary and exhausted not just from her travels but from her whole, entire life. All three and twenty years of it.

"Emma, darling, you're home!" her mother said, bursting into the bedroom where Emma moped while her maid unpacked and the servants drew a hot bath.

"Hello, Mother."

"Well, is it true that you have inherited everything?" Her mother asked this anxiously. Emma could tell from her voice, the way her brow furrowed, and from her clenched hands.

"I did not get the fancy china," she said flatly. Her mother appeared confused, which made Emma miss Blake terribly. He would understand. He would have shared the humor with her. Deadpan, he would have said, "Horrors" or "Tragedy" or "My life will never be complete without it."

"You shall buy a dozen more sets, or purchase it from whoever inherited it," her mother said. As if a china set *mattered.*

"Nor did I inherit the house, which was given to Blake," Emma said, and she was so glad of it, for Grey Manor belonged to him, truly. She could never have lived there without him.

"You shall still be mistress of it, once you marry. Awfully circuitous of her not to leave things to you two together. But she is known to have been . . . odd."

Emma had to ignore the slight to Agatha, for she didn't have the strength to persuade her mother of Agatha's brilliance. She hadn't just left money to her and Harriet Dawkins, she had given them a chance, a choice.

In giving Blake the one thing that really mattered, Grey Manor, she had ensured that they might marry for love. If they married. Emma sighed. No, she could not explain any of that to her mother.

"We are not going to marry."

"I beg your pardon? Not marry? Why on earth would you two not marry?"

Because he thinks I am a scheming fortune hunter,

thanks to the cursed letter that was never meant to be sent!

Emma regarded her mother, noting the lines etched into her forehead and the embroidered handkerchief clutched in her hands. Could what Blake had told her be true?

"Did you ever wonder, Mother, about the announcement that appeared in the newspaper?"

"Why do you ask?"

Emma hadn't wondered, for it was done, and to speculate seemed pointless . . . until now, when whomever had done so had set her up for a monstrously broken heart.

"Did it not strike you as odd?" Emma mused. "After all, the duke and I had never met. You knew I had no opportunity to have a secret, whirlwind romance. You knew I loved another."

Mother and daughter stood eye-to-eye in Emma's bedchamber. The maid busied herself with folding gowns. A hot bath was awaiting, steam rising.

"Rossmore's impoverished son you foolishly had your heart set on?" her mother said, laughing. "You couldn't marry him, Emma! He's too poor. And you could do better."

"Which does not explain how a letter found in this bedroom made its way to *The London Weekly*," Emma said, her curiosity growing when her mother did not deny it.

"I sent it," her mother said with a shrug. As if it were nothing at all. As if the truth, uttered so lightly, hadn't brought her heart to a complete standstill.

"You sent it."

"I did. And you are most welcome. Instead of throwing your future away on some poor, spineless boy, you have snared a duke. A duke! This family was desperate, Emma, and now we are saved."

"It's wrong! We do not deserve this money! The inheritance should have gone to someone in the family. Not me. Not a stranger."

As for Blake . . . her heart was still too raw, the hurt so overwhelming she could hardly breathe, let alone speak of him. She had loved and lost, twice, in little over a fortnight.

"I wanted you to be noticed, Emma. I was not sure how the duke would react, but I knew you would catch the attention of the ton. You never quite *took* even though you are so pretty and intelligent and a lovely girl. I wanted the world to know you as I do, Emma. I did this for you."

"But I am ruined now!"

"Nonsense."

"No, I love him, and he has left me because he thinks I have deceived him," Emma said coldly. She did not need to say *because of what you did*. The words, unspoken, were understood. Her heart was wrecked.

"Tell him the truth," her mother suggested. As if it were that simple! As if she hadn't tried to already!

"You tell him," Emma countered, her anger spiking. "You are the one who has created this whole epic disaster."

"Very well, I shall do so," her mother said. "If it will make you feel better. With your new fortune, you really can't marry below a duke anyway," she added, missing the point entirely.

"No! You have meddled enough as it is. Mother, how on earth could you do this?"

"I am sorry! I only wanted the best for you when you never wanted it for yourself!"

That silenced Emma. Because it was true.

"I gave her the letters, ma'am," the maid said, nervously interjecting. "I found them whilst straightening your room. I wasn't quite sure what to do with them, and you had gone off to Lady Olivia's home after the fire. "

"It doesn't matter now, Emma. We have the fortune now," her mother said, anxiously reaching out for her daughter's hand, which Emma snatched away.

But it did matter. Oh, it did. Because it wasn't about the money at all. It was about the love she never expected to know, and the love she had just lost forever.

"I'd like you both to go," Emma said coldly.

To her surprise, they listened. But then she recalled that she was now worth ninety thousand pounds and their livelihoods depended upon her goodwill toward them. Everyone would do what she said now.

Except for Blake.
Or would he?

The very next day
Emma's bedchamber

"More sherry?" Olivia offered the bottle to Emma and Prudence, both of whom held out their empty glasses. The three girls lolled about on the new carpet in Emma's bedchamber. Other than that addition, it was much the same in spite of everything that had transpired within its walls: stacks of romantic novels from the circulating library upon every surface, a four-poster bed, a window with a trellis leading up to it for the ease of burglars and devoted suitors.

"When you hear what I have in mind, you will need it," Emma said, holding out her glass. "Liquid courage, they say."

"I think that is whiskey. Or is it any strong liquor?" Prudence asked thoughtfully. "One can't quite picture a man downing *sherry* when he's off to face battle or fight a duel."

"Sneaking into the cordial is one thing," Emma said. "Stealing from my father's store of spirits is another matter entirely."

"You could just buy some," Olivia said. "You could buy lots. You could keep us drunk on sherry for weeks. Months. Years. Our entire Spinsterhood could be passed in a drunken haze."

"I could, couldn't I? But it feels wrong to

have this money. I cannot quite bring myself to spend it."

"That is tragic. What is the use of ninety thousand pounds if one cannot spend it?"

"I don't think there is an answer to that question."

"More sherry is the answer!" Olivia declared.

"Now to the matter at hand—" Prudence started, then stopped. "Is it true that your betrothal with Blake is finished?"

"They are saying you jilted him," Olivia said, with a dark glance at Emma suggesting she would be awfully disappointed if she had done so. "They are also saying he jilted you. No one can make heads or tales of the situation, which is not preventing anyone from gossiping about it extensively."

"My mother sent The Letter," Emma said, to the gasps of her friends. "However, Blake believes me to be behind it. He also has these ridiculous notions about us no longer needing each other. Thus, I have been jilted. Just as I feared. But worse."

"How worse?"

Emma paused, for she knew that that once she uttered these words, there was no taking them back.

"I fell in love with him. I made love to him. Because he thinks I am an awful but successful schemer, he told me to run off with Benedict. But I don't want to anymore. I could, and I don't want to! What kind of wretched twist of fate is this?"

"The heart wants what the heart wants," Prudence murmured.

"Emma, what are we going to do? There must be some way you can make him see the truth and that you love him."

"This is Ashbrooke we're discussing," Emma said with a weary sigh. "Lots of women love him and he's not concerned in the slightest."

"I really thought he loved you," Prudence said.

"I saw the way he looked at you. I'd do anything to have a man look at me like that," Olivia added.

"I thought he might love me too," Emma whispered. That was the worst of it all. The confidence he had inspired in her made it impossible for her to believe that his seduction had been a game. No, she would bet her fortune that his feelings of love for her were true. Now she believed in him—and herself. When it was too late.

"The question is, how do you win him back?" Olivia mused. "It goes without saying you must win him back."

"We're right back at the start again, are we not? Puzzling over how to force a man to propose," Emma said with a sad laugh.

"We managed that. Easily," Prudence said, grinning.

"Thanks to my scheming, meddling mother," Emma muttered. Her mother, with whom she had not spoken ever since her brazen confession to such a devastating crime.

No, Emma did not believe she was overreacting about it by locking herself in her bedchamber, save for her dearest friends and a bottle of sherry and a crippling heartache.

"If it isn't broke, why fix it?" Prudence suggested cryptically. Emma glanced at her friend nervously.

Olivia's eyes widened considerably. "Are you suggesting we send another engagement announcement to *The London Weekly*?"

"No, a *wedding* announcement," Prudence said.

Emma groaned. "Not this again!"

"Prudence, I don't know how you come up with such wicked ideas!" Olivia said. "I quite love it."

Prudence grinned. "It's the sherry. It inspires me."

"Perhaps you've had enough," Emma suggested. But to her horror, she didn't quite dismiss the idea of posting a wedding announcement, for she could see a certain poetry in the action. There was also a certain terror in the prospect.

"The duke must know that you have chosen him above *all* others," Prudence declared. It was clear that by "all others" she meant Benedict.

"That's awfully wise," Olivia said. "And terribly romantic."

"You have to act quickly, before Benedict's wedding," Prudence said, "Otherwise, Blake might think you are turning to him as your second choice."

"This is all so complicated," Emma said, heaving a sigh. She was weary from a sleepless night, tipsy from the sherry, and, quite simply, heartsick. She wanted nothing more than to crawl in bed with Blake and forget the world, but that was a silly dream. "Perhaps I shall take my fortune and retire to the country and read novels where other characters must bother with these sorts of troubles."

"The more I consider it, the more I am convinced that you should post a wedding announcement to the newspaper," Prudence declared, taking a hearty sip of sherry. "'The Duke of Ashbrooke will marry Lady Emma Avery at eleven o'clock in the morning on Saturday at St. George's.'"

"Ooooh," Olivia said softly. "Can you just imagine it?"

Emma could. She shuddered. And took a hearty swallow of sherry.

"There is only one problem with that plan," she said. "One horrible, massive, traumatizing problem. If he doesn't show up, I shall be jilted twice and publicly humiliated."

"I would die if that happened to me," Olivia said. "Honestly, I think I would just perish of mortification."

"Thank you, Olivia, for your words of encouragement."

"She's right to be afraid," Prudence said. "If the duke did not come, Emma would be the laughingstock of London. It would never be forgotten."

"And everyone would wonder why he jilted a woman to whom he'd been previously betrothed and who was worth ninety thousand pounds," Olivia said. "They would assume the very worst about you."

Emma's mouth dropped open in terror.

"Horrible, unspeakable things," Prudence concurred. Emma downed the contents of her sherry glass in one go.

"No one would marry you after that," Olivia added thoughtfully. "No one good, anyway. Not even Benedict."

"If you two are trying to be helpful, I'm afraid you are failing spectacularly," Emma declared. "I've half a mind to flee to the Continent already."

"But don't you see, Emma? No one would risk such grave consequences if not for true love," Olivia said simply, with an encouraging smile.

"Risking *everything* like that would be a testament to your love for him," Prudence said. "If he does love you, then he won't be able to resist your grand gesture."

"Oh, the romance!" Olivia gushed.

"Oh, the insanity!" Emma countered.

"He built the ancient ruins of a gazebo for you," Prudence said matter-of-factly, "which suggests his love for you is strong, and eternal and amenable to public displays of affection. Therefore—"

"The least you can do is plan a wedding," Olivia said. "And announce it in the newspaper."

"You do have the dress," Prudence pointed out. The three girls turned to look in the direction of the wardrobe, where one would find a beautiful ivory silk gown decked with seed pearls and glass beads. No one, not even the cruel dandy, Lord Pleshette, could scoff at her in that dress.

When Emma did not immediately and vehemently protest this new, absurd plan, Olivia declared, "I'll fetch the paper and pen," and started rummaging through Emma's desk.

"I will drink more sherry and pretend all of this goes away," Emma said, closing her eyes.

It did not go away. It was in the newspaper the next day.

Chapter 24

There are rumors that the Duke of Ashbrooke is dying, though his friends and physicians assure me that is not the case. Dear Readers, it's best left unsaid how I came upon that information.

—"FASHIONABLE INTELLIGENCE"
BY A LADY OF DISTINCTION,
THE LONDON WEEKLY

Ashbrooke House

BLAKE HAD BEEN suffering chest pains that ranged from a dull ache to hot, fleeting pangs that made him gasp. He found himself plagued with a shortness of breath; he feared suffocation. A general sense of malaise and ennui consumed him. None of his usual activities—flirting, fencing, making love, making merry, visiting his clubs, ballrooms or bedrooms, or reviewing calculations for the Difference Engine—kept his interest for more than a second, perhaps two.

He drank tumblers of wine or brandy. He brooded in rooms where the drapes were drawn tightly over the windows.

Sleep eluded him, thus depriving him of a few

sweet hours where he might not worry that he was dying. Was this how Agatha felt?

A consultation with the physician revealed that nothing was in fact wrong with him: His heartbeat was strong, his lungs sounded good.

Blake scoured medical texts in search of this obscure, devastating malady. Eventually, he was forced to conclude that he was sick with love. He told no one of this embarrassing condition.

The infamous Duke of Ashbrooke, laid low by love!

But there was no denying it, for his thoughts strayed constantly to Emma, for whom he still hungered in spite of everything.

"Your Grace," Pendleton intoned. With his white-gloved hands he presented yet another highly polished silver tray bearing yet another ivory vellum letter sealed with bright red wax. In the shiny silver, Blake saw the reflection of a man driven mad by pride, love, betrayal, and with a tendency to perhaps overreact.

He looked away quickly.

"This arrived for you," Pendleton said, presumptuously placing the letter upon Blake's empty breakfast plate.

"Where is the newspaper?"

Perhaps there would be news of Emma's elopement with Benedict, and he would know he'd lost his chance at love. Forever. Then he could move on with his life.

"I am withholding it, Your Grace."

Blake felt his temper spark, like the strike of a match.

"Withholding it? What the devil for? Are you seeking an early retirement?"

"It is my understanding that this letter will serve as an explanation."

Blake took the letter and glared at Pendleton while he sliced through the wax seal with a knife. A small clipping from the newspaper fluttered into his lap. Blake lifted it carefully. He read the words, vaguely aware that he was holding his breath. It was not usual for him to read outrageous, scandalous gossip about himself. Today he was not in the mood.

FASHIONABLE INTELLIGENCE BY A LADY OF DISTINCTION

This author has it on *excellent* authority that on Saturday, June 5, at eleven o'clock in the morning, Lady Emma Avery will trade in her title of "London's Least Likely" for that of the Duchess of Ashbrooke.

Blake pressed his mouth into a firm line, fighting an upturn at the corners that would indicate something like amusement, or hope, or appreciation. Not him, not lately. She couldn't just *do* things like this. She couldn't just declare something was so and that would make it so.

He was not quite sure which *she* he was referring to—Emma, or her scheming mother. But as he read *The London Weekly* snippet again, there was no mistaking that this was Emma's own wit and phrasing.

"That will be all, Pendleton."

"Are you certain, Your Grace? Are there any arrangements I might make?"

"No."

Blake then turned his attentions to the note itself, noting it was composed in Emma's handwriting. He recognized it from all of those false love letters. Which he might have saved. And read. And reread.

With his breath stilled and his heart carrying on tentatively, he focused on the letter in his hands.

Blake—

The reason I don't like sherry is because one night Olivia, Prudence, and I drank far too much of it. We discovered that it does, as Olivia's mother says, "make a lady forget herself." In our madness, my idle thought to draft a proposal to Benedict was spun into Prudence's very wicked idea that if I were to resort to such drastic measures to find myself a husband, I oughtn't settle for the likes of Benedict, but should set my sights on the most handsome and charming eligible man in town. You.

Prudence dictated the letter. Olivia wrote it. I foolishly drank another glass of sherry. In our haste to escape a kitchen fire, we forgot the letter. I learned from you that my mother had sent it.

He could, far too easily, picture those three girls three sheets to the wind on sickly sweet sherry. No wonder she refused to drink the stuff. No wonder she tried to refuse his proposal. She truly hadn't meant any of it.

Thus began our sham romance. Somewhere along the line came love. Then heartache. I still hope that it will lead to happily-ever-after for you and me.

However, I did write another letter, which I sent to The London Weekly. *You said you wanted our love story to be real, Blake. But would you like it to have a happy ending? I would . . .*

Meet me at the altar and make this love story true.

Yours (whether you like it or not),
Emma

A grin tugged at his lips, again. He fought it, valiantly.

She couldn't just do this—arrange a wedding, take matters into her own hands, control their fate. It was meddling and scheming and it broke the rules: She was supposed to be a damsel in distress, and he was supposed to save her. But this—she just expected him to arrive at the appointed time and place as if he had no say in the matter. Had Benedict married another? Had her mother pressured her into this? What the devil would he be walking into if he were to arrive at St. George's *today* at eleven o'clock?

A glance at the clock told him he had just an hour to make his decision.

He could leave her stranded at the altar, his

point very well made. She could take her ninety thousand pounds and buy all the sherry in England and post all the notices to the newspaper that she wished. But it wouldn't change the truth.

And the truth was . . .

Chapter 25

In all of my years reporting upon weddings of the haute ton, this author has never attended such highly anticipated and dramatic nuptials as today.

—"Miss Harlow's Marriage in High Life,"
The London Weekly

St. Peter's Church, London

Benedict stood at the altar awaiting his bride. In this, like everything else, he was unsure. But with the vicar behind him and his father beside him, there was no turning back. His fate awaited him—she was fussing over her veil and dress as women tended to do. She was a fate he didn't choose because he had been too slow to act, too blind to see the love waiting for him far longer than he deserved.

This was his last chance to escape this fate and seize another. For he had, once again, seen the devastating announcement in the gossip column.

The organ sounded, echoing in the stone chamber. Benedict's heart started racing.

This was his chance. If he ran now, he could possibly make it to the *other* church on time.

St. George's Chapel

Emma peeked into the church once more, taking care to keep herself hidden. Her father, mother, and a few others had eagerly taken their seats in the first pews and now were anxiously awaiting the wedding that was supposed to have started a quarter hour earlier.

Who knew a mere quarter of an hour could feel so endlessly, eternally, and infernally long? She did. She wished she did not.

"He's not here," Emma said. Again.

She took a deep, fortifying breath, which only served to remind her how blasted tight her corset had been laced. The satin gown, decked with pearls, weighed heavily upon her bones. She wanted to escape this dress and this horrid thing that was happening to her: taking a chance on true love and failing.

Prudence and Olivia, dressed in matching blue silk dresses, peered curiously at her.

"Call the carriage," Emma said, grasping at the neckline of her gown frantically. "I would like to be driven to the docks immediately. Perhaps someone would be so kind as to purchase me a one-way ticket to Paris. No, Italy. No, America. No, China. Yes, China should be far enough away—"

"Emma, it will be fine," Olivia said in a soothing tone of voice. "He will be here."

"Do you know that? How could you possibly know that?"

"Emma, you must have faith in the duke, and in true love," Olivia said.

She groaned.

"Easy for you to say! You are not in a wedding dress laced so tightly as to make it impossible to breathe, uncertain if your groom will arrive before suffocating to death. Though perhaps that would be preferable to life after being jilted at the altar."

"At least there is no one here. Other than us," Olivia said.

"And the mob outside," Prudence, ever logical and practical, had to point out. "Listen to them! They sound almost as eager as you to see if Blake arrives!"

Indeed. It seemed all of London had turned out to witness the unfathomable sight of the Duke of Ashbrooke marrying London's Least Likely. She had not considered that when she drunkenly assented to Prudence and Olivia's horrendous plan to send off the wedding announcement. Or when she wrote that letter to Blake explaining how, and why.

"This was a horrible idea," she cried, starting to pace about the room. "I'm never drinking sherry again. Ever! It is the devil's own brew and it makes a lady forget herself and all sense and reason. It should be banned! I will start a petition . . ." She paused when she saw her friends' nervous expressions. "Why are you two looking at me like that?"

"We'll have to return your wedding present, then," Prudence muttered. "I thought it was such a clever, romantic idea."

"A collection of sherry glasses," Olivia explained. "And we cannot return them."

"We had to get them engraved. One of a kind," Prudence said. Both girls smiled sheepishly.

"So I shall drink myself to a stupor in style. Since Blake will probably jilt me." Nerves got the better of her and the words started tumbling out in a rush of panic. "Everyone will know he jilted me, too, thanks to that blasted mob outside. I shall be mocked mercilessly for daring to think a man like him would care for *me*."

"Emma . . ."

"That is, if I don't die of embarrassment on the spot. Wait—weren't you going to fetch me a one-way ticket to America? No, China. I had settled on the Orient, had I not?"

"Emma!" Prudence shouted, finally managing to cut her off. "You must calm down."

"Calm down? *Calm down?*" Emma shouted back. Calming down was impossible. She had loved and lost not once, but possibly thrice in just one month! She was risking public mortification, her life and reputation in society, and most important of all, her already fragile heart.

"Calm down?" she said again, throwing her bouquet of Lady Grey roses to the ground. Prudence shrank back. "How could you tell me to *calm down* at a time like this?"

"One should never tell a woman to calm down," Blake remarked from the doorway. "It only infuriates them further."

"Oh, thank God," Prudence and Olivia exclaimed. Their relief was palpable. It did not compare to Emma's.

"Blake. You are here," she said, as if the words made it true. Honestly, she felt as if he might be a hallucination, a mirage, a fine example of wishful thinking.

"Hello, Emma," he murmured. She drank in the sound of his voice and reveled in the warmth it gave her. He was here! But did he mean to stay? His expression was inscrutable. Were his eyes dark with desire, or because he had awful news to deliver? Was that a hint of a smile upon lips or a grimace?

Her heart beat slow, steady, awaiting its fate—to race with joy or stop altogether?

"Perhaps we will leave you two alone," Prudence said, and with a firm grasp on Olivia's wrist, exited the room.

They were alone.

She had missed him.

Emma no longer cared about possible mortification, ruination, or any of that. He was here and she wanted nothing more than to wrap herself in his arms. Forever.

"You could have anyone," Blake said. "And not just because you are an heiress. You could have anyone because you are beautiful, intelligent, and fiercely true to yourself."

Her heart continued to beat, but tentatively.

"You could, too," she said. "You are legendary because you are handsome and charming. But you are also intelligent, thoughtful, and daring. Most of all, you have made me become a girl I never thought I'd be. It's you I want, Blake. You alone."

Blake pushed off the door frame he'd been leaning on and slowly crossed the room. Emma's heart pounded with every step he took closer to her. Blake wasn't leaving! But would he stay?

He placed his hand on her waist, possessively.

"Emma," he murmured, gazing down at her with his warm, dark eyes. Heat began to pool in her belly, like a slow, smoldering fire.

The heavy oak door leading to the chapel swung open.

Benedict had stepped out of the church a changed man, a determined man. For too long he had retreated from challenges, and in avoiding the wrong decision, had made none. He hadn't held on tight to the things—and people—whom he loved. He had strived to be a dutiful son. He saw now what all that duty and indecision cost him.

Emma. Love. Happiness.

He glanced at his timepiece. It was too late, though he suspected he'd missed his chance days, weeks, months, even years ago.

"Are you so bored of marriage already that you're looking at your watch?" Katherine whispered sharply, whilst smiling for their family and friends who had joined them on this day.

Benedict leveled a gaze at his *wife*. She possessed none of Emma's gentle disposition or sweetness. What she did possess was a fortune, which would go to his father's debts.

"Actually, I have somewhere to be."

"Our wedding breakfast? Do try to smile, even though you don't mean it. I am not exactly thrilled with the turn of events either, but I won't let them see it," Katherine said. She smiled fiercely.

"Later this afternoon I will be joining my regiment. I have purchased a commission," Benedict said. If it wasn't already too late, then it was high time he learned discipline, determination, and to fight for what he believed in until the bitter end.

There were certain times during which a man did not like being interrupted. Making love was one of them. Proposing to the love of his life, another.

"Oh, there you are, Duke!" Emma's mother cried, bustling in. "We'd begun to despair."

Prudence and Olivia scurried behind her, as politely as possible trying to remove the countess.

"Mother," Emma said, "we'd like a moment."

"Everyone is waiting and growing increasingly anxious," Lady Avery replied.

"We're fine. Everyone is fine," Prudence declared.

"My mother says ladies oughtn't interrupt the private moments of others," Olivia added.

"We'd best be getting on, then," Lady Avery chirped. "Are you coming, then?"

"Lady Avery, Emma has requested a moment of privacy. Therefore we shall have a moment of privacy," Blake said firmly, leveling a stare at his future mother-in-law. Really, he had to disabuse her of the notion that she could carry on meddling in their lives.

He stared. She stared. Finally, she retreated with Olivia and Prudence in tow.

"Now where was I?" he murmured.

"You were going to confess your undying love for me and declare how happy you were that I have arranged this wedding and how you cannot wait to marry me," Emma said. He burst out laughing.

"That's what I love about you, Emma. You know me so well. And," he said, smiling, "you aren't afraid to tell me about it. Or when and where I should do something about it."

"I only meant to show you how much I love you."

"It's just, if we are going to have a wedding, we ought to have a proposal."

"Another one?"

"A real one. And say yes this time," Blake said.

She laughed happily and said, "I will."

"Emma, I could list all the things I adore about you and go on for days," Blake said, clasping her hands in his. "I could paint a damn fine picture of our life together. But you know, just as I do, all the pleasure we give each other and all the little ways that we make each other better. Ever since the unusual circumstances of our first meeting, we've been on an adventure that I don't want to end. There is only one more thing to say." For this, he dropped to one knee and gazed at her earnestly, lovingly. "*Emily,* will you do me the honor of becoming my one and only beloved wife?"

LAKE WILLIAM PEREGRINE Auden, the ninth
uke of Ashbrooke, and Lady Emma Avery were
narried shortly thereafter. It is reported that
he duke played what might generously be de-
cribed as "musical notes" upon his flute as the
ride walked down the aisle. At the conclusion
f the ceremony, the large wooden doors of St.
eorge's were thrown open and the crowd let up
roar upon seeing that London's Least Likely had
nared her duke, thus giving hope to all the Wall-
lowers in London. Then he gave her a scandal-
usly passionate kiss that thoroughly put to rest
ny rumors that their marriage was anything but
love match.

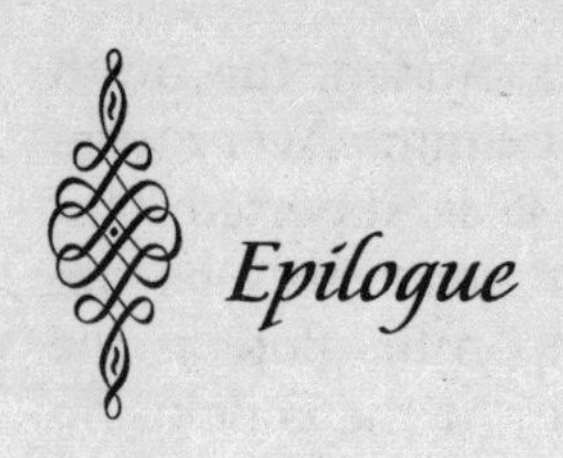

Epilogue

Lady Penelope's Anniversary Ball
London, 182
A few months later

FINALLY, *FINALLY,* THE moment Emma had both dreaded and anticipated in equal measure had arrived. Any minute now she would be announced at the anniversary ball celebrating one hundred years of Lady Penelope's Finishing School for Young Ladies of Fine Families. In the entire history of the school not one graduate had failed to make a match by the conclusion of her fourth season. Fortunately, Emma would *not* be the exception, as she had often feared during her first season. And second. And third.

Any minute now the butler would announce her not as Lady Emma Avery or the Buxom Bluestocking or even London's Least Likely to Misbehave. Because she had succeeded at the great husband hunt—beyond everyone's wildest expectations, including her own—Emma was now addressed as Your Grace.

"The Duke and Duchess of Ashbrooke," the butler intoned.

Heads turned to look at the sensational couple

The great Lady Penelope herself (great-granddaughter to the founder) beamed up at her former student. Emma held her head high and proudly smiled—even if it was a bit crooked. Her husband found it alluring, which was all that mattered.

"We must go find my friends," Emma murmured. Blake led the way through the crowd until they found Olivia standing off to the side.

"You look lovely, Olivia!" Emma exclaimed.

"Thank you. You look fine as well, although I'm not sure you have enough diamonds," Olivia remarked with an upturn of her lips as she eyed the diamond and sapphire necklace, earbobs and ring that Emma wore with her blue silk gown.

"A gift from Blake," Emma replied, smiling up at her husband.

"You mean a gift from your handsome, charming, utterly besotted husband," Blake said. He gave her a roguish smile, which *still* left her breathless.

"That's what I said," Emma replied. They gazed into each other's eyes. Neither Emma, Olivia, nor Prudence had been able to agree whether the duke's gaze smoldered or sparkled when he looked at his wife. Emma just knew that it made her feel very loved and wonderfully wicked.

"Have you seen Prudence?" Olivia interrupted anxiously.

"No. Have you not? She should be here by now," Emma replied.

"She cannot miss this ball," Olivia declared, glancing around through narrowed eyes at the

other guests—all graduates of Lady P's and a
with husbands.

"It's just not done," Emma murmured as Olivi
excused herself in order to seek out Prudence.

"Darling wife, would you care to waltz?" Blak
asked. Then furrowing his brow in concern, h
asked, "You *can* waltz in your condition, can yo
not?"

Emma barely had a chance to say yes before h
swept her into his arms and whirled her aroun
the ballroom. She felt lighthearted and light
headed, deeply happy in this moment and des
perately excited for what pleasure awaited whe
they returned home. Or perhaps sooner?

The duke waltzed them off the dance floor an
toward the open terrace doors.

"Blake, what are you doing?" That rogue of her
just smiled, making Emma's heart skip a beat.

Blake waltzed them across the terrace, to th
curious stares of the guests. Emma grinned as sh
guessed what he was about.

"The letters?" she asked.

"The letters," he murmured.

She knew what happened next because onc
upon a time they had written a dramatic and ro
mantic love story. It had been just pretend—unti
it was very, very real.

Scandalously, Blake waltzed them into th
darkened gardens, where they disappeared unde
the sparkling stars and moonlight for quite som
time.

The next day the gossip columns would compli

ment the duchess's gown and jewels—the Wallflower had blossomed quite nicely! They would also remark upon the Duke of Ashbrooke's devotion to his wife and the heart-melting smiles the young couple exchanged—as if they shared quite a secret.

A few months after that, the gossip columns would report the following:

> To the surprise of no one who has ever seen the Duke and Duchess of Ashbrooke's enormous affection for one another, the happy couple just announced the arrival of a healthy baby girl named Agatha. We hear she is already enrolled at Lady Penelope's Finishing School for Young Ladies of Fine Families.

Author's Note

THE DIFFERENCE ENGINE is widely considered to be the world's first computer. The inventor was the Englishman Charles Babbage, who had the idea in 1821 while reviewing a set of mathematical tables riddled with errors. "I wish to God these calculations had been executed by steam," he is said to have exclaimed. This brilliant mathematician, inventor, philosopher, and charming man about town spent thousands of pounds of his own money and government funds to design and build a machine to reliably perform mathematical calculations.

While Babbage is considered a pioneer of computing, he's also known for failing to build the machines he designed. The Difference Engine wasn't built until 1991—just in time for the 200th anniversary of Babbage's birth—when a dedicated team from The Science Museum in London endeavored to build it once and for all from the original plans—and to finally discover if it would work. (It did! Brilliant!)

I am completely indebted to Doron Swade's book *The Difference Engine: The Quest to Build the First Computer.* It was a marvelous and riveting account of Babbage's life and the modern-day quest to build the engine using Babbage's original plans.

As I embarked on a series of interconnected historical and contemporary romance novels (of which *The Wicked Wallflower* is the first), I was deeply pleased to learn that the computer—of all things!—could be a link between Regency London and modern-day New York City. Heroes of subsequent books in my Wallflower series will succeed where Babbage did not (because it's my fictional world and I said so). The hero of my contemporary series, *The Bad Boy Billionaire,* is a brilliant tech entrepreneur who, like so many men and women today, carry on the pioneering work of innovators like Babbage.

Keep reading for an exclusive excerpt from *The Bad Boy Billionaire's Wicked Arrangement,* the contemporary version of *The Wicked Wallflower.*

Discover the secret love story behind

The Wicked Wallflower!

Meet Jane Sparks. . .
She's a modern-day girl trying to make it in the big city—while writing a novel shamelessly based on her own romantic misadventures.

Do become acquainted with Duke Austen. . .
He's a bad boy billionaire with the kind of smile most often found on rogues in romance novels.

Be careful what you post on Facebook . . .
When a post appears on Facebook announcing their engagement, they do the unthinkable: play along with the ruse. And then the unexpected happens: they start falling in love.

An exclusive excerpt from

The Bad Boy Billionaire's Wicked Arrangement

The Bad Boy Billionaire's Wicked Arrangement

Hudson Bar and Books
New York City

@TechCrunch: Duke Austen's startup, Project-TK, files for 100 Billion IPO. Here's why it might not happen.

Is the third time a charm for Silicon Alley party boy Duke Austen? After the spectacular failures of his first two start-ups, he's on the verge of a major win—as long as investors can overlook his reputation for hard-partying and worries about him paying more attention to the hot supermodels instead of hot new products. Read More . . .

"THIS." I SET down the damned invitation on the bar.

"What is *this*?" Roxanna asked, looking up from her iPhone. We often met here after work for drinks and supper before returning to our microscopic, claustrophobia-inducing West Village apartment.

"*This* is the invitation to my tenth annual high school reunion. In other words, I have just been invited to a party to showcase what an utter failure I am."

"What are you talking about, Jane? You have ditched Bumblefuck, Pennsylvania, and your boring ex-boyfriend for the glamorous life of a single working girl in New York City."

"I'm working as a library assistant, which is a step down from my previous job as head librarian. I told everyone I was going to write a novel, but I have only a Word document that reads 'Untitled Romance Novel' and not much else. And I still love my ex-boyfriend, thank you very much. And he's been dating. I saw it on Facebook. I have *not* been dating."

"No, you're just having hot and heavy hookups with strangers. Much better if you ask me," Roxanna said with a grin. I had told her a little bit about what happened at the party last night, leaving out the most embarrassing bits. Which is to say, I left out most of the story.

"*One* hook up. Once. And while I was pawing at some random guy in the library like an adolescent, everyone else has gotten married and had children. Look—" I said, pulling out my iPhone and bringing up the list of my friends on Facebook, many of them from Milford High School. "Melissa, married. Has a baby. Rachel and Dan, married. *Two* children, when some people don't have any! Kate Abbott, who was totally horrible to me throughout high school, is 'seeing someone special.' And it's only a matter of time before Sam posts, Married! Baby! He keeps posting about dinners at all the romantic places around town."

"What, all three of them? You have to unsubscribe to his status updates," Roxanna said dryly.

"I don't know how," I grumbled. "Technology mystifies me."

"Here, let me see if I can do this on your phone," Roxanna said. I handed it over without a second thought. "I'll take care of this while you pine away for the days of card catalogues, horses, and bayonets."

"We were voted Most Likely to Live Happily Ever After," I said glumly.

"Aww, should we go home and look through your yearbooks?" Roxanna asked, pushing her red hair over her shoulder.

She was tough as nails and just what I needed. In return, since she was a disaster at things like laundry, cooking, and paying bills, I helped make sure she had clean clothes, Wi-Fi, and didn't subsist exclusively on bourbon and popcorn.

"No, it will only make me feel worse," I said with a sigh. I knew because I had already looked through them. It was all the inscriptions that slayed me. *Stay in touch. Don't ever change.*

Growing up, I had this idea of what my life would be like, and I did everything I could to make it happen. Good grades, good school, career in the library sciences, which would allow me some flexibility when Sam and I married and had kids.

We planned to get engaged after he finished his

dissertation. Then he'd get a job as a professor at Montclair University.

We planned to have a house on Brook Street—I knew just the one—with great bookshelves and a yard for the kids. Maybe a couch from Pottery Barn and . . .

Then BOOM—fired. Then BOOM—dumped.

Sam had coldly explained that he wanted to see more of the world. Date other people. Be with someone more adventurous. Someone who didn't have every detail of their life already preordered.

"Ah, this will make you feel better," Roxanna said, when the bartender set down our drinks: a glass of chardonnay for me and bourbon on the rocks for her. "Cheers."

"I just had this idea of what my life would be like by now,' I said as Roxanna messed around with my phone. "And so did everyone else. I had already planned my wedding on Pinterest. Now he's squiring some girl around town to all the romantic spots while I'm working at the low level job I had in college and I'm hopelessly single."

"Personally, I wouldn't give a fuck what my loser high school classmates thought of me," Roxanna said, sipping her bourbon and still messing around with my phone.

"I know. I'm seething with jealously."

Truly, I kind of was.

"But since you clearly do care, why don't you show up with a totally hot, successful date?"

I sighed and smiled. "It would make everyone jealous, wouldn't it? No one would ask me if I

nissed my old job, why Sam and I broke up, or
iow my novel writing is going. The problem is
'our plan requires me knowing a hot, successful
;uy. The only guy to ask me out since I moved
iere is José at the bodega."

"Speaking of hot, successful guys, *why do you
iave a friend request from Duke Austen?*" Roxanna
ooked up me, her blue eyes wide and her mouth
)pen in shock.

"Hey, why do you still have my phone?"

"Jane! Is this the guy you hooked up with?"
Roxanna held out my phone showing the Faceook profile of That Guy. All dark eyes, tussled
iair, unshaven. Like a pirate or a highwayman or
ome rogue up to no good. Yeah, that was the guy.

"I think so. It was dark. I had a mask on," I said.
figured he was just some charming but scruffy
;uy who was probably a struggling actor tending
ar at some hipster dive in Williamsburg. Totally
indateable.

"OMG," Roxanna said. Gasped, really. "OMG."

"What?"

"Jane, this is *Duke Austen,*" she practically
hrieked. Then she looked around as if someone
night overhear the conversation. As if he were
Somebody.

"I can see that. But who is he?"

"He's only the billionaire co-founder of Project-
TK. See, you do know someone hot and success-
ul. OMG do you ever!"

"He didn't look like a billionaire."

"Why? Cos he didn't wear a suit and gray tie

and wave around fat cigars and a bottle of fifty year Macallan? Welcome to the start-up world Jane. Where the billionaires look and act like the guys next door."

OMG, indeed.

"He caught me on my hands and knees," I whispered, horrified. "And shushing people at a party."

"And then he hooked up with you. I spent all day working on a story about him, in fact," Roxanna said. "His company is about to IPO but everyone is freaking out because he's a brilliant disaster and they're afraid it will affect the share price. He can code and he can sell anyone on anything. But then he's always getting wasted and missing work or getting embroiled in all sorts of scandals with models. And drugs. He's all kinds of bad news."

"Why can't I just find a nice guy with a steady job and benefits?"

"Oh, the romance. Oh, be still my beating heart," Roxanna said dryly. "I have an idea."

She grinned wickedly and started doing something on my phone. I reached for it, and she lunged away. "Hey, Jane, watch the drinks."

"Roxanna, what are you doing?"

"This."

She held out the phone.

Heartbeat: stopped.

Breathing: stopped.

My life: over.

FB STATUS: Jane Sparks is engaged to Duke Austen!

Everyone would see it. My mom, my dad, my ister. Everyone from Milford, my coworkers at he library, everyone I had ever known that had n Internet connection. Sam. He would see it.

And then all those people would see that it had een a joke, a prank, or the desperate and wishul thinking of a lonely girl. Haven't I had enough nortification?

I couldn't do it again. I couldn't answer all hose people saying sweetly (or not so sweetly), I thought you were with so-and-so. What hapened?" It hurt too much to always say *I don't now* when things kept going wrong.

Instead, I shrieked and lunged for the phone, nocking over my glass of chardonnay. It shatered, spilling all over the bar and dripping down nto my nude patent pumps. My life was in shamles. And there was wine in my shoe.

"What have you done?" I gasped.

"I just got you a hot date for your high school eunion. You are welcome."

"No, you just got me a fiancé!"

"Even better, right? I hope he gets you a giant liamond ring," Roxanna said dreamily. "Alhough, he's only a billionaire on paper. But don't vorry, I'm sure he's got a few actual millions ucked away."

"How do I undo this?" I frantically jabbed at he screen. It was so unsatisfying.

"I have no idea," she said with a shrug. "Faceook settings are impossible to figure out."

"Roxanna!"

My phone dinged with an incoming text message from a number I didn't recognize.

917-123-4567: Meet me at Soho House in ten minutes for celebratory drinks
Jane Sparks: Who is this?
917-123-4567: Your fiancé

Next month, don't miss these exciting new love stories only from Avon Books

he Pirate Bride by Sandra Hill
edana Elsadottir, known as the Sea Scourge, needs a few rile Vikings to help grow her female-only tribe. When ght strapping Norsemen come into her hands—and her iip's hold—she doesn't mind reaping the benefits, pecially with a godly specimen like Thork Tykirsson. iork doesn't mind being kidnapped by a beautiful pirate, it that doesn't mean he'll give in easily.

'ildest Dreams by Toni Blake
dvertising executive Stephanie Grant knows how to sell i idea, but she's never had to sell *herself* before. Walking to The Big Easy's most exclusive bordello, she's prepared do just that—until she meets *him*. Jake Broussard knows iis sexy blonde isn't who she says she is, and that she's aying with fire. Good thing he likes it hot . . .

uddenly Royal by Nichole Chase
s crown prince of Lilaria, Alex D'Lynsal is used to itoriety, but the latest scandal has sent him packing to merica and forced him to swear off women. That is, until : meets Samantha Rousseau. She's stubborn, feisty, and credibly sexy. Not to mention heiress to an estate in his untry. Sam can navigate the sudden changes to her life, it can she dodge her growing feelings for Alex?

#1 *NEW YORK TIMES*
AND *USA TODAY* BESTSELLER

TEN THINGS I LOVE ABOUT YO

978-0-06-149189-4

If the elderly Earl of Newbury dies without an heir, detested nephew Sebastian inherits everything. Newb decides that Annabel Winslow is the answer to his proble But the thought of marrying the earl makes Annabel's crawl, even though the union would save her family from r Perhaps the earl's machinations will leave him out in the and spur a love match instead?

JUST LIKE HEAVEN

978-0-06-149190-0

Marcus Holroyd has promised his best friend, David Smy Smith, that he'll look out for David's sister, Honoria. No easy task when Honoria sets off for Cambridge determi to marry by the end of the season. When her advances spurned can Marcus swoop in and steal her heart?

A NIGHT LIKE THIS

978-0-06-207290-0

Daniel Smythe-Smith vows to pursue the mysterious yo governess Anne Wynter, even if that means spending his with a ten-year-old who thinks she's a unicorn. And after y of dodging unwanted advances, the oh-so-dashing Ear Winstead is the first man to truly tempt Anne.

Give in to your Impulses!

These unforgettable stories only take a second to buy and give you hours of reading pleasure!

Go to ***www.AvonImpulse.com*** and see what we have to offer.

Available wherever e-books are sold.